FIND ME

ALSO BY TIFFANY SNOW

The Corrupted Hearts Series

Follow Me

Break Me

Find Me

The Tangled Ivy Series

In His Shadow

Shadow of a Doubt

Out of the Shadows

The Risky Business Series

Power Play

Playing Dirty

Play to Win

The Kathleen Turner Series

No Turning Back

Turn to Me

Turning Point

Out of Turn

Point of No Return

Blane's Turn

Kade's Turn

Blank Slate

FIND ME

A CORRUPTED HEARTS NOVEL

TIFFANY
SNOW

Montlake
Romance

This is a work of fiction. Names, characters, organizations, places, events, and incidents are either products of the author's imagination or are used fictitiously.

Published by Montlake Romance, Seattle

www.apub.com

ISBN-13: 9781542047845
ISBN-10: 1542047846

Cover design by Eileen Carey

Printed in the United States of America

For Erica. May I always be the mom you need me to be.

CH 1

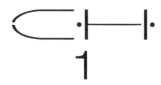

I had a boyfriend for Valentine's Day.

It was Valentine's Day, and I, China Mack, had a boyfriend.

My boyfriend and I were going on a date, on Valentine's Day.

No matter how many times and ways I said it inside my head, it still felt like a fairy tale. I was one of those people who ignored Valentine's Day. If someone brought it up, I shrugged it off as a "Hallmark Holiday." Then I'd go home and shoot up men on Halo. A *lot* of men (I was pretty darn good at Halo).

But tonight, there would be no first-person-shooter games for me, because I had a real-life boyfriend who was taking me to a real-world brick-and-mortar restaurant for a classic, romantic Valentine's Day date.

I'd even been promised roses and chocolates. (Yes, I'd asked for them, but still. He could've said no.) There would be flowers and candy and a boyfriend and wine and dinner and fantastic, toe-curling sex afterward with my amazing, wonderful, handsome, brilliant, and, did I mention rich? boyfriend.

It was going to be perfect.

As soon as I squeezed into my dress.

"Stop wriggling," Mia complained. "You're going to get your skin caught in the zipper, and that'll hurt like hell, trust me."

"It itches," I complained.

"So what? You look amazing. You're wearing it, and I don't care if it itches. Now hold your hair so it doesn't get caught in the zipper. And be careful! I worked hard on those curls."

Mia was my sixteen-year-old niece who'd gotten all those "girl" genes that had skipped right over me. My hair was coal black, thick, and long. Usually, my hair style of choice—and ability—was a ponytail. Tonight, Mia had spent an hour with various heating and styling implements to turn my hair into a work of art. And I had to say, she'd succeeded.

Long curls in an artful disarray streamed down my back, while the sides were pinned up behind my ears. Some twisting strands were left loose and framed my face, making my jawline appear delicate and feminine—two adjectives I had trouble pulling off on the best of days.

My usual attire was jeans, a T-shirt, and a button-up shirt layered over that because I was perpetually cold. Tonight, I was guaranteed to freeze because the dress Mia was currently zipping me into had less fabric than my summertime Endor *Star Wars* pajamas.

I had one "real" dress (Mia's description) in my wardrobe, bought for a work-related-undercover-kind-of-thing. Though in reality I had four—if you counted the Dalek dress I'd had specially made for Halloween, my Uhura miniskirt dress from *Star Trek*, and Princess Éowyn's wedding gown from *The Return of the King*. I'd wanted to wear the work dress for tonight. Mia had firmly vetoed that plan.

"Jackson's already seen you in that dress," she'd said.

I didn't see why that was a reason for Jackson—the aforementioned boyfriend—not to see me in it again, but I'd been hauled out to the shopping mall despite my quite logical argument that if I continued with this "rule" of not rewearing garments Jackson had seen, I'd soon be out of space in my closet. Mia had ignored me.

She'd chosen this dress, and while I'd been skeptical, she was right. As usual. It was a deep midnight-blue, which she said "brought out" my eyes, which were also blue. Silver threads were woven through the fabric (and were the source of the itching), but weren't visible until light hit them in just the right way, so no matter which way I turned, I sparkled. It was a cap sleeve with a V-neckline that showed more cleavage than I usually displayed. And since I usually displayed none, I hoped Jackson appreciated the view, because it was darn cold. Since I barely topped five foot two on a good day, Mia said I needed a short hem, which was the only part of the dress not clinging to me like a second skin. Floaty and overlaid with a filmy blue fabric, the skirt stopped an inch above my knee and flared when I spun in a circle, which I'd done too many times to be appropriate for my age. I was twenty-four, not six.

So, the bottom line was that the woman looking back at me in the mirror when Mia was (finally) through with my makeup looked nothing like the China Mack (that's me) that I saw every day, which I suppose was the point. It was a holiday, after all, even if it was just a Hallmark one. Not for the first time did I wish I could handle wearing contacts instead of glasses, just to show off Mia's mad makeup skills.

I slipped on the silver ballet flats Mia had made me buy to go with the dress—I'd put my foot down at the mention of heels, literally—and eyed the silver clutch purse she was holding.

"It's not big enough to carry anything," I complained. I never used a purse. A backpack was much more practical, and easier.

"All you need is your phone." She put it in the purse. "Your keys." Those went in, too. "Lip gloss and powder." She handed the clutch to me. "All set."

"When do I put on the makeup?" I didn't usually wear the stuff, having never quite gotten the hang of "smoky eyes" and "pouty lips."

She rolled her eyes. "I've told you. After dinner, in the bathroom. Don't ever touch up makeup at the table, and you can reapply the lip gloss more than just once—hint, hint."

"For as much as it cost, I'd better." The little tube had been almost forty bucks.

"Jackson is going to flip when he sees you," she said with more than a little satisfaction, looking me up and down. "I am *so* good."

I laughed outright. "And modest, too," I teased, but she just shrugged. "You look stunning. Let's take a selfie."

Thus began about ten minutes of her posing us and posting on various social media platforms, at one point turning us both into puppy dogs via Snapchat. Mia's long, blond hair and Barbie-perfect face—even without makeup—were a stark contrast to me, and usually I felt dumpy next to her statuesque beauty. But not tonight. Tonight, I felt *pretty*.

I kept glancing at the clock. Jackson was never late, and I was anxious to see him. He'd been out of town for a couple of weeks, and though we'd FaceTimed every day, I'd missed him. Missed his arms around me, his warm kisses, and his smile that was just for me when we were alone together.

It was straight-up seven o'clock when the doorbell rang. My stomach flipped over in anticipation, and I was across the living room and foyer of my duplex in three seconds flat, my cheeks hurting from the huge grin I couldn't help.

I threw open the door and stopped breathing.

Jackson Cooper was six feet of pure male perfection, with thick, wavy hair the warm shade of chestnut and eyes the golden brown reminiscent of Edward's "vegetarian" diet in *Twilight* (without the special effects, of course). His shoulders were wide, his waist narrow, and his body lean, lithe muscle. Said body was currently wrapped in an immaculate tuxedo that I knew had to be designer and tailored. Jackson wasn't shy about liking nice things, and since he could afford to buy them, he did.

"Wow," I breathed. If I'd been a cartoon character, my eyes would've morphed into red hearts.

He didn't say anything at first, and his eyes widened. He looked me down, then up, then made the journey all over again . . . slower. When his eyes met mine, there was a gleam in them that made my tummy flip again.

Shy under his silent scrutiny, I went for my nervous tic of reaching up to tighten my nonexistent ponytail.

"Don't touch it!" Mia called out sharply, making me jump. I'd forgotten she was in the living room behind me.

I yanked my arms back down.

Jackson cracked a smile, his low chuckle warming the air between us. "I see Mia's been making you even more beautiful than you already are," he said.

And the man could turn a phrase. Jackson ticked all the boxes on the Man of a Woman's Dreams list and then some. Lucky for me, he was *my* Dream Man . . . and my Valentine date.

"Doesn't she look awesome?" Mia popped up over my shoulder.

Jackson's gaze was still on me. "Indeed, she does." His voice held an undertone of promise that made my cheeks grow warm.

Mia snickered.

He suddenly brandished a small bouquet of pink mini-roses and offered them to Mia. "Happy Valentine's Day," he said.

She squealed with delight. "Awesome! Thanks!" Then she was off, padding into the kitchen to put them in a vase.

I waited, expecting more flowers. But his hands were empty.

Oh.

Well, that was okay. Flowers were technically already dead once they were cut. Really, it was an illogical expenditure. Still, though, no one had ever bought me flowers before.

"Are you ready?" he asked. "It's cold. Let me get your coat."

He brushed past me and retrieved my one dress coat from the closet. It was also a new expenditure—a cream wool swing coat that was warm and didn't make me look short. He held it for me to put on, his fingers brushing the back of my neck as he lifted my hair free of the collar. A shiver went through me at the light touch.

"You might want to check the pockets," Jackson said. "I thought I felt something in one of them."

I pushed my hands into the pockets, and sure enough, one of them had a small box in it. Puzzled, I pulled it out. It was a black box, to be precise, with an elaborate "HW" imprinted on the top. I glanced up at Jackson, who winked.

"Open it," he said.

Carefully, I lifted the lid, then stared in shock at the diamond tennis bracelet inside. I'd never had a piece of jewelry in my life, much less diamonds. I had no idea how much this had cost, but it sure must have been a heck of a lot more expensive than flowers would've been. And diamonds were significant in a relationship (I'd been reading back issues of *Cosmo* lately). Any kind of jewelry was a Big Deal.

"Jackson, I don't know what to say . . . ," I finally managed, unsure how to react or what his gift meant. "You didn't have to spend so much money on me." Maybe he'd bought it just because he could. Though I made a good salary—a really good salary—I wasn't even close to Jackson's league when talking about net worth.

I'd grown up on a farm north of Omaha, and money had always been tight. I'd made my way through my three undergrad degrees and MIT by scholarship, so landing a job that paid six figures was a welcome relief. And even though I'd bought some pretty expensive things—my life-size Iron Man Mark IV replica suit hadn't been cheap—I was relatively sure I could've bought a half dozen Iron Men for what Jackson was currently fastening around my wrist.

"Of course I didn't have to," he said. "I wanted to." He pulled the edges of my coat, making me step closer to him, slipped off my glasses, then leaned down and pressed his lips to mine.

Now this was what I'd missed . . .

Jackson's lips were warm and his tongue hot. My hands slid up his shoulders to his neck as I melted into the kiss. I stretched up to my toes, trying to get closer to him, and felt his hands at my waist inside my coat.

He smelled good, and his jaw was freshly shaven, the skin soft to the touch. His hair was cold and slightly damp, the strands like silk against my fingers. The kiss was deep and languid, making me rethink the whole idea of leaving rather than dragging him up to my bedroom.

When he broke the kiss, it took me a moment to come back to earth from the cloud I'd been on. Nothing else seemed to matter when I was with Jackson, and when I finally met his eyes, there was more than desire in their depths. Warmth and softness radiated from him as he lifted a hand and tucked a stray curl behind my ear, then slid my glasses back up my nose.

"Aww! You two are so sweet!"

Mia's words were an abrupt reminder, and I hastily stepped away from Jackson. She was standing in the entry from the kitchen to the living room, vase of roses in her hands, and gazing at us with the expression of an adoring puppy.

"Time to go," Jackson said, and I figured it was probably the only time in his life he'd ever been called "sweet." *Forbes*'s Ten Most Eligible Billionaires list had used words like "sexy," "aloof," "mysterious," and "genius" to describe him, not *sweet*.

I expected his usual car when we went outside, but instead, there was a shiny black stretch limo in my driveway. I'd never ridden in one before, and as a car aficionado, I immediately itched to see inside.

"I thought I'd go all out," he said. A driver was waiting by the car door and opened it for us as we approached. I didn't recognize him.

"Where's Lance?" I asked. Lance was Jackson's man and took care of the household and drove for him.

"It's Valentine's Day. I gave him the night off. The rental came with a driver anyway."

The inside of the limo was gorgeous black leather with sparkly lights that looked like stars on the ceiling. I gasped when I saw not one, not two, but three huge bouquets of red roses placed strategically around the interior. Their sweet scent permeated the limo.

I scooted over on the back seat, wide-eyed, as Jackson climbed in next to me. The driver closed the door behind him, and we were alone.

I felt overwhelmed. No one had ever done something so romantic for me before. "I feel like Cinderella," I said.

"You're much prettier than Cinderella," Jackson replied, his fingers grazing my jaw.

I turned toward him and it hit me then, how much I'd missed him. Two weeks had felt like an eternity.

Reaching up, I pulled him down to kiss him again. This time it wasn't languid. It was urgent and wet, and I wanted him desperately.

"We should've stayed at my place," I murmured against his lips.

He didn't answer. Instead he pushed my coat off my shoulders and dragged me onto his lap. I knelt, straddling him, still kissing. Then his hands were on my bare thighs and sliding up underneath my skirt, sending a rush of heat between my legs. Two weeks was too long.

He suddenly froze and pulled away, a strange look on his face. "What are you wearing underneath that dress?"

I remembered then, and grinned. "Oh, just a little something I picked up." I lifted my skirt so he could see my black satin bikini panties. They had words printed on the front in large white letters.

"Use the Force," Jackson read, then burst out laughing. His laugh made me smile wider. I loved hearing it, especially when I was the one who'd amused him. Amusing him *on purpose* was even better.

I squealed when Jackson picked me up and reversed our positions, kneeling in front of me. His smile turned wicked as he tugged the panties down my legs.

"Wait, what are you doing?" We were in a car, for crying out loud. Yes, a limousine, but still. The driver was *right there* up front, even with the divider separating us.

"I thought I'd head downtown first."

Usually euphemisms went over my head, but it was hard to mistake Jackson's meaning when he spread my knees and put his mouth between my legs.

My eyes slammed shut at the touch of his tongue. I bit my lip to stay quiet, but Jackson moaned, pressing closer. His . . . enthusiasm . . . for this particular activity translated into an awesome benefit for me.

I stopped caring about where we were and who might hear about five seconds after he slid a finger inside me. I opened my eyes and watched him. The sight of his head between my thighs sent my pulse into overdrive. His eyes had been closed, too, but now they looked right at me, watching me watch him kiss the most intimate and sensitive part of me.

It was enough to send me over the edge. I clutched his head and came apart.

The look of smug satisfaction on his face when I was able to open my eyes again was enough to make me chuckle.

"You look mighty pleased with yourself," I said.

"Considering how loud you were, I think I have the right," he murmured, pressing his lips to the inside of my knee.

But instead of being sated, I wanted more. Leaning forward, I tugged at his bow tie.

"Please tell me wherever we're going is far away," I said.

"It's however far you want it to be."

Good enough.

I yanked his jacket off his shoulders and discarded it along with the tie. Then I pushed at his shoulders.

"Up there," I said, motioning to the long seat that ran along the length of the limo. "I want you up there."

Jackson's lips twisted at my bossiness, but he did as I said, leaning back against the seat and looking much too sexy for a man who wrote computer code for a living. His tie was gone and I'd managed to get the top three buttons undone on his shirt, showing an enticing glimpse of his chest that made my fingers itch to touch him. His eyes were at half-mast, watching me, his lips slightly swollen from our kisses.

If I sold a picture of him looking like this, I'd make a fortune. Good thing I was too focused on stripping him to grab my phone.

I got the rest of his shirt unbuttoned and tugged it from his slacks, not bothering to push it off his shoulders. I could get to his chest now, and I spent some time admiring the view. I traced the muscles of his pectorals and abdomen with my fingers, his skin warm to the touch. Then the length of his erection straining at his slacks caught my eye.

Since I'd been partly satisfied, I took my time, teasing him. Slowly unbuttoning his trousers and carefully lowering the zipper. When my fingers touched him, he sucked in a breath, and I smiled.

"Miss me?" I asked.

"You have no idea."

Being short had its advantages, so when I straddled him, I didn't have to bend my neck to not hit my head on the roof. I looked into his eyes as he guided himself into me, and it felt as though more than our bodies connected.

I kissed him, and he grasped my hips, lifting me, then letting me slide back down.

"Oooooh," I breathed. "That feels . . . nice."

He grunted. "Nice? Really? Just nice? I guess I'll have to try harder."

Taking me with him, he moved to the opposite seat, effectively switching our positions. I clung to him with my arms and legs, sucking the skin covering his clavicle. I really didn't care what position he wanted us in. I just didn't want to miss a moment.

However, having sex in a limo isn't as easy as it sounds. He couldn't quite get enough leverage or the right angle, and at one point, my skull cracked against the ceiling. But the rest of what he was doing felt too good for me to care. We were both too into each other to mind if it was awkward or that we had to adjust a few times. I giggled when he muttered a curse under his breath, then he must've found a sweet spot because he was thrusting inside me so fast and hard, I didn't care if I bonked my head another half dozen times.

I bit into his shoulder when my orgasm hit, stronger than the first, and his body jerked into mine. We'd never had a simultaneous orgasm before, and I thought it was just a myth . . . until now. And OMG. It was worth all the hype and Harlequin odes of joy.

"Best . . . Valentine's Day . . . ever . . . ," I panted into his ear.

His soft chuckle made me smile as his lips pressed against my neck. "God, you feel good," he said.

I didn't know if he was referring to holding me or to where his penis currently resided, but I decided against asking for clarification. It might ruin the moment, which was pretty darn good.

"Was it the diamonds or the sex?" he asked.

"If you have to ask, then you must be in need of affirmation of your sexual prowess."

"Unless you're a really good actress, I believe I've had all the affirmation I need," he drawled.

I laughed, then we got on with the business of putting ourselves back together, though the only lighting we could figure out was how to turn the roof lights into a flashing rainbow. Six college degrees between us and we couldn't figure out the control panel. Finally, we were clothed again and I was digging in my purse.

"Yes!" I pulled out the small bottle of antigerm gel that Mia knew me well enough to include. "Hand me some of those cocktail napkins," I said.

I squirted some gel onto the napkins Jackson handed me.

"What are you doing?" he asked, watching me.

"I'm sanitizing," I explained, carefully wiping the seat where we'd . . . enjoyed each other.

"Of course you are."

I didn't think that required a response, so I continued with my task. A few moments later, I heard a champagne cork pop behind me.

"I think Valentine's Day requires champagne," Jackson said, handing me a flute filled with sparkling golden fluid.

I set aside my napkins, sanitation accomplished, and accepted the champagne while he poured his own glass.

"To an amazing woman who makes me miss being home," Jackson said, clinking his glass against mine.

"To a man who's made my first Valentine's Day super special," I replied, and took a sip of the champagne.

Jackson frowned, not taking a drink. "What do you mean, your 'first Valentine's Day'?"

"I mean, I've just never had a boyfriend before on this particular . . . holiday."

He smiled. "Well, then, I guess I'd better make this night one to remember." He set aside his flute and reached for one of the vases of roses, removing a small box from behind it. He handed it to me.

"What's this?"

"Something to make the evening memorable."

I rolled my eyes. "Um, I think two orgasms has already made the evening memorable, especially since we were in a moving vehicle at the time and violating all kinds of seat-belt laws."

"I'm aiming higher," he said, nodding toward the box I held.

Slowly, I lifted the lid. I hadn't received gifts for Valentine's Day since my mom was alive and had given me a teddy bear that sang "P.S. I Love You" when you pressed its paw. I'd been five years old at the time. I still had that bear.

I sucked in a stunned breath when I looked inside the box. A pair of eyeglasses was sitting on black satin. But not just eyeglasses. These had wire rims and perfectly round lenses. My hands turned cold, and there was a buzzing inside my head.

"Jackson . . ." I trailed off. I had no idea what to say. "Is this . . . ?" I couldn't say the words out loud.

"It is," he said. "It took some convincing for Dan to part with them, but he has another pair. Or more. He was a bit cagey about that. Plus, it wasn't as though he could turn down a very sizable donation for Demelza House."

"That . . . that's his favorite charity," I stammered. Jackson smiled.

"I know."

I looked back down at the glasses. The diamond bracelet was beautiful, but *this* . . . this meant something more to me, and that Jackson knew that about me made tears spring to my eyes. I wasn't the crying type, but being given Harry Potter's glasses was worthy of taking a moment.

"I-I don't know what to say."

"I told him you'd take very good care of them."

I carefully replaced the lid on the box and set it aside, then I threw myself at Jackson.

"Thank you thank you thank you!" I squeezed him as tight as I possibly could, and he hugged me back.

"You're very welcome," he wheezed. I abruptly loosened my grip.

I didn't know how I could possibly thank him enough, but I thought he understood what I couldn't put into words, because his smile was soft.

The car slowed to a stop, and I glanced outside. We were parked in front of a fancy restaurant, and the valet opened the door for us. I wasn't about to leave the glasses behind, so I emptied the makeup out of my little silver purse and carefully put them inside.

He held out a hand to me, and I took it.

I expected we'd be seated at a table, but instead we were led to a private room in the back. When I walked through the door a waiter was holding open for me, I gasped.

Jackson had re-created the Yule Ball from *Harry Potter and the Goblet of Fire*.

I stared in wonder. Everything was covered in ice and dripping with icicles. A huge tree stood at the far end of the room—it had to be at least twenty feet tall—its branches laden with snow. Arches of ice gleamed above us—tiny lights, like stars, twinkling through.

Jackson swung a warm fur around my shoulders and pulled me close. "Is it everything it should be?"

I looked up at him, my jaw still agape. "I can't believe you did this. It must've cost—"

"The cost doesn't matter," he interrupted. "Now, may I have a dance before dinner?"

Music swelled and I recognized it from the film as he turned me around on the floor, which actually wasn't ice, but somehow looked as though it was. It must've been frosted glass, maybe? I was living my own fairy tale at Hogwarts, complete with a Champion to open the Ball.

I felt as though I were floating as Jackson led me to a table. Dinner was wonderful and perfect, and they didn't serve me anything weird like oxtail or anything that swam (I wasn't a fan of fish). Just good ol' Omaha beef and the best macaroni and cheese I'd ever had. Jackson ordered wine, and we shared a dessert that was made tableside and included flames. At first, I'd argued they shouldn't use fire in a room full of ice, but the engineer had come out and explained to me that it would be okay. Only then did I let the poor waiter finish making the crêpes suzette.

It was the most perfect evening of my entire life, and I had to pinch myself. How did I, China Mack, end up with arguably the Best Boyfriend Ever?

I was pleasantly relaxed from the wine and lethargic from the food when I returned from the ladies' room to the table. (Thank goodness the ice hadn't extended to the toilet seat.) Jackson was waiting for me and I slid in next to him. His hand rested on my knee and I cuddled close to his side. I was sure that if I'd been watching us, I probably would have hurled at the sappiness of the scene, but I couldn't help it.

"I have one more thing for you," Jackson said.

I looked at him in disbelief. "If the Batmobile is outside, I'm going to pass out."

He laughed and shook his head. "Not this time. It's something quite a bit smaller."

He slid out of his chair and I watched in dawning realization as he knelt in front of me on one knee.

"Oh my God," I whispered, my eyes widening.

"China, I want to ask you something," he began.

I stopped breathing.

"I love you and can't imagine my life without you," he continued. "Will you marry me?" He reached inside his jacket and pulled out a small box. He opened it, revealing a diamond ring that elicited audible gasps from the waiters hovering nearby.

I froze. We hadn't discussed marriage since our disastrous argument on Halloween when he'd talked about the future as though he was "off the market," then had gotten upset when I wasn't as sure about us as he was. But people were watching, most of them already smiling, and now it was starting to get weird because I hadn't said anything. I couldn't breathe and the walls were closing in. The ring stared up at me the same way everyone around us was.

Marriage. It wasn't the institution that frightened me so much as its . . . permanency, and expectations, and so many unknowns. And he'd just sprung it on me out of the blue. *Spontaneous* and *surprise* weren't in my vocabulary.

"China?" he asked, his brows gathering into a frown as he looked up at me.

Suddenly, someone burst through the door. Another waiter, though this one not clad in Hogwarts attire. Jackson stood, shielding me as if the man was a threat.

"What are you—?" Jackson began, but the man shouted over him.

"The president's been shot!"

CH. 2

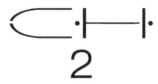

It took a moment for me to process what he'd just said.

"I need to get in to work," I said, jumping to my feet.

An unusual thing to say, but then again, I had an unusual job. I was in charge of Vigilance—a super-secret-I'll-have-to-kill-you-if-I-tell-you government agency that reported directly to the president. We were the eyes and ears and everything in between for connecting the dots between what people did on the Internet, what they did in meatspace, and what they were *going* to do . . . especially if it was something Bad. Since something really, *really* Bad had just happened and we hadn't known anything about it, I thought I'd better get my ass in to work and find out everything we could.

Jackson said nothing for a moment, his expression unreadable. He was still holding the ring box, but now it was closed. "Okay. Let's go," he said at last.

He wasn't supposed to know what I did for a living, but since he'd been the main developer of the algorithms that turned Vigilance from just monitoring software into thinking and predicting software, he had the inside scoop.

My phone rang as Jackson hustled me into the waiting limo. "Is he alive?" was how I answered the call.

"Yes. They said he's in surgery," said Derrick, the night-shift manager.

"What happened?"

"All the news has at this point is that he was speaking at a campaign event and that it was a sniper shot. They've practically shut down DC, trying to find the shooter." Derrick was usually calm and collected, but I could hear the shock in his voice as we spoke.

"I'll be there in twenty," I said, ending the call.

A few decades ago when the Cold War raged and the threat of nuclear weapons loomed, Raleigh had built a sprawling Underground. It had flourished for a while, then gone dormant, only to have a brief resurgence in the eighties when it was filled with restaurants and a vibrant music scene, all taking place six stories below. Then that had died off, and most had forgotten the area even existed, which was why it was the perfect place to hide a secret government-surveillance facility.

There were only two entrances to Vigilance: one via a parking garage, and the other a more hidden and obscure one I'd overseen myself. While Jackson knew of the former, he didn't know the latter, so when I told the limo driver to stop outside a worn-down Chinese-takeout joint, he gave me the side eye.

"This entrance is closer," I explained.

"Through a Chinese restaurant?"

"Yes," I replied curtly. It would take too long to explain, and I didn't have that kind of time.

"I'm coming with you," he said, stepping outside the cab with me.

"You can't." I stopped him. "I'm sorry, but you just can't."

"I've been in there before," he argued.

"And Clark shouldn't have brought you," I said. "I promise, I'll be fine. I'll call you soon." Stretching up on tiptoe, I quickly kissed him, then ducked into the Chinese place. Jackson still hadn't looked pleased, but there wasn't anything I could do. I had to go to work. He wasn't allowed inside.

"I'd like a Whopper, please. With everything." My order to the man behind the counter would've made anyone else look twice, but he took it without so much as blinking.

"We only serve Big Macs," he said.

"Then super-size mine."

Putting down the giant ladle in his hand, he turned and headed back into the kitchen. I followed. He stopped in front of the door to the walk-in freezer and punched in a code on the number pad affixed to the wall. The door lock released and opened with a whoosh of chill air.

"Remember, only fifteen seconds," he said.

I nodded. As if I needed reminding that I had a finite amount of time to authenticate my identity before I'd become freeze-dried China.

He closed the door behind me and I hurried to the opposite wall. The freezer was empty save for another door on the opposite side with a more complex control panel.

"Authentication China Mack," I said, my teeth chattering, and pressed my palm to the flat, slate-gray screen. A green light scanned my palm, and an electronic voice said, "Voice recognition incomplete."

Shit.

I gritted my teeth to stop the chattering and tried again. "Authentication China Mack." We hadn't bothered programming in my real last name, since it was fifteen letters and had way too many consonants to be something that just rolled off the tongue. I'd gone by "China Mack"—a shortened form of my middle name, Mackenzie—for as long as I could remember.

This time, without the teeth chattering, it worked, and the door slid open with a hiss. Since the internal clock inside my head was nearing ten seconds, I rushed through to the stairway beyond, and the door swished shut behind me.

Three-flights-down later and I was stepping on the steel-terraced walkway that led to my office, then past that to another set of metal stairs down to the main floor of Vigilance.

Screens dominated the wall opposite, stretching from about six feet off the floor to the ceiling, twenty feet up. The screens were molded to the concave wall. Facing the wall was a three-tiered curved platform with workstations side by side on each level. Usually at this time of evening, only a third of the spots would be filled, but more people were trickling in. The shooting had brought everyone to work.

Derrick was huddling with Mazie, our head of perimeter network security. He saw me and they both shifted in my direction.

"Get the heads of every department in, if they're not here already," I said. "Meeting in the conference room in fifteen minutes."

They both nodded and scattered. I headed for The Black Box, which is what we called the room that housed backups of backups for everything we did. It wasn't a large room—only twenty by twenty—but it was lined with shelves holding hundreds of drives. Shepherd was on duty, and he looked as frazzled as ever. If the sky wasn't currently falling, it was always only a matter of time, according to him. And since currently the sky *was* falling, Shepherd was a wreck.

"Holy bejesus, boss, did you see? How could we have missed this? Do you think it was just a crazy person or maybe a terrorist? I bet it was Russia. It's like JFK all over again, only it's the Russian Mob instead of the Mafia. And I have the backups uploading already to our tertiary recovery cloud, just in case. Should I activate the emergency wipe procedure? Because I can, I—"

"Stop!" I had to interrupt him or I wouldn't get a word in edgewise. He was six foot five and as thin as a string bean. With wild, untamed curly hair and glasses a half-inch thick, he perpetually looked as though he didn't quite know what was going on. But he was meticulous in his job and took the backups as seriously as though the future of his own next breath depended on them.

"I just need you to upload all data centering around that area of DC from the last twenty-four hours," I said. "Surveillance footage from any shops, dashcams, stoplights—all of it. Look for patterns, the same people showing up, suspicious packages, the works."

"You got it."

"Thank you, Shep." I left him scrambling to do my bidding, and knew he'd have the uploads done in less than thirty minutes. Shepherd also had a one-track mind and was dizzyingly fast.

I'd compartmentalized my feelings from my work, but now I had time to think as I waited for people and information. I'd met the current president a few months ago, and had been a fan of his and his family ever since they stepped on the national scene.

President Blane Kirk was a no-nonsense kind of guy. Former Navy SEAL, trial litigator, and senator, he'd been elected to the highest office in the land two years ago. His wife, Anne, was America's own version of Kate Middleton and as close to gracious royalty as it was possible to be without an actual crown. They had twins, a boy and a girl, who were as adorable in person as they were in their photos. The thought that those kids might now be fatherless made my heart hurt.

I had a red phone in my office, which was a total cliché, but you couldn't mistake its meaning. A direct line to the president, fully encrypted. My goal was for it never to ring. A goal that was shattered by the shrill sound it suddenly emitted.

I grabbed the receiver, irrationally hoping to hear the president himself on the other end.

"What information do you have?" was how the conversation opened, and I didn't recognize the voice.

"Who is this?"

"Someone with access to the president's phone. You can call me Kade. Now start talking."

Now I knew who he was. Only rarely did anyone ever actually see Kade Dennon. He was rumored to be close to the president and have his confidence. We'd done a quick background on him a while back, just to be thorough, and there hadn't been much to find.

Outside the political scene entirely, Kade was not only drop-dead gorgeous, he had a look that made the Terminator appear to be as friendly as a flop-eared bunny by comparison. I didn't know what he'd done before becoming a close friend to the president. I just knew I'd never wanted to draw his attention or his ire.

"Um, shouldn't I be talking to the vice president?" Technically correct.

"He doesn't even know you exist," Kade snapped. "Now, someone took a shot at the president. Tell me you know something."

"We're working on it," I said. "How is he?"

"He's in surgery, but they say he'll be okay. I want to know who the hell did this."

"Sir, I understand how you feel—"

"You can't possibly," he snapped. "I want answers. Sooner rather than later." The line went dead.

An ass-chewing from the commander in chief's BFF. Hadn't been on my bucket list, and now I knew why.

My phone buzzed. It was Mia.

"Oh my God, have you heard?" she asked, her voice tight with strain. "I've been trying your cell for ages."

"I know, I'm sorry," I said. "I'm at work now and might not be home until late, so don't worry."

"Okay. I love you, Aunt Chi."

The phrase made me pause. Mia and I had grown close over the past six months that she'd been living with me, and I was suddenly glad that she could say something like that to me. "I love you, too. Get some rest. I'll see you in the morning."

When I arrived at the conference room, almost everyone was already there. I took a deep breath and settled into my chair.

The next hour was spent pulling together what information we had and piecing together surveillance video. The police and FBI had access to the same footage and were already broadcasting grainy shots of a figure wearing a hoodie whom they suspected of being involved. No one had a clear shot of his face, though.

"So there was no chatter, no warning, and nothing afterward?" I asked the room at large. We'd exhausted all our resources and had basically come to the same conclusion. "This was someone off the grid entirely?"

A truly nightmare scenario. Vigilance was excellent software and could comb through millions of terabytes of data to find the proverbial needle, but it could do nothing if there was no data to be had.

"The only talk I'm seeing is those just like us, speculating on who it could be and why."

"Okay," I said. "Let's get back to work. This gets a red-flag priority. We need to find who did this. I want everyone to set aside whatever else they're working on and devote all our resources to this."

Chairs scraped against the floor as everyone got up and left the room.

I was bone-tired and no new information was coming in. The adrenaline had worn off, leaving me feeling like a limp rag doll. After telling Derrick to notify me the moment anything of import was found and scheduling a meeting for first thing in the morning, I caught a cab home.

Mia was long since asleep, and the house was quiet. I hesitated to call Jackson this late and just sent a text instead, letting him know I was home and that I'd call in the morning.

Responsibility lay heavy on my shoulders as I passed through the darkened house. Weak winter moonlight filtered through the blinds. My thermostat was on a strict energy-conservation schedule, so it was also freezing. I shivered as I opened the refrigerator. Though I was tired, I knew I wouldn't sleep without a little help, so I poured myself a glass of white wine.

I didn't want anyone to get hurt—much less the leader of the free world—not when I was in a position to prevent it. But *being* in that position had never been something I wanted. My sole career goal had been to learn more and be on the cutting edge of technological development. I loved learning and creating. Writing computer code might not seem creative, but I begged to differ.

Now, I was no longer in the business of creating. I was in the business of law enforcement. And I didn't like it. Not one little bit. My path out was clouded with uncertainty, not least because the life expectancy while doing this job was questionable . . . at least, under the previous chief of staff. Now that I reported directly to the president, maybe he'd just make me sign my life away and move to Montana if I wanted to quit. I heard it was peaceful in Montana.

All of this was on my mind, as well as the dangling marriage proposal that Jackson and I had conspicuously *not* discussed earlier, as I climbed the stairs to my bedroom. My Doctor Who TARDIS nightlight shone bright enough to see by as I carefully slipped off my shoes and filed them in my closet. Setting my glasses on the bathroom counter, I wriggled out of my dress and washed the makeup off my face.

All I wanted was to go to work, do my job, and come home. Assassins and terrorists were beyond me. It had been bad enough when I'd been the target of terrorists and made to wear a suicide vest, then kidnapped and tortured by the Chinese—events that still haunted my nightmares. Maybe wanting to retreat into my little shell sounded selfish. I didn't know. I just knew that I felt how I felt.

My bra was a black satin demi-cup to match my bikini Use the Force panties, and I took a moment to sigh at the blurry image in the mirror. Limousine sex notwithstanding, this hadn't been how I'd envisioned my first Valentine's Day with a boyfriend ending.

I paused in the bathroom door, sliding my glasses back on and letting my eyes adjust to the darkness. The TARDIS sent pale light past me. I pushed my fingers through my hair, finding pins in it that I'd forgotten. I sighed and began removing them, the curls Mia had worked so hard on falling down my back. I rubbed my scalp when I was done, groaning a little. Who knew taking your hair down could feel so good?

"Okay, any more and I'm going to hell."

I yelped, my eyes flying open. Panic closed my throat at the sight of a dark form. I hadn't seen it before, but someone was in my room. Yet even as my pulse skyrocketed, a lamp flicked into life.

"Between that outfit and the metal bikini costume, I'm starting to think you have a serious sci-fi sex fetish."

"Clark," I breathed, grabbing onto the doorjamb to keep my suddenly jellified knees from collapsing.

Clark Slattery, my erstwhile employee and partner, who'd up and quit his job three months ago. I hadn't heard from him since, though he'd crossed my mind often. A dedicated loner who operated both inside and outside of the law, depending on which best suited him at the time, he'd saved my life on more than one occasion. A fact that didn't exactly endear me to him, since he'd rather not be responsible for anyone's well-being, least of all mine.

"Is that you?" I asked when he didn't reply. It would've been hard to mistake Clark for anyone else. He was the best parts of all the Hollywood incarnations of the Man of Steel, in one six-foot-two, musclebound, raven-haired, blue-eyed package. He even had the dimple in his cheek when he smiled, which wasn't often and certainly wasn't now.

"You terrified me," I said, my heart still racing.

"I wish I could say the same."

His words and the strange note in his voice made me scrutinize him more closely. He looked intense and . . . hungry.

"When was the last time you ate?" I asked, suddenly concerned. Had he lost weight? Maybe. It was hard to tell with him sitting, slouched like that with his knees spread. "Can I get you something? I have leftover Chinese. Mia got takeout even though it's not technically Chinese night—"

"I'm fine," he interrupted, his lips twitching in a wry smile. "I'm not really into . . . leftovers."

I grimaced. "I'm not either, but it's such a waste otherwise. They refuse to cut down their portions no matter how much I argue that it's physically impossible for someone of my size to consume that much food."

He didn't respond, just looked at me. A shiver fluttered across my skin.

"Do me a favor," he said. "Slide your glasses down your nose, look over the top, and say, 'You've been naughty, Mr. Slattery.'"

I looked at him, utterly confused. "Why would I do that?"

He shook his head. "Never mind," he said, getting up from his chair. He had on a leather jacket that he shrugged off. "Since you don't seem like you're going to put clothes on anytime soon, let me help."

I'd totally forgotten that I was standing there in my underwear, Clark's sudden appearance taking me so by surprise. I grasped his coat, grateful for the warmth. It still held the heat from his body.

"I can put my pajamas on," I said. "I was just distracted."

Clark grimaced. "That makes two of us."

"Why are you here?" I asked, pulling the edges of the jacket around me. The hem reached his hips, but was midthigh on me. "What's going on? Why haven't you called?"

Clark sighed and moved past me, leaving the bedroom and heading downstairs to the kitchen. I followed, the wooden floor cold on my bare feet.

"What are you doing? Are you leaving?"

He glanced back at me, his gaze running from head to toe before he answered. "No." Reaching into my refrigerator, he pulled out the bottle of wine I'd just opened and poured himself a hefty glass. Then he drank half of it in one long swallow.

I watched his throat move, his Adam's apple prominent, and the skin of his neck. He wore a black, long-sleeve, V-neck T-shirt that stretched across his shoulders and chest, outlining the curves of muscle beneath. Dark jeans covered his legs, and I could see a wide leather belt in the front where his shirt was tucked in, though the tail had come out.

I cleared my throat and lifted my eyes to his. Frowning, I stuck my hands on my hips. "Are you going to knock off the Man of Mystery thing or what? Because it's not like I don't have better things to do than play Twenty Questions with you."

"I need a place to crash tonight," he said.

"Why? Why can't you go home?" That gorgeous cabin/mansion in the woods that I'd been lucky enough to see. Once.

He finished his wine before answering. "Because someone's trying to kill me."

CH 3

Trying to kill me.

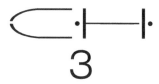

The words kind of hung in the air like a noxious odor. When I finally found my tongue, I asked, "What do you mean?"

Now, most might wonder why I'd go with that query, rather than the Who, What, and Where. But I knew Clark was perfectly capable of defending himself with lethal force, and had done so before. And for the record, his prowess in killing people wasn't something I usually dwelled on. What he *didn't* usually do was a) let himself get caught, and b) not finish the job.

"Let's just say that there was almost a nasty 'click-click-click' . . . hmm . . . 'click-click-click . . . boom' with my car."

"Boom? You mean your car blew up?"

"Would've. Luckily, the 'click-click-click' warned me in time."

Clark had almost been blown up. One part of my brain tried to process that while another part went through the ramifications. "Who's after you? And why? Was this the first time something like that has happened? Wait . . . someone's trying to kill you and you came *here*?" My voice rose as each question only panicked me more.

He winced. "Okay, only dogs can hear you. Take it down a notch."

"I won't take it down a notch," I argued, lowering my voice anyway. "You realize that Mia, *my niece*, lives with me. If you've put her in danger—"

"Relax," he interrupted me. "You should know I wouldn't do *anything* to put you or her at risk."

The sharpness of his reply silenced me, and his sincerity eased my concern. But still—

"Who is it? Who's after you?"

He shook his head. "I don't know. I'd tell you if I did, trust me."

That struck something inside that had been hurting ever since he'd walked out of my life three months ago.

"Trust you," I retorted. "Trust you? You left with barely more than a 'Have a nice life.' I thought we were friends. Partners. Then you . . . you . . ." *Kissed me* was on the tip of my tongue, but I was still in heavy denial about that particular incident, so I skipped right to Stammering Incoherence. "And now you just show up here in the dead of night and expect me to welcome you with open arms?" I was proud of using that last idiom correctly. I'd been working on my idioms and colloquial phrases, since I had a tendency to take people's words literally.

Clark set his wineglass on the counter. "If you want me to go, I'll go. But I don't do apologies. And I don't explain myself to anyone. I like it that way. So just say the word and you'll never have to see me again."

The part of me that had ached at the sight of him now gave a sharp stab of pain at his last sentence. *Never have to see me again.* It made something anxious flare inside. My hands fisted in the folds of his leather jacket, holding it tighter.

"I didn't say you had to leave, just that I didn't have to be overjoyed at your presence," I said stiffly.

"Well, that's good, because you don't *seem* overjoyed." His dry tone and the roll of his eyes clued me in to the sarcasm. He retrieved the bottle of wine from the fridge and emptied the rest of it into his glass. "Got anything stronger?"

"You know I don't drink much," I said, reaching inside the cabinet for my ever-present package of Fig Newtons. I was in need of my nightly fix. I bit into one and offered the package to Clark, who grimaced.

"No, thanks. Doesn't go with the wine."

"So what exactly do you want from me?" I asked, finishing off exactly two Newtons. I wanted a third but limited myself to two.

"Just need a place to crash for tonight," he said with a shrug. "I won't be in the way."

I seriously doubted that. "I don't have another bedroom, and my office doesn't have a bed in it." Mia had taken the one remaining room and converted it into a teenage girl-cave.

"Couch will work. I'm not picky." He quirked an eyebrow at me. "You're not going to start getting all twitchy on me, are you? Upsetting your routine?"

"Don't be ridiculous. And I don't twitch." Not unless he started using *seen* instead of *saw* or demanded I change the scent of my laundry detergent.

Opening the linen closet underneath the stairs, I pulled out a set of sheets, a thick blanket, and a pillow. Heading to the couch, I said, "Don't touch the thermostat and hang up your towels."

"Gotta say, you've become pretty flexible." He glanced at my fish tank. "You've even managed to keep the Doctor alive, I see."

I flinched at the mention of the lone goldfish swimming in the depths and started tucking a sheet over the couch cushions. "Ah, well . . ."

He quirked a dark eyebrow. "Which number are we on now?"

Rubbing my forehead, I mumbled, "Nine."

Clark's low chuckle made me smile a little, too. It was almost impossible not to. He looked as though he'd stepped from the pages of my favorite Superman comic. Except the Man of Steel didn't have the wicked glint in his eye that Clark sported in his baby blues.

It felt good to have him back. As bristly as his personality was, he was one of only two people I considered to be my close friends.

"Fresh towels are under the sink in the bathroom," I said briskly, returning to my task. "You're free to help yourself to anything to eat if you're hungry. Watch TV if you want. Just don't delete any of my recordings." I was two episodes behind on *Castle*. "Please use the Poo-Pourri before any BMs, and I don't like dirty dishes left on the counter."

"The poo what?"

Not wanting to go into details of the exact chemical reaction that occurred when using the product, I just said over my shoulder, "It's in the bathroom. You can read the instructions."

The corners were tight and I started tucking the blanket in, leaning over to reach the far side.

"Enough."

The sudden sharp word startled me upright, and I spun to face Clark. He'd moved up behind me, and the look in his eye made my breath freeze in my chest.

"The striptease earlier was bad enough," he said, his voice low, "but I don't need more reminders of . . . *Star Trek*."

He was close enough that I could see the pulse beating underneath his jaw, and I had to tip my head back to meet his gaze. I could smell the slight tang of his skin, and his eyes were so very blue. It hurt to look at him, he was so beautiful. When I was caught off guard—like now—he took my breath away.

"Um, it's *Star Wars*," I managed, nervously pushing my glasses up my nose. "Not *Star Trek*." An unforgivable sin, confusing the two, not that Clark looked like he'd heard a word I said.

"You're like a piece of candy that's just out of reach," he said softly. Now I felt a soft touch on the outside of my thigh, his fingers sliding up underneath the hem of the jacket I wore to skim the skin at the edge of my panties.

Surprise froze me and I had to swallow from a suddenly dry mouth. "Don't," I managed to say. "We're partners and friends. That's all." I still remembered the wry finality in his voice when he'd said those same words to Jackson. "That's all we'll ever be. Remember?" I didn't think I sounded bitter, but he winced ever so slightly.

"Shhh. I'm just stealing a moment. Something I can replay inside my head when I'm alone." His hand cupped my cheek, and not the one on my face. I could feel the heat of his touch through the thin satin. "I'm alone . . . a lot. I never thought it would bother me." He sounded vaguely surprised.

"Everybody needs friends."

"Do you?"

"Of course I do," I replied, trying to ignore his touch. I sidled away a bit and his hand dropped. "I need to be needed, just like anyone else."

Clark's brows drew together. "A need to be needed. That helps you get up in the morning?"

"My alarm clock gets me up in the morning," I said. "But Mia needs me, and Bonnie needs me—since I'm one of her only friends who'll test her lackluster cooking skills. My job needs me." I paused. "*Jackson* needs me." The reminder of my boyfriend made Clark's gaze narrow. "Whereas you obviously *don't* need me, because you left without a backward glance."

He stepped away to sit on the couch. Elbows on his knees, he pushed a hand through his hair, which fell perfectly into place. How he'd gone this long without a long-term relationship, I had no idea. Women probably fell all over themselves to get at him. When he didn't reply, I headed for the stairs, unsure what else to say or do.

"I do."

His words froze me on the second step. I glanced over to where he sat. The room was shadowed with just a lamp lit, and I couldn't see the expression on his face.

"You do what?" I asked.

"Need you."

I didn't move and neither did he, though the air between us felt heavy with unsaid things. Our gazes were locked, and I searched for something to say.

"I don't understand you, Clark," I said at last. "And I don't know what you want from me. Why are you here, really?"

He took a deep breath. "I need your help."

Something inside me crumpled, deflating like a balloon after a few days until it was shriveled and shrunk. For a moment, I'd thought . . . well, I didn't know what I'd thought. But Clark was my friend, and he'd just admitted to needing my help. To my knowledge, the only time he'd ever done so. I went back down the steps and took a seat beside him on the sofa.

"Talk to me."

Clark settled back against the cushions, rubbing his jaw with one hand while he stared into space. "It was a long time ago," he said. "Or at least, it feels like it."

"Why? What happened?"

He glanced at me, his eyes flicking down to my bare knees and thighs, then looked away. My cheeks warmed and I thought I should probably run upstairs and put some clothes on, but then he started talking.

"I used to be in the Army, which you know. What you don't know is that some of what I did was in special ops. There was a job I did about six years ago. There were five of us who were tasked with getting into Bab al-Azizia."

"Where?" My geography wasn't as good as my math skills.

"It's in southern Tripoli," Clark clarified. "And was Muammar Gaddafi's headquarters."

Ah. Okay. Gaddafi. Tyrant of Libya until his execution in 2011. "Why did you have to go there? Wasn't it dangerous?"

Clark gave me a look that said he still had doubts as to my IQ, despite the fact that I'd shown him my score numerous times. "Just a little," he deadpanned. "Our mission was to get in and steal documents and secret recordings that proved the United States had helped keep Gaddafi in power. Between him or Al Qaeda, we came down on the side of the lesser evil."

"Why did it matter who kept him in power?"

"Because he killed and tortured thousands of his own people," Clark replied. "It would have looked very bad had the United States been seen helping to prolong his rule. Especially in light of the Arab Spring going on at the time. Effectively, we helped keep him in power two years longer than it might otherwise have been."

"So did you get what you went in for?" I asked.

He nodded. "Yeah, but it went to shit. The tech guys were supposed to shut down the security system, but they only did half their job. We barely made it out." He paused. "Not everyone did."

My eyes widened. The regret and sadness on his face was unmistakable. Reaching out, I tentatively touched his hand. "I'm so sorry."

He shrugged and cleared his throat. "It's in the past. The problem is that someone knows about it, that mission, and I think they're . . . hunting . . . us. Killing the remainder of the team, one by one."

Clark's eyes met mine and I went cold all over. The idea of someone hunting him down—

"What can I do to help?"

"I need to find the rest of the team and who else knew about the mission. Only you have the kind of access and skills it'll take to get that information."

"It'll be classified. Probably Top Secret."

"I know."

"I could be fired."

"That's a distinct possibility."

We stared at each other. As Clark was someone who tried never to depend on anyone or ask for anything, I understood that this was a Big Deal for him. He prided himself on being a one-man show. When he'd left Vigilance, he'd told me it was because he didn't want to have to worry about someone else, a partner, and fail.

"Why didn't you tell me this right away?" I asked.

"I hadn't decided whether or not to ask you."

"Why not? I'm your friend. Why wouldn't I help you?"

"It's not that I didn't think you would," he said. "It's that I didn't want to ask it of you." He hesitated. "I'm . . . unused to needing anyone, as you put it."

He looked so pained at having to admit that, I almost chuckled. Instead, I squeezed his hand, slotting our fingers together, and smiled.

"I'm glad you asked. And of course I'll help you. No one's going to kill you on my watch." I said it lightly, but I meant it with every fiber in my five-foot-two-inch body. If Clark needed to know who was after him, then by God I'd find out.

"You can't tell Coop," he warned. "The fewer people who know, the better."

I squirmed a little on the inside at the idea of keeping something like this from Jackson, but I nodded. "Okay."

"You are still together, right?" he asked. "Or did you dump him for some hot personal trainer?"

I laughed at the thought of trying to maintain a conversation with a personal trainer. "Right. Please. Yes, we're still together." I hesitated, then added, "Tonight he even . . . proposed." It was the first time I'd said it out loud, and it felt very strange.

Clark's face took on an expression I couldn't read, though I was familiar with *happy*, and it didn't look like that. "Wow. I guess I should say congratulations, then." He extricated his hand from mine and pushed his fingers again through his hair. "So, um, when's the big day?"

"Actually, I haven't answered yet." A minor detail, that.

"You're going to say yes, right?"

"Um, yeah. I mean, I should, so I guess I will."

Clark snorted. "You might want to muster up a little more enthusiasm when you talk to Coop."

"I know, it's just . . ." I struggled to put my feelings into words, always a painful task. "I never really thought about getting married. Unlike the cliché, I haven't been planning my wedding since I was six. Jackson is in such a hurry to settle down, I don't know what he expects from me. I mean, will I have to stop working? Is he going to want kids right away? I don't even know if I *want* kids. What if they turn out just like me?"

"You say that like it would be a bad thing."

I looked at him. "I wouldn't want to inflict the kind of childhood I had on my own kid. My mom was the only one who understood me, and she passed away when I was eight. Having a kid, being a mom . . . I just don't know."

"I take it you and Coop haven't had this discussion."

I shook my head. "It hasn't come up."

"Maybe you should have that conversation before answering his proposal."

Just thinking of doing that made my palms sweat and my ears ring. "I-I can't do that."

"Why not?"

"Because," I said, "we might not agree. And this isn't the kind of difference of opinion like which Chinese restaurant is the best or who's the best Doctor." David Tennant, obviously. "This is something that could end our relationship."

"And if it does?"

That anxious panic I'd fought earlier returned with a vengeance. "Jackson is a fixture in my life. I can't just go and . . . *change* that. I've gone through too much to get here. I never even had a boyfriend before him. What if we break up and there's no one else who likes me again, ever? I don't want to be alone."

"China—"

"I don't want to talk about this anymore," I interrupted, jumping to my feet. "I'll start looking in the morning to see what I can find. Just write down any details that could help me." I hurried to the stairs.

"Wait, China—"

"Oh yeah. Sorry. Here you go." I tossed his jacket to him, and he caught it, then I turned and ran up the steps.

I changed into my winter *Star Wars: Hoth* pajamas and climbed into bed, pulling the blankets up underneath my arms just so. Time to go to sleep. Except I just stared at the ceiling.

◆ ◆ ◆

The next morning, Mia was waiting for me in the kitchen. "You do know that Clark is here, right?" she asked, sliding a plate of scrambled eggs and toast in front of me.

"Yes. He came by last night and needed a place to stay." I glanced around. "Where is he?"

"He's in *my* shower," she complained. "Getting boy germs all over it."

"I told him about the Poo-Pourri," I said, sitting down opposite her.

"Thank God," she grumbled, shoving a forkful of eggs into her mouth.

We ate in companionable silence. Mia, I had found, could make amazing scrambled eggs. She said her secret was that she didn't rush them, letting them cook slowly as she stirred them to fluffy perfection. I'd thought about telling Bonnie about Mia's cooking secret, but Mia had assured me that Bonnie wouldn't appreciate the advice.

I opened the paper and pulled out the Lifestyle section, handing it to Mia, who passed me the front page of her paper. They all carried the story of the assassination attempt last night, and said the police were still searching for the suspect but that the president would recover. We ate and read in silence.

"So how was last night?" she asked when she was finished. "I mean, up until the president was shot."

"Oh my God, I just remembered." I scrambled out of my chair and grabbed my silver clutch, opening it and carefully removing the velvet case inside. "Jackson gave me these."

My smugness must've clued her in that it was something big because she eased open the lid as though expecting to see the Hope Diamond inside. It took her a moment of shocked disbelief, then she clapped a hand over her mouth. She looked at me, her eyes as wide as saucers.

"Yep. It's really them," I assured her.

"This is so amazing . . . wow. Best Valentine's gift ever, right?"

I nodded. "I couldn't believe it either." Taking our plates to the counter, I rinsed them off. "And he proposed, too." The dishwasher was nearly full, but I saw just enough space on the bottom rack—

"What?"

I nearly dropped the plates at her sudden shriek.

"Jackson *proposed*? And you didn't lead with that?" She was still talking really loud.

"Well, I—"

"You're getting married!" She threw her arms around me. "That's amazing! I'm so happy for you!"

I didn't know what to say, even if I could speak. She was squeezing me so hard, it was difficult to breathe. "Can't . . . breathe . . . ," I managed. Mia let go immediately.

"Can I be a bridesmaid? Please?" she begged.

"Um, yeah, of course, but—"

"Awesome!" Another rib-cracking hug. "Just wait until Granny hears. She's going to be tickled pink. But don't worry. I won't spoil it.

I'll let you tell her." She glanced at her phone. "Oh, crap. I'm going to be late for school. Jen's picking me up."

With an air kiss and a flurry of blond hair, she was past me and out the door, a cloud of flowery perfume left in her wake.

"Choosing bridesmaids already? I thought you had to say yes first."

I glanced up at where Clark stood at the top of the stairs. He had a towel around his neck, another around his waist, and that was all.

Wow, was the first thought in my head, which was really the only correct response to a near-naked, damp Clark. The next thought was, *Isn't he cold?* Which was the one I ended up voicing.

"Aren't you cold? It's February."

"I take very hot showers."

That provoked more images I didn't need. Shaking my head, I firmly set my gaze back on the dishes that still needed loading. I had a boyfriend, maybe even a fiancé. I didn't need to be drooling over another man, no matter how drool-worthy he might be.

"So, when you gonna talk to Coop?"

I jumped, startled. How he'd come up behind me without me hearing anything was beyond me. For a big guy, he could move as silently as a cat. I mean, I assumed cats were pretty quiet. I'd never owned one, but that was one of those idioms again.

"Um, I, uh . . ." I struggled to focus on what he'd asked. Clark was currently pouring a cup of coffee for himself, and he'd left one of his two towels in the bathroom. I had a brief flash of regret that it had been the one around his neck. "I mean, yeah . . . at some point. There are more important things on our plate right now."

He was leaning against the counter, one hand braced on the edge, the other holding his coffee. The morning light dappled across his chest, and I suddenly found a pressing need to reorganize the utensils in the silverware drawer. Mia had put the soup spoons with the regular spoons, which was wrong wrong wrong.

"So you're just going to keep him in suspense?"

Salad forks didn't belong with dinner forks . . .

"I doubt he's in suspense," I said, moving cutlery. "Men don't usually ask that question without knowing the answer. I would guess he assumes my answer is the affirmative."

"But it's not."

"I didn't say that."

"You didn't say yes either."

A knock at the door interrupted the conversation I didn't want to be having anyway. I hurried to look through the peephole. I jerked back and clapped my hands over my mouth.

"Mmph," I mumbled.

"Who is it?" Clark asked, coming up next to me. He'd left the coffee behind and now held a gun. I had no idea where he'd gotten it. Not a lot else could possibly fit underneath that towel.

"It's Jackson," I hissed. "He can't see you. Not here. And especially not like . . . *that*."

Clark's lips twisted. "I didn't think you'd noticed."

The knock came again, more insistent. "China? Are you there?" Jackson called through the door.

"You have to hide." I grabbed Clark's arm and pulled open the coat closet. "In here."

"You've got to be kidding me," he groused.

Jackson knocked again, harder. "China?"

"Just get in!" I put my palms on his chest and pushed, which was a mistake. The minute my skin touched his, I sucked in my breath and froze. His flesh was warm and his muscles rock hard. I was standing too close and we were both inside the closet, shrouded in darkness. His eyes seemed to glow in the low light, his gaze locked on mine.

For a moment, I didn't breathe. I could only think of how close he was and how very little he was wearing. There had always been an energy between Clark and me, but it had transformed into a friendship and partnership. Now it was morphing again, and I wasn't ready.

Jerking away, I slammed the door in his face, then spun to open the front door. Jackson looked worried, then relieved, when he saw me.

"S-sorry," I stammered, pushing my glasses up my nose. "I was . . . upstairs." I took a breath. "What are you doing here?"

His brows lifted. "Seriously? After last night, did you think I was just going to let you go to work today?"

I stared at him, flummoxed. "What else am I supposed to do?"

"Come with me."

"Come with you where?"

"Nebraska."

Surely I'd misheard him. "Nebraska? What's in Nebraska?" I asked.

"Your family."

Okay, that shut me up. Jackson must've read the confusion on my face, because he said, "I thought, if we're getting married, we need to meet your family."

So much was wrong with that sentence, I couldn't process it all at once. "I'm not going to Nebraska. I have to go to work."

He sighed. "I figured you'd say that. Fine. I'll take you. We'll discuss it on the way."

Yay.

"Let's go," I said, grabbing my backpack and coat from the chair by the door. I followed Jackson out, leaving a nearly naked Clark hidden in my closet. I decided that my routine wasn't just *off* today—it was descending into soap-opera territory.

CH 4

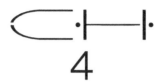

"I can't do this right now," I argued with Jackson on the way to Vigilance. We were in the back seat of his car, and Lance was driving. "There's too much to be done. The president's . . ." *BFF* didn't sound right. ". . . staff will want an update, and I have to have something to give them." Anything to avoid the topic of marriage.

"Any thoughts on who might have done it?"

"Not yet. But I'm hoping the Secret Service and my staff will have more information today."

Jackson pulled me over so that I straddled his lap. "I missed you last night. It wasn't exactly how I'd planned on ending our evening. So, which fandom are you wearing today?" His hands were on my hips and he spread open my coat so he could see my T-shirt. *"Team Moose,"* he read.

"It was either this or my *Wibbly Wobbly Timey Wimey* one," I said. "I went for simple. And Mia freaked over the glasses." I laughed. "I think you've earned sainthood in her book."

"That'll be the only book where I earn that particular designation," he said wryly.

Jackson looked good today, going casual with jeans and a navy sweater layered over a striped button-down shirt. His hair was a bit askew from running his fingers through it. Unlike Clark's hair, which always fell perfectly back into place when he did that.

Clark. Not a good thing to be thinking about right now.

"You look yummy," I said, forcing my thoughts to the here and now. Leaning in, I kissed him. A slow, sweet, good-morning kiss that smelled of his aftershave and tasted of coffee.

"Yummy?" he asked when we parted.

"Yep. I could eat you up. I mean, not literally, but I've been working on idioms and euphemisms."

"Excellent work."

"Thank you," I said, pleased at the compliment on my progress. "So where are you going to be today? Cysnet? Or working from home?" His "real" company that did "real" work, as opposed to SocialSpeak, the social network he'd invented that had made him a multimillionaire.

"Yes. I have several meetings, and work that can't be done remotely."

"Okay. Text me later." I kissed him again as the car pulled to a stop. I hopped out, but Jackson snagged my hand, stopping me.

"You forgot this," he said. And before I knew it, he'd slid the diamond ring onto my finger. It fit perfectly. Jackson's smile was brilliant.

"Right," I said, forcing my fake smile. "Gotta go."

Lance had dropped me off at the "official" entrance to Vigilance via the parking garage. I had to swipe my ID, my palm print, then be scanned for physical anomalies that didn't match the profile on record before being allowed inside. Not wanting to answer anyone's questions, I slipped the engagement ring into the pocket of my jeans.

Meetings and e-mail consumed my morning, though the reports were dismal. No one could find a digital footprint that led to the perpetrator, and the Secret Service wasn't sharing any information that they had.

"So basically, we're no better off than we were last night," I said to the room at large. All the department heads were gathered around the conference room, and we'd spent the better part of three hours going through stacks of information that all led to the same place: nowhere.

"Sorry, boss," Roscoe said, looking even more droopy than usual. Eeyore was his spirit animal.

It was frustrating to be in such a position and not know what to do next. Vigilance was a secret organization that had no public profile. We didn't show up at crime scenes and investigate. We collected and analyzed data, then handed over what we found to those who took care of such matters. When Clark had worked there, we'd had a quasi-military arm that he'd directed. I'd closed that division down once he'd left, uncomfortable with replacing him, especially since the legality of those kinds of operations was rather dubious.

"Has the FBI discovered anything?" I asked Tessa, our liaison between Vigilance and other government offices.

"Forensics is working on it, but nothing yet," she said.

"Okay, then, unless something else comes up, it's business as usual." I got up and everyone else began gathering their things as well.

I headed back to my office, hoping Scary BFF Kade didn't call me again. Maybe I could earn my salary by helping Clark, starting with the list he'd given me.

It wasn't much to go on. He'd written down six names. Logging on to my computer, I went to work.

Hours later, my searches came back with mixed results. They weren't easy people to find, and it wasn't as though I was just Googling. I had access to not only Vigilance, but FBI databases and municipal law enforcement, too. I stuffed my research inside my backpack so I could take it to Clark. Some of it wasn't good and only increased my worry for him.

I rubbed my eyes underneath my glasses. I was tired and starving. I'd worked through lunch and hadn't stopped except to snag a Red Bull from the break room's fridge. Speaking of which, it was time for another one.

I was in the break room when it happened.

Loud noises, shouting, lots of booted feet on the metal staircase. People were here who weren't supposed to be.

Instinctively, I yanked open the supply-closet door and tucked myself inside. It wasn't big, but then again, neither was I. Crouching down amid the stacks of paper towels and cartons of coffee creamer, I listened and waited, my heart in my throat.

I could hear loud arguing, but no gunshots. Lots of footsteps went by, the steel mesh staircase and suspended walkways reverberating with the traffic. I pondered what to do. My cell was on my desk and there was no phone in the break room.

It grew quiet and still I waited. It had felt like forever, though the clock inside my head said more like twenty-three minutes. I couldn't stay here all night. I needed to get back to my desk and my phone.

My office was one corridor away, but it felt like a mile. Every step I took had me wincing, waiting for someone to hear me. The normal hubbub of a full office was absent, giving the whole place the menacing quality of an empty high school at night.

Someone was already there, in my office. I could see the light was on as I hesitated at the corner. A man's arm, resting on my desk, was visible from my vantage point, but nothing else. I stood for a moment, then made a decision. This was *my* department and that was *my* office. Whoever had usurped it and terrorized my staff would have to answer for it.

Stiffening my spine, I stopped creeping and marched to my door and swept inside. I faltered for only a second when I saw who sat at my desk.

"About time you showed up," the president's BFF said to me. He hadn't even bothered to glance up from the computer monitor. "Have a seat." He gestured to the two chairs opposite him.

"You're in it," I retorted, folding my arms over my chest.

He did look up then, and the coolness in his gaze made me rethink my minor rebellion. Kade Dennon wasn't someone you crossed, I bet. At least, not twice. I sat.

"We have a bit of a situation," he said.

"We were working on it, until your men cleared out my people."

"I'm not a fan of kid gloves when dealing with terrorists."

"We're not the guilty party here," I protested.

"No, but you employed one. Maybe more."

That stopped me. I frowned in confusion. "What are you talking about?"

"We have intelligence that Clark Slattery was behind the assassination attempt."

I stared at him, trying to process what he was saying. "That . . . that's impossible. Clark is military—"

"Ex-military," Dennon interrupted. "The best kind for wetwork."

"I know him," I said. "He would never do something like that. I don't know what intelligence you have, but I would seriously consider the veracity and reliability of your source."

"Right now, you should be more worried about how reliable I find *you*." He leaned back in my chair and folded his hands, surveying me, the look in his eye glacial. My mouth went dry.

"What is that supposed to mean?"

"It means, you've had unprecedented access to a great deal of information. Just a few months ago, you were in a situation with a nation known for their hostile intentions toward the United States. How do we know you weren't compromised?"

Anger surged inside me and I gripped the arms of the chair to keep my control. "The Chinese beat and threatened me," I gritted out. "Now you're accusing me of working for them?"

"Pain and threats work," he replied evenly. "Or else no one would use them."

I took a breath. "I see." My voice was icy. "So now not only are you accusing Clark of plotting to kill the president, I'm under suspicion, too?" Nice to know I was valued.

"You're dangerous," Dennon said with a shrug. "And my job is to protect the president."

"Isn't that the Secret Service's job?"

His sharp gaze narrowed. "I take a . . . personal interest in his safety."

"I'm not planning anything, nor am I working for anyone who is," I said.

He flicked a switch on the computer in front of him and swiveled the screen so I could see. It was grainy security footage. I saw the same figure we'd seen before, only this time, he turned and I got a glimpse of his face. The picture froze on the screen, then enlarged, showing someone who looked very much like Clark in the black-and-white footage.

"That-that can't be," I stammered, staring at the grainy image. "Clark would never do that. He'd never try to assassinate someone."

"Then what am I looking at?"

"I don't know, but that can't be him. Or . . . the footage has been altered somehow. But Clark would never try to kill President Kirk."

"Trust me," Dennon said. "With the right incentive, anyone will do anything." Something about the way he said that made me think he had personal experience.

"So, if you think Clark's the sniper, why are you shutting us down? We can find him."

"I don't trust you, or that Vigilance hasn't been compromised. Until we find out, you're closed for business."

"And how am I supposed to prove that I'm one of the good guys? Take a lie-detector test?" Which was beatable, but still.

He rolled his eyes. "Please. As if I'd trust that thing. No, you're going to prove you're not involved by finding Clark Slattery and handing him over. To me."

I went still. "Hand him over to you . . . for what?"

"That's above your pay grade. Just do as you're told."

"And I won't get hurt?" I added.

Dennon smiled, but it wasn't a friendly smile. "I didn't say that. Just do your job."

"How? You've taken away the best tool we have."

"You're a smart girl, China. You'll figure it out."

I left Vigilance through the "front" door, escorted by two men with guns. The locks clicked shut and somehow I doubted my ID card would get me back in. I had the heebie-jeebies. The Men in Black hadn't exactly been friendly or chatty.

My phone buzzed with a text message, and I picked it up.

Meet me across the street. Usual place.

Okay, the number was one I didn't know, and "usual place" was ubiquitous. I texted back, Who is this?

I used the Poo-Pourri.

Ah. Clark.

Okay.

The sun had long since set, which meant I went to work and came home in the dark. I jogged across the street to the little Italian eatery, grateful for the tomato-scented warm air that enveloped me when I stepped inside. Clark was sitting at the far-corner red-and-white checked table with his back to the wall. I hurried over, pulled out the spindly wooden chair, and sat down.

"I ordered for you," Clark said. He was in his usual jeans, T-shirt, and leather jacket. I wondered if he had several leather jackets that were all the same and he alternated, or if it was just the one.

"I haven't told you what I wanted," I said. "How could you possibly order for me?"

His eye roll was epic. "I've never seen you eat anything but the same kind of pizza. I took a guess."

Just then the waitress arrived, setting a cola and a cannoli in front of me.

"I can't eat this first," I protested. "It's dessert." But she was already gone.

"Have dessert first," he said. "Life's short."

I looked at him, then the cannoli, then him again. I picked up the fork.

"How'd the search go?" he asked. His eyes flicked beyond me, constantly moving and watching. His posture looked casual, but I knew he was tense and alert.

"I have some bad news, and some worse news," I said through a mouthful of cannoli. "Which do you want first?"

"You pick."

"Two of the men you listed are deceased."

There was a moment before Clark replied, which I supposed was all the emotional response he was going to give.

"Who?"

"Taggert and Williams," I said. "Taggert a month ago. Williams two weeks ago."

"How?"

"Taggert was a car wreck. Williams drowned."

"He drowned? That makes no sense. He was a Navy SEAL."

"It's what the police report said." The cannoli was nearly gone.

"What about the other two?" he asked.

I shoved the last of the cannoli in my mouth, then dug in my backpack, pulling out the stack of papers. "One is still in the service and currently deployed. One, William Buckton, runs a security firm." I spread the papers on the table.

"Where is he?" he asked, picking up a stack and flipping through it.

"Omaha."

"And what about the operation?"

"There's nothing about any kind of infiltration into Bab al-Azizia," I said. "It's nonexistent. There was nothing anywhere, not even a whisper or trace. If there are any records, they're on paper only, or very well hidden."

Clark grimaced. "That's unfortunate."

The waitress arrived with our pizza, and I cleared a place for it. It was half-and-half, with my half being just pepperoni and Clark's half being every meat they had in the place.

"What's the other news?" he asked.

I slid a dripping slice onto my plate. "The Secret Service has video footage and thinks you're the sniper who tried to kill the president."

That got a reaction. He'd been reaching for his own slice and stopped.

"Excuse me? What did you say?"

"I don't know how, but your face is on security footage of the building the sniper fired from."

"I'm not a sniper."

"I guess they think otherwise," I said through a mouthful of cheese. "The footage has probably been doctored, but he wouldn't let us examine it. Apparently, I'm under suspicion, too. If I find you, I'm to turn you over to them."

"Is that what you're planning to do?"

I took another bite. "Of course not," I mumbled. "Proving your innocence after they already have you in custody would be pretty difficult."

Leaving the edge of crust on my plate, I reached for more, then noticed Clark still wasn't eating. "Did they make it incorrectly?" I asked. "We can have them make it again. I only ate one slice."

He shook his head, his lips twitching in an odd sort of smile. "Sometimes you surprise me, that's all." Finally, he took a slice of pizza and bit off a chunk.

"Because I don't meet your expectations of my behavior?"

"Because you exceed them."

I wasn't sure what to say to that. It sounded like a compliment . . . but Clark didn't give compliments. I decided a change of subject was the best response and the one I was most comfortable with.

"Do you think one of the other members of the team is after you?" I asked. "It can't be a coincidence that two of the names you gave me are deceased so recently."

"I don't know. Maybe. Though why they'd wait until now is a mystery. It's been six years." He picked up a second slice and demolished half of it with two bites.

My cell buzzed. Jackson was calling.

"Where are you?" he asked when I answered.

"Eating pizza," I replied. "You still at work?"

"It's not pizza night," he said. "And, yes, I need to work late tonight, but I didn't want you stranded at work."

I sucked down some Coke before replying. "It's fine. I'll have Mia come get me." I'd finally allowed her to start driving my Mustang occasionally. So long as I wasn't with her at the time, I could handle it.

"So why the break from routine?" Jackson asked. "You never have pizza on a Friday."

"Uh . . ." The reason was something I couldn't tell him—that I was with Clark and he'd been the one to choose the restaurant. "I guess I was just craving pizza." I winced. It didn't matter if I was craving something. My nightly dinner schedule was printed on card stock and laminated. For real. Luckily, Jackson seemed to accept that.

"Okay, well, I'll call you later. Text me when you get home, please. I want to make sure you get home safe."

"Will do. Bye." I ended the call, going back to my pizza. Clark was studying me.

"What?" I asked. "Do I have sauce on my chin?" I dabbed my mouth with a napkin.

He shook his head. "I thought you would've told him."

"About you?" I frowned. "You told me not to. Why would I tell him?"

"Loyalty."

"I don't understand," I said, a bit exasperated. "You think I'm being disloyal to Jackson because I'm keeping my promise to you? That makes no sense."

"I don't mean it as a bad thing," he said, reaching for more pizza. "I just didn't think you'd pick loyalty to me over loyalty to Coop."

I started on my third slice, mulling over what he'd said. This wasn't my usual pizza place, but it was pretty good. "The consequences of disloyalty are much higher for you at the moment. My decisions are logical."

"Yeah, that's what I was thinking," he said, deadpan.

I studied him as I chewed, trying to figure out what he was thinking, and failed. "Shouldn't you be in hiding or something? Especially if someone is after you and already knows you're here in Raleigh. And now the government is after you, too."

"Thought you might need a ride home from work. And I've left a false trail out of here, heading west."

"So now what? You're just going to run forever, hiding?"

He looked at me as though I'd just asked him to wear a miniskirt and hula hoop. "Of course not," he said. "I'm buying time. I need to speak to the guy you found, see what he knows. I'll head to Omaha tonight."

Alarm shot through me and I put down the pizza I was about to take a bite out of. "By yourself?"

"I work alone. You know that." He sat back in his chair, apparently finished eating.

"I don't think you should go by yourself," I said, shaking my head.

"You offering to ride shotgun?"

I wiped my hands on my napkin. "It's not a bad idea."

"I'd be hard-pressed to think of a worse one."

I glared at him. "Listen, I just helped you out. And chances are, I could help you more if you take me with you. I'm not asking to be Robin to your Batman. Just that it's not always best to work alone. Maybe you should rethink your policy."

"My policy keeps you safe," he said.

"Unless you're planning on locking me inside a bubble, I'm not safe. No one is. Not really. I have a higher likelihood of a heart attack than being killed just because I'm with you."

"That's debatable," he argued, picking up the check the waitress dropped off and reaching for his wallet.

"Here," I said, digging in my backpack and handing him a twenty. But he didn't take it, instead focusing on my wallet.

"What does that say? Slayer?"

I looked at my black-and-white wallet. "Yeah. I got it off Etsy. See? The zipper pouches inside have Spike's image all over, and it says *Slayer* everywhere else. Cool, right?"

Clark's expression was pained.

"What? Are you okay? Do you need some Tums or something? Sometimes the tomato sauce gives me heartburn, too."

But he just waved my concern aside. "Never mind. And keep your money. I can at least buy you dinner after you let me crash at your place last night."

"Oh." That made sense. "Okay, then." I stuffed the money back into my wallet, and wallet back into my backpack. "Take me home?" We could argue there about my going with him.

I followed Clark outside, where he led me to a motorcycle. I looked at him.

"You've got to be kidding."

He grabbed a helmet and tried to hand it to me. "Am I laughing?"

"Listen, I'll just take an Uber home—"

"You're scared of riding a motorcycle?"

"Absolutely. Anyone in their right mind would be. The fatality rate of motorcycle crashes compared to passenger vehicles is over five times higher." I'd planted my feet on the ground and grabbed onto the light pole just for good measure.

"I'm not letting you out of my sight, so you have no choice," Clark said, taking off my glasses.

I grabbed for them, but missed. "What are you doing? You know I can't see."

He slid them inside his jacket. "It'll be better this way."

"No. Clark, I do not want to ride a motorcycle." I latched onto the pole with both hands now, which he began peeling away, finger by finger.

"You'll be fine. I promise. You just hang on to me and close your eyes."

I was breathing too fast and spots started appearing in my blurry vision. "No, Clark, I can't. Please." All I could see was an image of my body being thrown from the back of his bike onto the hard asphalt, which would rip through my clothes and skin like cheese through a grater.

"Okay, okay, calm down. Look, I'm not touching you, okay?" He'd suddenly stepped back, away from me, putting his hands in the air as if I were arresting him. "It's cool."

Something zinged past me, hitting the brick wall of the restaurant, then my cheek suddenly stung. I couldn't see anything but Clark right in front of me, who plucked me from that pole as if I were the size of a toddler. A moment later, we were on his bike and he'd fired up the engine.

"Hold on to me," he said, pulling my arms around his chest. "And don't let go."

CH 5

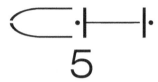

Terror streaked through me, and I screamed as the bike leaped forward. My hold on him seemed desperately inadequate as the street sped by. Fear took my breath, and I couldn't scream anymore, could only pray for this to be over.

It went on forever. The longest ride of my life, and that was counting when my brother had tricked me into getting on the Mummy ride at Universal Studios theme park. I tried to recite the periodic table in my head so I wouldn't think about it . . . but it was impossible *not* to think about it. The wind pulled at my clothes, and I could hear other cars as we passed them.

I focused on Clark instead. He was warm and solid and didn't move, unlike everything else around me. His jacket was soft and I could just smell a bit of his aftershave mixed with the leather scent of his coat. It was a comforting smell. One I associated with him.

I breathed deeply and calmed somewhat. At least I didn't feel as though my heart was about to leap from my chest and run off screaming in the opposite direction. Anatomically impossible, I knew, but the image struck me as appropriate to my previous level of panic.

We were slowing, but I didn't dare look up from where my head was buried against Clark's back. I was holding him so tightly, my fingers were beginning to cramp, but I didn't care. I wanted solid ground underneath my feet more than I wanted my next breath.

Finally, we stopped. Clark turned off the engine, and the sudden quiet left my ears ringing. Much as he had done earlier, he had to pry my fingers one by one from the death grip I had on his jacket, then he lifted me from the back of the bike and set me on my unsteady feet. I glanced around, vaguely recognizing the surroundings. My neighborhood. My house. My driveway.

"Are you okay?" he asked.

The question hit me like a slap, and the wave of rage that washed over me had me actually *seeing red* for the first time in my life. I'd thought that was just an idiom, too, but apparently it was based on a real anatomical reaction to overwhelming fury.

"How could you do that?" I yelled at him. My vision was blurry and it wasn't just because I didn't have on my glasses. "How could you do that to me? I *told* you I didn't want to ride that thing and you . . . you . . . *forced* me to!"

"China—"

"Without even a helmet!" I kept going. "I was *terrified*! And I could have fallen off and been . . . been torn *apart* on the asphalt!"

He stepped closer to me and grasped my arm. "China—"

"Don't touch me!" I jerked my arm out of his grip. "Just-just . . . get *away* from me." I shoved him and he stumbled back a half step. "Go on, *go*!" I shoved again, harder. "You could've killed—"

Clark suddenly grabbed me by both arms and hauled me into him. Then he was kissing me, cutting me off midtirade. He wrapped both arms around me, and I couldn't move a muscle. His mouth pressed hard against mine, almost bruising.

It shocked me, blanking every thought from my mind except that . . . Clark was back, when I thought he'd be gone forever, and he was kissing me.

So I kissed him back.

It wasn't an elegant kiss, or sweet, but messy and wet and bumping noses and nothing like the movies. But it didn't change how I felt. How *it* felt for him to kiss me the way he was . . . as though we could be standing in the middle of a freeway and neither of us would notice the cars careening around our locked bodies.

He tasted just like I remembered, dark and forbidden. Harlequin would have a field day describing how Clark tasted. My feet weren't even on the ground anymore. He'd lifted me up, loosened his grip enough so I could wiggle my arms free and wrap them around his neck.

We'd learned each other by now, and the kiss turned from frantic and fumbling to deep and intense. Time passed, and for once I had not even a remote idea of how long it had been. I memorized each second, each touch. The feel, taste, and smell of him.

He ended the kiss sweetly, with long, lingering kisses on my lips that moved to my cheeks. He rubbed his nose alongside mine, and I heard him inhale deeply, squeezing me tighter in what was now closer to a hug than a restraining hold. Finally, he pulled back enough that I could see his eyes.

I didn't have the faintest clue as to what to say, and even as the seconds ticked by, reality was crashing in around me. I'd just kissed another man. Perhaps the kiss months ago I could ignore because I'd been so taken aback and Clark had left right afterward . . . I'd never thought to see him again, so I'd convinced myself it didn't matter.

This. Mattered.

I'd just cheated on . . . my . . . my fiancé. On *Jackson*. The man I loved. I could feel myself get light-headed as the blood drained from my face. I was a liar and a cheat—

"Jesus, China," Clark said, his lips twisting. "I just wanted to shut you up for a second."

I gasped in dismay, the meaning of his words sinking in like knives. Pain lanced my chest, and for a moment I couldn't breathe. I found myself back on my feet, Clark studying me. His lips were still in that infuriating smirk, but his eyes . . . I couldn't read what was in his eyes. But the smirk was enough.

I hadn't even realized I'd slapped him until I felt the nasty sting on my palm. The crack of the strike echoed, but I'd achieved my aim. When he looked back around at me, the smirk was gone.

"I don't ever," I said, my voice trembling, "*ever* want to speak of this again. Do you understand?"

"Yeah."

His mumbled reply sent my fury spiking again. "I said, *do you underst—*"

"I got it," he bit out, cutting me off. This time I could definitely read the look in his eyes, and under any other circumstances, I'd take a step back. But I was too angry to care.

I headed for the front door. When I got there, I realized that he hadn't followed me. I turned in irritation. "Are you coming, or what?"

Without a word, he followed me inside.

Mia was sprawled on the couch, watching TV. She looked at me when I walked in, then did a double take.

"Oh my God, what happened to you?"

I stopped, confused. Could she tell I'd just kissed Clark? She bounced off the sofa and hurried to me. "You have blood all over your cheek."

Lifting my hand, I touched my face, then looked at my fingers. They were stained red. I glanced at Clark, confused.

"Someone shot at us," he said. "I'd just stepped back or it would've hit me. Instead, it hit the wall. Bits of brick flew and cut you."

Oh. That was why he'd grabbed me and put me on the Machine of Death. He'd been running. And he'd tried to tell me, but I'd been so angry, I'd just yelled and yelled at him . . .

"I—"

"Get the first-aid kit, Mia," Clark interrupted. "Your aunt needs tending."

Mia jerked a quick nod and ran off. I was left staring at Clark. Neither of us spoke. His eyes were blue, so very blue. And gave away nothing. Not for the first time did I curse my lack of insight into human interactions.

"I don't understand," I whispered.

"I know."

Mia was back, fumbling with the first-aid kit, and began dabbing alcohol on my face. It stung and I winced.

"Come sit down," she said, pulling me toward the couch.

I saw Clark head upstairs out of the side of my eye but didn't question it. I was just glad that he was out of the room for the moment.

Mia tended me in silence. After she'd cleaned the scrapes and applied ointment and tiny bandages, she spoke.

"I saw you, you know. Kissing Clark."

I sucked in my breath, her face inches from mine as she placed the bandages. She carefully avoided my gaze.

"I didn't mean to," she said. "I just heard the motorcycle outside and went to the window . . ."

I didn't know what to say. I was . . . embarrassed . . . I realized.

"It . . . I didn't mean . . ." I stammered.

"You don't need to explain," Mia said. Finally, she looked at me. "I just think that . . . if you can kiss a man like that . . . then maybe you're not as in love as you think you are." She shrugged. "I'm not judging, Aunt Chi. I just want you to be happy. With . . . whoever can make you happiest."

I gave a short nod, looking away from her gaze that was too penetrating.

"I love you," she said, giving me a quick hug. "No matter what you decide."

Decide? There was nothing to decide. Clark had offered me nothing but shame and regret. His words still echoed inside my head. *"I just wanted to shut you up."*

Mia didn't give me a chance to reply. She rose and put the first-aid kit away, then headed up to her room.

I got unsteadily to my feet and walked to the powder room. Flicking on the light switch, I examined my reflection. I had been cut. More than I'd thought. Mia had done a nice job patching me up, but I looked as ragged on the outside as I felt on the inside. I tugged out my ponytail and ran my fingers through my hair with a sigh. Clark still had my glasses.

The house was quiet and still. I turned off the lights downstairs and ascended to the second floor. The ring was burning a hole in my jeans pocket. I reached in and retrieved it, sliding it back onto my finger. The diamond glittered, even in the semidarkness.

A glance in my office showed that Clark had made up the futon, but wasn't in there. The light around the closed bathroom door gave away his location. I passed by and went into my bedroom, changing into my pajamas. After a brief hesitation, I left the ring on my finger. It was a good reminder. I loved Jackson, and Clark was my friend, not the other way around.

I really wanted my glasses, but my reluctance to see Clark again was greater. So, I climbed into bed and pulled the covers up just so. The clock said bedtime was still seven minutes away, but I didn't mind going to bed early.

My phone buzzed. Jackson. With a start, I realized I'd completely forgotten to text him.

"Hey," I answered. "I'm so sorry I didn't text."

"I was just about to come over there," he said, irritation edging his tone. "I was worried about you. I just got home from work myself."

"Wow. Long day."

"Yes, and I want to revisit what we discussed this morning. I'd like to meet your family. Your father and brothers."

"Why?" A valid question. Jackson was my first boyfriend. I'd told no one but my grandma in Florida about him. My father and older brothers didn't think I even had a social life, much less a boyfriend.

"China, we've been dating for months. In case you've forgotten, we're engaged. It's time."

Ouch. There it was. The engagement that I hadn't actually agreed to. The huge elephant in the room. "You really want to go to Omaha?" I asked, avoiding the elephant. I'd grown up on a farm north of the city and close to the river. Not exactly a Happening Place.

Jackson sighed. "We're not going for a vacation. I want to meet your family, and I'm sure they'll want to meet me."

My silence must've clued him in, because he said, "China . . . they *do* know about me, right?"

"I'm sure Granny told them," I hedged. "Or Mia." Mia was sixteen. Gossip was as second nature to her as putting on makeup and curling her long, blond hair into perfectly tubed ringlets.

"When was the last time you even spoke to your dad?"

"I don't know. A few weeks ago." I shrugged. "We talk every now and then." Which was true. Maybe three or four times a year. Enough to keep in touch. Not enough to be close. "He talks to my brothers more often."

"Oslo and . . . ?"

"Bill. Named after Billings, Montana. Oslo is the oldest, Mia's dad," I explained. "Bill is the middle, and he's eight years older than me."

"That's a big age difference."

"Yeah. Mom and Dad thought they couldn't have any more kids, even though Mom really wanted a girl." My family made me anxious. I'd gotten used to not having to work so hard to find something to talk about with people. The only thing I had in common with my older brothers was blood.

"China." Jackson's tone had me holding my breath. "I can't help but feel that you're acting as though you really don't want me to meet your family."

The hurt in his voice was painful to hear. It made my heart ache. The last thing I wanted to do was hurt Jackson. I needed him, something I couldn't have foreseen six months ago. I loved him. But I didn't know if I was ready to spend my life with him. How did you know when it was The One? How did Jackson know I was his The One? Trying to put those feelings and doubts into words was the hard part. And the kiss with Clark tonight only made things more confusing.

"I do want you to meet my family," I said. "It's just that . . . things with my dad and me have always been a little strained. Ever since my mom died."

"How did your mom die?" he asked. "You've never said."

I cleared my throat before I spoke. "Um, well, that's because when she died . . . it was partly my fault."

"What are you talking about? You were eight years old. How could it have possibly been your fault?"

"I was with her, in the car," I explained. "It was snowing out and the roads were bad. She'd picked me up from a weekend camp at the University of Nebraska. They sometimes had stuff for brainy kids, and I'd insisted on going to this one.

"Anyway, she'd picked me up and we were driving home Sunday night. A tractor trailer slid on the ice, and we slid into it. There was a huge pileup, and our car was smashed. People started helping each other, and I was little enough for them to get me through a window." I paused. The memory of that day and those moments was something that I'd never forgotten. "But Mom . . . she was wedged too tightly. There was a fire and . . ." I stopped, unable to go on.

"I'm so sorry," Jackson murmured, his voice low and soothing in my ear. "I had no idea."

"It is what it is, and it's certainly in the past," I replied. "There was nothing the rescuers could do when they got there except put out the flames. Dad has never said anything about it being my fault, but it's always been there between us. A giant chasm. And he's right. If we hadn't been on the road that night, Mom might still be alive."

"You can't know that," he argued. "And it wasn't your fault. You were a child. Your mother was the adult. And accidents happen. It's no one's fault."

"Logically, I know that's all true," I said. "But emotions aren't logical." A huge understatement. Guilt gnawed at me, and part of me wanted to confess what had happened between Clark and me, but the other part didn't. I didn't want to hurt Jackson, or for him to know how awful a person it appeared I was at heart. He'd never understand.

"Why don't I come over?" Jackson said. "I miss you, and last night ended so terribly."

I was on the verge of agreeing—it would be so comforting for him to hold me at the moment—when I remembered. Clark was here.

"No," I blurted, then realized how that sounded. "I mean, I'm really tired and I'm already in bed. I'll come over there tomorrow. How does that sound?"

"Are you sure? It's really no bother. I can just crawl in beside you and go to sleep with you."

That sounded really, *really* good, but I knew it was a Bad Idea. "No, it's fine. I'll call you in the morning."

"Okay, then," he said. "Sleep well, pretty girl. I'll talk to you tomorrow."

"Good night."

"'Night."

I ended the call and set the phone back on my nightstand. As I set it down, I noticed my glasses were on the table, too. At some point while I'd been talking to Jackson, Clark had come in and left them for me. I wondered how much, if any, of my conversation he'd overheard.

◆ ◆ ◆

Morning came too bright and too early. I debated what to wear, finally settling on my *I Survived Helm's Deep* T-shirt with my usual uniform of jeans and a long-sleeve shirt over it. I'd switched to cozy flannels for the winter months and was just brewing my coffee when my cell rang.

"Morning, Granny," I answered. My grandma and I always spoke on Saturdays, when I got to hear all about her latest misadventures in the retirement community in Florida where she lived.

"Good morning, China-girl," she said, her perky voice and southern lilt making me smile. Suddenly I felt a thousand times better. This was normal, this was routine, this was my Granny. "You'll never guess what happened to me last night."

I hesitated. It could be anything from being arrested for operating an underground poker game to TPing her neighbor Helen's condo (Granny viewed Helen as a stick-in-the-mud fuddy-duddy ever since it had come out that she'd been the one to report Granny's poker game to the cops).

"Probably not," I answered. "What happened?"

"Well, Harvey had come round to take me to dinner—that man is such a romantic, I have to say—and he'd somehow found an old Ford Model T! He thought it was somethin' else, but I have to tell you, they didn't make them with air-conditioning, and I wasn't about to sweat my way through this Florida heat. I'd put on my fake lashes and pantyhose! And honey, you know what wearing pantyhose in the heat will do to you."

I didn't, since I'd never worn any kind of nylons before, but I made agreeing noises as though I knew exactly what she was talking about.

"Well, anyway, we took my car to dinner instead, and can you believe it? He proposed!" She laughed in delight. "Gracious, I didn't think I'd ever get one of those again."

I'd stopped pouring my coffee. "Wow, Granny! That-that's wonderful. Congratulations."

"Oh, China-girl, I didn't say yes," she chortled. "Heavens to Betsy, I've had enough of marriage since your grandpa passed. I'm not about to give up my freedom to be someone's maid and cook again, no sirree."

"So you told him no?" I couldn't fathom how it could be socially acceptable for someone to say no to a marriage proposal. "How?"

"Why, I simply told him how flattered I was, and how special he was to me, but that marriage wasn't something I wanted. I must say, he took it well. He was a bit crestfallen, but then we danced for a while and he perked right up. Of course, it also helped that I still let him come inside for a nightcap afterward."

"That's great," I interrupted before she could go further into explaining what she meant by "nightcap." I got the gist.

"What's going on with you?" she asked. "How's my boy Jackson doing?"

Now was the time, if I was going to start telling my family. "Um, well, it sounds like we had very similar experiences." I took a deep breath. "Jackson proposed on Valentine's Day."

I yanked my earbuds out and winced at the shriek that followed.

"That's fantastic! I knew he was special. Have you set a date?"

I got the last part of that when I tentatively put my earbuds back in. "Um, well, actually . . . I'm not sure I want to get married."

Granny was quiet for a moment, and when she spoke again, her voice was serious. "Talk to me," she said. "Do you not want to get married? Or do you not want to marry Jackson?"

"It's just that . . . how do you know?" I asked. "How can either of us be sure that we're . . ." I searched for the right term. ". . . marriage material? What if he just really wants to get married, and any compatible woman will do? How do I know that he loves me more than he'll ever love anyone else? How do I know the same about him?"

"Well, honey, those are all really good questions, and I don't think any bride-to-be hasn't asked herself the same thing."

"You knew you *didn't* want to get married again," I said. "I should know with as much certainty if I *do* want to get married, right?"

"China-girl, nothing in life is a hundred percent certain, not when it comes to love. That's the point. Some things have to be taken on faith and trust and hope. You trust that Jackson loves you and have faith that you're both making the right decision. Then you hope that the future is kind."

The idea of trusting the rest of my life and happiness on ephemeral things such as faith, hope, and love made me sit in the nearest chair and put my head between my knees.

"You all right?" Granny asked when I didn't reply.

"Yeah," I said, breathing in through my nose and out through my mouth. "Just practicing my coping techniques."

She chuckled.

"But it's not just that," I said, lowering my voice. I glanced toward the stairs, but it was still all quiet upstairs. Mia was getting her Saturday-morning beauty rest, and I hadn't heard a peep from Clark. "There's . . . there might be . . . another man." I flinched even as I said the words.

"Oh my! Hold on, honey, I need to put some whiskey in my coffee for this." I waited for a few moments, then she returned. "Okay, go on ahead. Spill it."

I told her, as succinctly as I could, about Clark and how he'd kissed me a few months ago when he'd gone away, but how he was back now and then he'd kissed me again last night and said other things before that . . . suggestive things that even I had picked up on as sexual innuendoes.

"And now I've cheated on Jackson, and I don't know how to tell him," I said. "He's going to hate me."

"First of all," Granny said, "he's not going to hate you. Don't be silly. Second, there's no need to tell him a thing. If there's one thing I know about men, it's that what they don't know, won't hurt 'em. Unless you're plannin' on dumping Jackson and taking up with this Clark. Are you?"

"No, of course not. It was just a weird one-time . . . two-time . . . thing."

"Then I wouldn't worry about it," she said. "It sounds like this Clark fella has a thing for you, but he's never made a move before now, and now . . . you're taken. Some men find that easier. Takes them off the hook, so to speak. They don't have to pony up and commit to a woman, which is what Jackson's doing. I think you should decide what you want with Jackson, without letting the idea of Clark influence you."

That was really good advice. And *so* much easier said than done, I found once I'd hung up. I'd never been so confused before. It felt strange, not to know my way forward. I'd always had my future mapped out and made decisions logically and quickly. But logic wasn't playing much of a part here, because as much as I should logically want to marry Jackson—and I did—I still couldn't stop thinking about Clark and that kiss last night.

CH 6

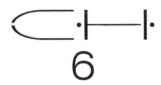

I left a note on the kitchen table for Mia—who'd likely sleep until noon—that I was going to Jackson's, then I crept out of the house. I shouldn't have bothered. Clark's motorcycle was gone.

That made me stop for a second. Had he gone to Omaha to see the remaining member of his old team? He hadn't left me a message or a text. Automatically, I reached for my phone, then stopped myself. If he wanted me to know where he was, he would've told me. For all I knew, he wasn't coming back at all.

Which would probably be a good thing. Maybe not for my career, but certainly for my peace of mind.

Lance let me into Jackson's house, the foyer of which was larger than the entire first floor of my place. The chandelier hanging above us was undergoing a cleaning, and I could tell by Lance's grimace and curt greeting that he was cranky. Frankly, if I had to clean that thing, I'd be cranky, too.

"Where's Jackson?" I asked.

He motioned down toward the east wing. "His office." Then he began climbing the huge ladder he'd obviously abandoned to answer the front door. The height was dizzying and I couldn't watch.

Jackson was indeed in his office, talking on the phone. I poked my head in, and he smiled, motioning me inside. I listened with half an ear to his conversation as I wandered around the room. I had chair envy of the ergonomic state-of-the-art throne that he sat in to work. Right now, he sat in a normal chair behind a normal desk. But on a raised dais was the chair where he coded. It held screens with one arched metal arm while the keyboard was on another, and could recline at various degrees, all while holding the workstation safely. It was awesome . . . and incredibly expensive.

I had just decided to climb up into the chair when he ended his call.

"Good morning," he said, coming around from behind the desk to kiss me. "How'd—" He stopped, taking my chin in his hand. "What the hell happened to you?"

I had my excuse all ready. "Um, yeah. Cat."

"Cat?"

"Yeah. Mia brought her friend's cat over, and it didn't like me. Scratched my cheek all up."

Jackson eyed me, frowning. He opened his mouth to speak.

There was a television mounted on the wall, and it caught my eye. It was always tuned to a cable news channel and muted, but what was on the screen now made my blood freeze.

"Oh no," I breathed, the imaginary cat forgotten.

Jackson dropped his hand and turned to see what I was staring at so fixedly.

Clark's service photograph was on the news. The caption said "Manhunt Under Way."

Jackson reached for the remote and turned up the sound.

". . . search for what the Secret Service and FBI are calling 'a person of interest' in the assassination attempt on President Kirk," the anchor was saying. "Clark Slattery is an Army veteran and should be considered armed and dangerous. Authorities are asking people not to intervene themselves, but to call this number, should they spot him. Sources tell us that Slattery was last spotted in the Raleigh-Durham area of North Carolina."

Jackson turned to me. "Did you know about this?"

I tore my gaze from the television. "I didn't know they were going to do this," I said. "I know they suspected him, but I didn't believe them. Clark wouldn't do that."

"Has he contacted you?"

I hesitated, remembering my promise to Clark. "Why would you think he'd contact me?" My tried-and-true way of avoiding answering a question . . . ask another.

"Clark strikes me as the kind of guy who wouldn't hesitate to use what connections he has to get himself out of a jam."

Jackson's wry comment hit a little too close to home. But I still wasn't ready to break the promise I'd made. Clark's life was on the line—not only from whoever was hunting him and the former members of his team, but from whatever the government would do to him if they got their hands on him.

"They shut Vigilance down," I said, not wanting to pursue a conversation about Clark.

"What?"

"Last night. This guy, special adviser to the president, came in with an armed team and shut us down."

"Special adviser to the president?"

"Yes. He said his name was Kade Dennon. He told me I had to find Clark and turn him over."

"Turn him over to him?"

I nodded.

"Why him? Why not the Secret Service?"

I swallowed. "I, um, kind of got the impression that Clark wouldn't be having his day in court, if you know what I mean. That guy meant business, and not the kind that involved due process and defense attorneys."

"He can't do that," Jackson argued. "I don't care what kind of special adviser he is."

"That wasn't the worst part." I took a deep breath. "He also implied that I might be a part of Clark's plans. To prove my innocence, I have to turn Clark over. I mean, if I can find him," I added.

"If he's on the run, then the likelihood of us being able to catch him when all the powers of the US government are also searching for him is between slim and none," he said. "How can you be sure he didn't do it?"

I gave him a look. "You can't be serious. I know Clark isn't your favorite person, but something like that is utterly out of character for him. Surely you know that."

He shrugged. "Who knows why anyone does anything? People change, and he may have motives you know nothing about. But it doesn't matter. We need to find the real person behind it if we're going to clear your name."

"What do you mean, 'we'?" I asked.

Now it was his turn to give me a look. "They want to put my fiancée in jail," he said. "That's not going to happen. They've shut you out of Vigilance, so the best resource you have is me. Between the two of us, we can find out what they have on Clark and counteract it. If he didn't do it, someone else did, obviously."

"You're friends with the president. How is he?"

"Friends might be pushing it," Jackson said, taking my hand and leading me from the office. "But from what I've been able to find out, the news is correct. He'll be all right. The bullet cracked a couple ribs, but the ricochet didn't hit anything vital. He's very lucky. He's also a tough son of a bitch. Used to be a SEAL, you know. He's no stranger to bullets."

I followed him toward the kitchen, guilt dogging me. I was keeping so much from Jackson. It wasn't something I was used to doing. I didn't like secrets and wasn't a good liar, which was why I tried to avoid answering direct questions.

Jackson still held my hand, and his thumb brushe I wore. "You know, you probably think I didn't notice actually answered my question."

I stiffened. Emotional territory instead of facts an plan—it was riddled with land mines. "Events precluded n to give adequate attention to your . . . proposal. You had o a lot of time and thought into the evening."

He was still looking at the sparkling diamond. "I've neve to a woman before. I was quite nervous." Finally, he looked am, China."

My smile was too wide. "Why would you be nervous? E ding jitters?" My laugh was too forced. It wasn't a surprise whe didn't even crack a smile.

His eyes were a warm, honey brown that glittered in the s streaming through the kitchen windows. They were solemn, t and he moved closer to me. He took my other hand in his, too.

"China," he said, and it was hardly more than a rasp of sound you marry me?"

I looked at him, really looked. He had the same expression Mia had had when she'd asked if she could live with me. Hopeful, afraid at the same time. Was he afraid of the embarrassment if I tur him down? Or did he fear something else?

"What are you afraid of?"

His gaze searched mine. "Being without you."

And I melted. I mean, not literally, that would be impossible. And painful. But in the Harlequin meaning of the word.

"Yes," I said, reached up to cradle his cheek in my hand. His skin was smooth and soft from shaving this morning. "Yes. I will marry you."

Jackson's eyes were suddenly much shinier than usual, and he smiled. He took my face in his hands and pressed his lips to mine.

It was a Moment. Even I could recognize that this was something that didn't come along every day: the moment Jackson and I decided

spend the rest of our lives together. I memorized the feel of his , the warmth of the sun against the back of my neck, the scent of kson's aftershave mixed with the heavy aroma of coffee and citrus in kitchen.

When he lifted his head, neither of us spoke. I found my eyes were t, too. My hand was still on his cheek and he held my face in his lms.

My phone buzzed in my back pocket. I ignored it. It buzzed again.

"You should get that," he said, taking a step back. He turned away reach for coffee mugs in the cabinet while I grabbed for my phone.

"Hello?"

"Don't say my name," Clark warned.

I cursed inside my head, turning toward the windows so Jackson wouldn't see my face. "What do you want?"

"Have you seen the news?"

"It's hard to miss." I glanced toward Jackson, but he seemed busy with the coffee.

"I got a lead on who might be setting me up," he said. "We're supposed to meet today."

"How do you know it's not a trap?"

"I don't."

My eyes slipped closed. *Damn it.* "This isn't a good idea."

"Do you have a better one?"

I didn't. Still, "Where is this meet?"

He snorted. "Like I'm going to tell you. I don't need you sticking your neck out for me anymore. You've done enough."

My hand tightened on the phone. That sounded a lot like a precursor to a goodbye.

"So," he continued, "I guess I just wanted to say . . . thank you. And about last night—"

"It's fine," I cut him off through lips gone numb. I'd been right. "You're leaving, aren't you?" And I really didn't want a rehash of that disastrous kiss, not with Jackson standing not ten feet away.

"That or die trying," he joked, which fell flat. When I didn't respond, he said, "Gotta go. Catch you later, Mack."

"Wait—" But he'd already gone.

"I'm going to kill him," I hissed under my breath, angrily shoving my phone back into my pocket.

"What's going on?"

I squeaked and jumped. Jackson was right behind me. His smile was crooked as he observed my antics, then handed me a cup of coffee. Since I'd taught him how to make it correctly, it was perfect.

"Oh, just work problems," I said, shifting my eyes away at the lie.

"Can you talk about it?" he asked.

"Not really." Jackson had always been pretty good about accepting when I couldn't discuss things with my job, and it went both ways. Much of what Cysnet was involved in was also classified or proprietary, so work usually wasn't our first topic of discussion. But his easy acceptance now only made my guilt ratchet higher.

I remembered what Granny had said, that he didn't need to know. Clark was leaving again, so it wasn't as though there would be a repeat. Of course, that's what I'd told myself last time . . .

"Let's celebrate our engagement," Jackson said. "Retread is calling your name."

It took me a second to realize he wasn't being literal. Retread was my favorite store, and stores obviously couldn't speak. "An idiom," I said. He grinned.

"I hear they had a whole new stack of used Harlequins come in. You know, for *Granny*." His smile grew wider and he winked.

"Good," I said, ignoring him. "She'll love that." And if I read a few of them before shipping them off to Florida, then I was just getting my money's worth. Going to Retread was normal and routine for my

Saturday schedule. Routine was good, especially when I was powerless to help Clark. Plus, if I *didn't* go, Jackson would know something was wrong.

"I have something else to show you," he said. "Follow me."

We went out to his garage, which was big enough to house ten cars. Jackson had thought it was "cool" that I had a thing for cars—something I picked up so I had a topic of conversation with my dad and brothers—and recently he'd taken me shopping for a new Jaguar. He'd let me pick out all the bells and whistles and ordered it.

"Look what came," he said, flicking on the lights.

I squealed in delight. "It's here!" I clasped my hands in glee, wanting to jump up and down. I ran over to it, lovingly running a hand over the curves of the hood.

"Jaguar F-Type SVR Coupe 5.0 all-wheel drive, supercharged, with five hundred seventy-five horsepower under the hood. Can go zero to sixty in three point five seconds, with a top speed of two hundred miles per hour. Exterior color of Firesand, with a panoramic glass roof and no rear spoiler because it would slow down the top speed by fourteen miles per hour."

Jackson dangled the key fob in front of me. "All yours. Consider it an engagement gift."

There was nothing like the promise of speed and power under the hood to turn me on. I pushed thoughts of Clark aside. Jackson was right. Today was special, and I'd been having *all the feels*, as Mia would say, before he'd called.

Taking a fistful of Jackson's shirt in my hand, I pulled his head down for a kiss. A deep, I-want-you-here-and-now kind of kiss that had him backing me up against the side of the car.

"Let's christen it," I whispered against his lips.

He needed no persuading. Still kissing me, he undid the button and zipper on my jeans and shoved the denim down my legs. Locking his hands on my waist, he lifted me up to sit me on the hood of the car, my legs dangling between the front wheel and the driver-side door. Toeing off my shoes, I kicked my jeans aside. The metal was cold underneath my thighs, but it didn't bother me one little bit.

I went to work on his belt and the fastening to his slacks. His mouth moved from my lips to my jaw, then my neck. Wedging himself between my knees, he pushed apart my thighs and touched between my legs.

I sucked in a breath, losing track of where I was regarding the status of his zipper.

Jackson had pianist's fingers . . . on the thin side, but long. He made up for this by using two at a time.

I clutched at his shoulders and gasped. "Oh God," I moaned. "You looked at that article I sent you, didn't you?" His fingers bent, sliding and stroking inside me.

"You mean the article on the 3-D clitoris?"

Speech was beyond me, so I just jerked my head in a nod.

"It was very informative," he said, pressing a kiss to my neck. His fingers moved deeper and faster. "And knowledge is power, right?"

I moaned again, it ending in more of a mewling sound than a proper moan. I think it even echoed in the garage, not that I cared.

My orgasm was quick and powerful, making me send even more echoes off the walls. Then I went to work getting to the part of Jackson I wanted most at the moment.

"You know, some might think you want me just for my cock," he teased as I shoved his slacks down his hips, freeing his thick erection. My mouth watered at the sight.

"Not true," I said, brushing my thumb gently over the tip. I was gratified at the sound of him sucking in a breath between his teeth. "I'm quite fond of Mr. Happy's life-support system."

It took him a second to catch on, then he laughed. Our lips met on a smile, which is one of the best ways to start a kiss.

Bending my knees to plant my feet on the hood, I leaned back on my elbows, then cocked an eyebrow at Jackson.

"Do you need an invitation?"

"I think your body language is invitation enough."

He guided himself into me while I watched. It was an erotic sight, especially given our location. After years of seeing bikini-clad models posing on cars, I felt like I was in their same league. Screwing a really hot guy on the hood of an equally hot car.

Jackson held my hips and was quick, thank goodness, because after the orgasm and heat of the moment had passed, the metal was darn uncomfortable and verging on slippery. And what wasn't slippery was skin stuck in a not-so-good way.

His breath in my ear was a good sound, and I smiled as I crossed my ankles behind his back.

"Best new car ever," he said, pressing a kiss to my mouth.

"Ditto."

We put ourselves to rights, adjusting clothes, and I hopped on one foot then the other as I pulled on my tennis shoes.

"Do I get to drive?" I asked, redoing my ponytail.

"Of course." He tossed the key fob to me, and I slid into the driver's seat. I immediately grumbled about how far I had to move up the seat and raise it, but eventually I was situated.

"Buckle your seat belt," I said. "Time for me to give *you* a ride." Sex joke! Ha ha ha.

Buddy, the owner of Retread, greeted us when we walked in. The musty smell of attic and basement that clung to the items filling every nook and cranny of his store assailed me. It was a comforting smell. I'd visited this place every weekend since I'd discovered it upon moving to Raleigh.

"Got anything new for me?" I asked, pushing my glasses up my nose.

"Yeah. Uma dropped by a whole trash bag full of paperback romances." He jerked a thumb. "Over there."

"Uma?" Jackson asked me as I headed in that direction.

"Oh. She's this little old lady who looks like what Uma Thurman will look like in forty years. We call her Uma."

"Does she know this?"

I paused, glancing up at him with a frown. "I don't think so. Do you think we should tell her?" It was only then that I caught the twitch of his lips. "Oh. You were joking."

He touched his nose with his index finger and winked. "You're getting better."

I pawed through the latest in paperback drop-offs while Jackson drifted through the store. It was empty of any other patrons, and I never knew how Buddy stayed in business. My personal theory was that his family was independently wealthy and let him pursue his hobby without requiring it to turn a profit.

I had an armful of books when I found Jackson in a neglected alcove, holding a metal lunch box.

"What did you find?" I asked, peering over my stack.

"A Buck Rogers lunchbox," he said, showing me. "I had one of these in kindergarten. I loved that show."

"Who didn't? Twinkie was awesome."

He popped it open. "Look, it even still has the thermos."

There was such little-boy delight in his voice, I couldn't help smiling. "Okay, since you got me the Jag, I guess I can buy you the lunch box."

We ended up leaving with more than two dozen dog-eared romances plus the lunch box. I was already eyeing one called *Falling for the Highlander,* with a bare-chested kilt-clad hot guy on the cover. I had a thing for the Highlander men and had watched *Outlander* season one at least half a dozen times.

After we'd stored our purchases in the trunk and I slid behind the wheel, something caught my eye.

"Jackson, what's that?"

We both looked at the metal talisman, hanging from the rearview mirror. I could have sworn it hadn't been there before.

Jackson reached out, slowly removing the object from where it hung. I scrutinized the symbol.

"That . . . isn't that a Roman numeral?" I asked. It looked like the number two, with two vertical lines and two horizontal, one above and one below.

"Yeah, it kind of looks like that," Jackson said, turning it over in his hand. His face was pale, which alarmed me.

"Jackson? Are you okay? What is that?" But he just shook his head.

"Nothing. It's nothing. Someone playing a prank, that's all." He smiled, but it seemed forced even to my untrained eye. "Let's go."

"I didn't leave the doors unlocked," I persisted. "And who would possibly play a prank like that?"

"Drop it," he said. "I don't want to talk about it."

Okay. Red-flag warning. "Jackson—"

"I said, drop it."

I almost didn't, but Jackson's lips were pressed tightly closed, and he was looking out the window now, the talisman clenched tightly in his fist.

"Fine," I muttered, backing out of the parking space. I started home, but after a couple of miles, Jackson spoke.

"I think we're being followed."

I automatically glanced up in the rearview mirror. There was a big pickup, an F-150, right on our tail. As I watched, it inched closer, then put on a burst of speed, slamming the Jag in the bumper.

The wheel jerked and I struggled to keep control. Then we were hit again.

"Get away from him," Jackson said, twisting around to look out the window behind us.

There was an exit ahead. I hit the accelerator.

While the Jag might have been able to go from zero to sixty in three point five seconds, I didn't go that fast, not least of which because I didn't want to black out from the g-forces.

The engine purred, growling like its namesake. The tires gripped the pavement as the trees on the side of the road flashed by in streaks of brown and green.

"Did he follow us?" I asked.

"Yes, but you're losing him. Keep going."

I accelerated coming out of the next curve, gaining more speed, then tapped the brakes as another curve came up.

Nothing happened.

I pressed the brakes again. Still nothing.

"Jackson," I said, trying to remain calm.

"Yeah?"

"Um, well, there's no easy way to say this. The brakes are out."

I saw his head swivel my direction, but I kept my eyes on the road. We were going more than a hundred miles per hour with no brakes. I didn't dare look away.

"Okay, well, lay off the gas," he said.

"I'm not pressing the gas," I gritted out. "But we're going downhill." The car was going faster and faster. I didn't dare try to downshift, not knowing how badly the transmission would react.

There were cars ahead, including a semi in the passing lane, and we were coming up on them fast.

"Jackson . . . ," I warned.

"I see them."

There was no way around it. We were either going to smash into the back of the semi going more than a hundred miles an hour, or the back of the SUV it was passing. Neither option was good for them or us.

Very carefully, I began to steer the Jag onto the shoulder. It was notched pavement, meant to warn and wake up sleepy drivers drifting from the road. But when my wheels touched the bumps, it took all my strength to hold the wheel that threatened to jerk out of my control.

I was terrified, part of me unable to believe this was even happening. And even as our speed began to slow, we were nearly on top of the cars in front of us, and I had to make a decision. Ramming into them going this speed would certainly slow us down, but we might not survive. Not to mention the poor, unsuspecting drivers.

Or I could steer off the road to where the ground was thick with dead grass and weeds, and pray that slowed us down to a stop.

There was no choice. "Brace yourself," I told Jackson.

I turned the wheel slowly, driving us off the road, and saw Jackson grip the dash out of the corner of my eye.

We bounced down the ditch and up, becoming airborne for a split second, then landed with a teeth-shattering crash. The tall grass and undergrowth became tangled around the wheels, and the steering wheel wouldn't respond. We were still going over seventy when, to my horror, I saw a deer flash by in front of us.

The impact was deafening, the windshield shattering as blood and gore splattered, and the world turned upside down as an airbag exploded in my face.

CH 7

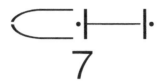

Vague impressions of screeching steel and lots of voices. My body hurt all over, and I couldn't see properly. My left arm was numb. I closed my eyes as hands lifted me from the seat. I smelled fresh air and burned rubber. Lots of people talking and yelling. Sirens screaming in the distance.

I was on the hard ground now, the only still thing in the midst of commotion all around. Forcing my eyes open, I saw gray sky above me. It took every ounce of will I had to turn my head to look around.

Jackson. They were just laying him on the ground a few feet away from me. He was unconscious. At least, I prayed he was unconscious.

I blinked, turning my head again, and saw a blurry face standing above me. I blinked again, squinting and trying to bring the features into focus.

"Clark?"

But then he was gone, replaced by paramedics who asked me questions I was too tired to answer, so I closed my eyes again.

◆ ◆ ◆

Mia was hovering like a mother hen, fussing over me. Did I need more water? Were my pillows okay? Was I cold? Was I hot? Did I need something to eat?

"I'm fine," I reiterated for the tenth time. "I have bumps and bruises, Mia."

"And a broken wrist," she reminded me.

"A sprained wrist," I corrected her. "I only need to wear the brace for a couple of days."

"At least it was the left arm and not the right." She spread a blanket over my lap and adjusted the couch cushions.

"It could have been so much worse." Images of the accident flashed through my head. The pictures I'd seen afterward of the mangled wreckage from which Good Samaritans had pulled us free. Jackson had escaped major injury as well, thank God, but his life was insured so heavily, they called the hospital and required him to stay overnight for observation.

As it was, I looked like I'd been in a fistfight . . . and lost. Bruises spotted my face, torso, and arms. But all of it was surface and temporary. Not that it had been meant to be.

Someone had tried to kill us.

I'd told the police about the truck chasing us and that I hadn't gotten a look at the driver. There had been little they could do, and I wondered if they'd even believed me, and that I wasn't just making excuses for losing control of the car while driving at high speed. They would need to tear apart the car to see if what I'd said about the brakes was true.

I took a long, hot bath, which helped with my aches and pains. My cell rang while I was soaking, and I smiled when I saw who it was.

"Desperate to get out of there?" I asked Jackson.

"You have no idea."

I laughed at the pure frustration in his voice. "It's good that you're staying. An accident like that . . . I'm shocked that we weren't seriously hurt."

"Thanks to you," he said. "Your driving was nothing short of phenomenal. If that deer hadn't been there, we would've been fine."

"Yeah. I bet he'd say the same, if he could." At least it had been a quick death for the poor creature.

"How are you feeling?"

"I'm fine," I said, resting my head on the back of the tub. My glasses were fogging up, so I closed my eyes. "Bumps and bruises. I guess we can advise Jaguar that their safety features in that model work very well."

There was quiet for a moment. "I wish I could be with you. I need to hold you."

The tears I'd fought all evening stung the backs of my eyes. "Me, too."

"Lance dropped off my car, so I'll come as soon as I'm discharged in the morning."

"Okay." I pushed my glasses up my nose even though they were too foggy to see out of properly. "Jackson . . . someone tried to kill us. Or you. That-that's a pretty big deal."

"I know."

"Why?"

"I don't know."

"That thing in the car. You have no idea what that was or who would have put it in the car?"

"I told you that I didn't." He sounded irritated. But I didn't believe him, and that bothered me. A lot.

"Is Mia taking care of you?" he asked, changing the subject.

"Of course." I cleared my throat. "She's been force-feeding me Fig Newtons and hot tea while watching *Supernatural* episodes back-to-back."

"She knows your love language."

I smiled. "True. She cares about me. I don't know what I'd do without her."

"Is she like a sister? Or a daughter?"

That was a meaning-laden question, given our lack of discussion about children. The ring on my left hand slipped and slid around my wet finger. I looked at the glittering stone. "Both, kind of. I've never really seen myself as a mother. Most of the time, I barely see myself as an adult."

"I know we haven't discussed it, but you should know that I'd like children. At least one. Preferably two." There was a pause. "What about you?"

I took a deep breath and let it out on a sigh. "Honestly, I haven't thought about it very much. I don't feel ready for that. Not yet."

"We don't have to have kids right away. I just want to know it's not something you've already ruled out."

"Of course not. But I'm . . . relieved that you want to wait awhile. I think it's going to be an adjustment. I've never considered or imagined being a parent before. It'll take me some time to wrap my head around the idea."

"We certainly don't have to decide anything now," he said. "My pain meds are kicking in anyway, putting my ass to sleep."

That snorted a giggle from me. "Get some sleep. I'll see you tomorrow."

"Okay. Good night."

"'Night. Love you."

"Love you more." He ended the call before I could get in the last word.

Kids again. The last thing on my mind was having children. I was still focused on the fact that Jackson and I had barely escaped with our lives today. And had that really been Clark that I'd seen, standing above me? It seemed like a dream now, though I could've sworn . . .

But I hadn't been wearing my glasses at the time, and I'd just been in a horrible crash. Maybe I'd hallucinated him. Or thought one of the people helping us had looked like him.

Speaking of Clark, I wondered where he was. If he was okay. It had been wishful thinking that I'd thought I'd seen him. I was worried, that was all.

"Well, this is a sight worth dying for."

My eyes snapped open and I jerked upright in the bathtub. Water sloshed onto the floor as I yanked off my fogged glasses.

"Clark?"

I wasn't hallucinating this time. It was him. Standing in the bathroom. With me.

And he was bleeding.

"Oh my God, Clark!" I jumped up, ignoring the aches and pains protesting in my own body. "What happened to you?"

I caught him just as his knees gave out, my wrist sending a stab of pain through me, making me wince. Clark's weight was twice mine, and I strained to keep him upright. His knees hit the floor, taking me down with him. I landed on top of him on the bathroom floor.

"This was worth waiting for," Clark murmured. His eyes were shut and his face was white. But his hands were on my bare ass.

"What happened?" I scrambled to the side, ripping open his jacket. Blood stained his white T-shirt. It froze me for a second, then I ripped his shirt from neck to hem.

A bullet hole—an honest-to-God bullet hole—was in his upper torso. I didn't know what to do. *Pressure.* I grabbed a towel and held it over the wound, pressing hard.

"Fuck," Clark groaned, his eyes popping open. "That hurts."

"Good," I snapped. "You get shot and then you show up here? Why didn't you go to the hospital?"

"Can't," he gritted out. "I'm kind of a wanted man. Remember?"

Oh yeah. There was that. If I took him to the hospital, they'd patch him up, then arrest him.

"I don't know what to do," I said. "I can put pressure on it, but that's all. The only medical training I have is CPR."

"I wouldn't mind some mouth-to-mouth, but that's not going to stop the bleeding."

"No shit," I snapped.

"You just need to get the bullet out," Clark said between hissed breaths. "Use tweezers. It didn't go through."

I scrambled to my feet. Tweezers. Mia had made me buy a pair for my eyebrows, not that I plucked them. It hurt. She did it for me when she was able to run me down.

Top drawer on the left. Yes, there they were. And I had my first-aid kit in the lower cabinet. I poured the rubbing alcohol over the tweezers with hands that shook. Alcohol splattered on the counter.

I dropped back down to my knees and pried open the kit. Saline solution. Gauze. Tape. Clark had closed his eyes, but they slitted open when I took away the towel.

"Do you want something to bite down on?" I asked.

His brows drew together in a frown. "What?"

"In the movies. They always give the hero something to bite down on when there is no anesthesia available. I may have a leather belt—"

"First," he grunted, "I'm not the hero. Second, I'll take my chances. Third, don't tell me details about the leather belt. Let me use my imagination."

I still hesitated. What if I messed up? What if I made it worse?

"Do it," he said sharply. "It's not going to climb out on its own."

"Okay." I squeezed the tweezers tight in my hand. "I'll be as quick as I can."

My glasses were clear now, thank goodness, and I had to block everything else from my mind as I looked into the wound.

I didn't know much about medical practice, but I knew if he'd been hit somewhere vital, he'd be in a lot worse shape. By some rainbow that seemed to follow Clark like a blessing, he'd been shot in the shoulder, which I'm sure hurt like hell, but it had hit muscle rather than organs.

I eased the tweezers into the hole, opening it further, until I saw a glint of brass. The bullet. It was intact and in one piece. I sucked in a deep breath. My glasses were sliding down my nose, but I couldn't take a moment to push them up. Clark was in pain and losing blood. And he'd come to me to help him.

The bullet was slippery and it took too long for the tweezers to grab hold of it. I was near tears of frustration when I was finally able to move it. Holding my breath, I pulled it out, moving more slowly and carefully than I ever had about anything. When it was clear of Clark's flesh, I let out my breath in a huff of relief. The tweezers and bullet fell from my suddenly numb fingers, and I thanked God again that my left wrist and not my right had been injured.

The adrenaline drained out of me as I pressed the towel again to the wound, now oozing fresh blood. My glasses had slipped so far down, I just tossed them away. I was crying, but just now realized it.

"Shhh, it's okay," Clark said, putting his uninjured arm around me. "You did good."

I wanted to yell at him and hit him and hug him all at once. I settled for collapsing on top of him, still holding the towel to the wound. I needed to bandage it, too, but couldn't rally the energy at the moment. The adrenaline was gone, leaving me limp and weak.

Neither of us spoke. His arm was still around my waist, and tears still leaking from my eyes fell onto his chest. It was utterly silent. All I could hear was the sound of his breathing and the rhythmic thud of his heart beating inside his chest.

Clark moved, reaching for another towel, and dragged it over me. "You're shaking," he said.

I nodded, sitting up and wrapping the towel around me. I wiped my wet cheeks with the back of my hand, put my glasses back on, and took a deep breath.

"Why do you look like you've been moonlighting as a bouncer?" he asked. The words were rough, but the knuckle he dragged along my cheek was gentle.

I grimaced at the reminder. "Car wreck. Today. We were lucky."

"We?"

"Jackson and me. He's in the hospital overnight, but we both walked away. I'll tell you all the details later, but for now you need to conserve your energy."

"Thank you," he said. "For helping me."

"You didn't leave me much choice." And I wasn't done yet. I checked the wound, and the bleeding had finally stopped. I poured some saline solution into it, hopefully washing away all the bad stuff, then carefully packed and bandaged him. All the while, he remained still on the floor, watching me.

"I expected that you'd pass out," I said.

His eyes were brilliant and I focused on them. My hair had come free from the loose bun I'd put it in for the bath, and he reached up to play with the tendrils, draping them over my bare shoulder.

"I had a distraction," he said, his finger sliding down my arm.

The look in his eyes wasn't one of pain, and I hurriedly glanced away.

Getting to my feet, I said, "You can't lie on the floor all night. Let me help you up." I kept one hand on my towel, where I'd tucked in a corner so I wouldn't lose it, and held out my other to him. He took it, and with a grimace and a few curses under his breath, stood. He promptly swayed, and I grabbed him around the waist.

"Don't you dare fall," I said. "You'll hit your head, and I'm not strong enough to carry you."

"God, you're bossy," he groused, but he was steadier, and we made it out of the bathroom and into my bedroom in one piece.

Leading him to the bed, I sat him down and went back into the bathroom to retrieve his jacket and ruined shirt. When I returned, he still hadn't moved from where he sat, clad in only his jeans and boots.

Dried blood was smeared on his chest and bicep, and his eyes were closed. He looked as though it was all he could do to remain upright.

Hurrying into my closet, I threw on my *Hoth* pajamas, then got a package of wet wipes from the bathroom. My hair was already a mess, so I pulled out what remained of my bun and set the hair tie aside.

I knelt on the floor by Clark's feet and began undoing the laces of his boots. He must've been sleeping while sitting up because he jerked, startled, when I tried to tug one off.

"What're you doing?"

"You're not getting my sheets dirty with your shoes," I said, tugging harder. It was hard to do one-handed, and they were a snug fit.

"I can do that." He brushed my hands aside and removed his shoes himself, though his movements were slower than usual.

"Okay, then lie down," I said once the offending footwear was discarded. I gently pushed him sideways and he obediently fell back onto the pillows. Scrambling onto the other side, I knelt next to him and started cleaning off the blood. This time, I'd found my latex gloves in the med kit and put those on. If I'd been thinking more clearly earlier, that would've been a smart thing to do.

"What's with the latex, doc?" he asked.

"Precautionary," I said. "I should've had them on earlier."

"You're safe. I'm not carrying any cooties." He was watching me again, in that way that made me want to look anywhere else but into his eyes.

I focused on my task: cleaning the blood from his skin. Clark's very soft, very well-muscled body, with just the right amount of hair across his pectoral muscles. It was very . . . manly . . . though I didn't consider myself someone who liked chest hair. Jackson's chest was virtually hairless, which I'd always considered a plus.

Clark's bicep was bigger than both of my arms put together, and he wasn't even flexing.

"Did you know that the word *cootie* actually comes from a Malay word meaning 'dog tick'?" I asked. "Supposedly, British soldiers from World War I brought back the word and used it to refer to the lice in the trenches that multiplied and spread terribly."

Clark said nothing, just watching me in that steady way of his while I prattled on. There was blood smeared on his stomach, too. The skin below his pecs was smooth and hairless until right above his navel.

"Of course, people don't often know that 'cootie' is also used in the phrase 'cootie catcher,' which is something I'm sure you've seen—"

"I usually call them something else," he drawled.

I paused. "Really? They've also been called a paper fortune-teller, a whirlybird, a chatterbox, or a salt cellar. The origami method is simple, which is why most children are the creators of cootie catchers." I resumed my task. He was nearly clean now. Just some on his side by his rib cage. "I never played with one, of course, but I've seen many children do so."

He frowned. "Why didn't you play with one? You said it was easy to make."

"Well, yes, I did *make* a few, but you have to have someone to play it with, and I didn't really have any friends." It was long ago and I said it matter-of-factly. My life history was no secret to me. But Clark had a weird look on his face.

"I mean, I didn't really *want* to anyway," I hastened to add. I didn't want him to think I was a loser when I was a kid. "There were only four fortunes in it, no matter how many times you worked it. Pretty boring, actually."

I'd just finished when there was a knock on the door. *Mia.*

"Don't say anything," I hissed to Clark. "Just a second," I called out.

"Are you okay? You've been in the tub for a while," she said through the door. I hurried over and opened it a crack.

"I'm fine. Just going to bed, actually."

"Do you need anything?" she asked. "I can make you some more tea or something—"

"No, no, I'm fine. Just going to take my pain meds and conk out." I smiled, which I shouldn't have done, because when I try to smile, it's very fake and painful-looking. I'd practiced, but it was never going to be a skill I mastered.

Mia gave me a look. "Um, okay, if you're sure?"

I nodded. "Thank you. I'm fine."

She began to back away from the door. "Just text me if you need anything."

"I will."

I waited until I saw her disappear down the stairs before closing and locking the door. We couldn't afford for anyone—not even Mia—to know Clark was here. She didn't hold any credence to him supposedly trying to assassinate the president either, but as of now, I was harboring a fugitive. Mia didn't need to be a part of that.

"Good decision," Clark said when I returned.

"Are you going to tell me what happened?" I asked. "I take it the lead you had turned out to be not so friendly."

"We had a slight disagreement."

"I hope he fared worse than you." Anger burned inside my stomach that someone had taken a shot at Clark.

"You could say that," was his response, and I didn't ask for further clarification. Sometimes it was best not to know the details.

I was exhausted and crawled underneath the covers on the other side of the bed. "Someone was chasing us today," I said, pulling the covers up. "Then the brakes went out. We would've been okay, I think, but a deer made a really poor decision."

"Ouch. You hit Bambi?"

I twisted onto my side to look at him. "I don't think it had a name," I said with a frown.

Clark tapped the tip of my nose with his finger. "Joke," he said softly. He touched my left hand, which was resting between us. "I see you overcame your doubts."

I looked at the ring. "Yeah. I think so. I mean, my grandma said that it takes a leap of faith sometimes. That you can't know with one hundred percent certainty."

"I bet that made you twitch all over."

I laughed at the wry comment. "It goes against my nature, yes. I'm still . . . coming to grips with the idea."

"Jackson is a lucky guy," Clark said at last. His voice was rough, but I didn't look at him, my gaze still on the ring.

"Can I ask you something?"

"You just did."

I smiled a little. Clark using my own logic against me. "Why would you say something so . . . cruel . . . last night? After . . . you know." I didn't know if I'd have to be more specific. The incident stood out in my memory like a gaping black hole with capital letters: The Kiss.

"Because I knew you'd take responsibility and beat yourself up. I thought you should channel that anger outward rather than inward."

"That doesn't make sense," I said. "It wasn't just you. I was an . . . enthusiastic participant." It was difficult to say, but the truth was the truth. "I'm engaged to another man, and I kissed you. It's wrong."

"It was . . . spur of the moment," he said. "Adrenaline fueled. Don't worry about it."

"You seem pretty eager to brush it off, dismiss it," I said.

His finger brushed underneath my chin, forcing me to look at him. "There's not much else I can do, is there." It was a statement, or perhaps a rhetorical question. In either case, I didn't know what to say in response. Our faces were inches apart and I tried to read what was in his eyes. He looked . . . a little sad. A lot resigned.

A grimace of pain crossed his face, and I jumped up. "I have pain pills that the doctor gave me. They'll help." The bottle was in the bathroom, and I filled a glass of water.

"Here," I said, handing him a pill along with the water. He took one, then I did. "At least we'll sleep well tonight."

"I wouldn't count on it," was his muttered reply, but I didn't ask for clarification. I was tired and my body hurt all over.

I grabbed a blanket from my closet and handed it to Clark. "It's probably best if you stay on top of the covers and use this." He took it without comment.

Switching off the light, I climbed back into bed and pulled the bedcovers up. There was a good eighteen inches of space between us. I sighed and closed my eyes, feeling my whole body relax into the familiar softness of my bed.

I was just drifting off, the medicine doing its job, when I heard Clark speak.

"I know I should apologize for kissing you," he said, so softly I wondered if I might be dreaming. "But I can't bring myself to. You could've died today. Or me. And I would've always regretted not making sure."

He didn't say anything else, and I was too groggy to even open my eyes. "Make sure of what?" I mumbled.

"Whether what we have is more than just friendship."

Alarm bells sounded inside my head, clearing away the cobwebs. "And?"

I heard a rustling beside me but didn't move. Clark and I were in the same bed together. If I moved . . . *that way be dragons.* I remained still.

"I think you know the answer to that," he murmured. "Maybe you just don't want to face it."

I swallowed hard, gradually falling to sleep with his words echoing inside my head.

CH 8

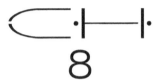

I was even more sore when I woke, and I didn't want to move from where I was warm and cuddled. I snuggled deeper into the arms that surrounded me. They were muscled and wrapped all around me—one under my head, the other over my waist to meet in the middle. A palm had slipped inside my pajama top and cupped my breast.

Wait a second. Jackson was in the hospital. Clark had been shot. Clark was the one in my bed, touching me in a totally inappropriate way.

My eyes popped open. Everything farther than fifteen inches away was blurry. I was frozen, unsure what to do. From the steady breathing in my ear, Clark was asleep. He must've come closer in his sleep. I had no memory of it. The pain meds had knocked me out.

I moved a scant inch, thinking to ease out of his grip, but he sighed deeply and tightened his grip. His thumb brushed over my nipple, and I sucked in a breath. Then he began gently massaging my breast.

"Clark," I said, wriggling in his arms. "Wake up."

He mumbled something and started kissing my neck, sending a shiver through me.

"Clark," I repeated, louder this time. He was still playing with my breast, the nipple growing erect under his touch. Another shiver went down my spine, and my mouth was dry.

"Mmmm, baby," he murmured against my skin.

Baby. The endearment went right through me to my mushy center and set up camp, which was bad bad bad. I grabbed his wrist. "Wake up, Clark."

That produced more of a response, and he stopped kissing me and stopped stroking my breast.

"Good morning," he said in my ear.

"Your hand—"

"Yeah. Right." He slipped his hand out of my shirt, and I let out a breath.

I was up and out of the bed like a shot, grabbing my glasses and rushing into the bathroom. I was flustered and still reacting from his touching me.

My world was shaken. Something was wrong with me. I couldn't possibly be in love with Jackson if I reacted with anything other than shock and revulsion to Clark's . . . advances, for lack of a better word. But revulsion had been the last thing on my mind when we'd kissed, or this morning when he was touching me.

The thought of losing Jackson made my heart squeeze painfully in my chest, and I doubled over, bracing my elbows on the sink. But what else was I to do? I'd betrayed him—not once, but twice. And not with just anyone. With the one man he felt threatened by: Clark.

I didn't know what to do, which wasn't something I was often faced with. What my head said I needed to do was drastically different from my emotions, and I instinctively cringed at the thought.

So I lapsed into routine, the one thing that was a solace to me. The comfort and normality of showering, drying my hair, and putting it up in a ponytail. I wrapped myself in a towel before exiting the bathroom to choose my clothes. I could see from the corner of my eye that Clark was sitting on the side of the bed, head down, elbows braced on his spread knees.

I said nothing as I picked out my clothes, first grabbing a *Make Love, Not Horcruxes* T-shirt. My eyes widened and I shoved it back, pulling out an *I Suspect Nargles Are Behind It* shirt instead, a random long-sleeve shirt, and a pair of jeans. I went to my bureau to choose my bra and underwear, acutely conscious of Clark coming up to stand behind me.

His hands settled on my bare shoulders, and I stiffened. "I'm sorry," he said softly. "I didn't mean to make you uncomfortable."

"Then what did you mean?"

"We have something," he said. His thumbs brushed my skin. "I know I can't be the only one who feels it."

I spun around and shoved him away. "How dare you?" I hissed. "How dare you do this? You were very clear that there would never be anything between us, and then you *left*. And now . . . now it's too late. I'm *engaged*, Clark. And you trying to . . . to . . . *seduce* me, is only making me feel like shit."

His face was wiped of expression, though he was paler than usual. "Well, excuse the fuck out of me for hoping that I wasn't too late." He stalked to the bathroom door, then glanced back. "Sometimes it takes longer than you'd think to realize you've made the biggest mistake of your life." The door closed behind him.

I heard the shower come on, so I dressed quickly, trying not to think of what he'd just said.

◆ ◆ ◆

Mia was already in the kitchen, leaning against the counter, mug in hand, waiting for the coffeepot to finish brewing. She glanced up when I came down.

"Good morning. How are you feeling?" She reached up into the cabinet for another mug. Her pink Hello Kitty pajamas were half-hidden by a fluffy pink robe two sizes too big for her. She had matching fuzzy slippers, too.

"Like I was in a car wreck," I said. "You're up early for a Sunday."

Mia covered a massive yawn with her hand. "I know. But I promised Shelly I'd go to church with her."

My eyebrows flew upward. "Church? I didn't know you were a believer."

Mia shrugged. "I think there's something larger than us, bigger than us, out there. I'm not sure what it is, but hey, better safe than sorry, right?"

"Hedging your bets?"

"Being pragmatic," she corrected with a wink. "Remember what they say—there are no atheists in foxholes. Anyway, she'll be here in half an hour, and I'm pushing it as it is." She poured coffee into her mug and headed back to her room. "I think we're going to breakfast afterward, FYI," she called back.

"Okay, have fun." My response was automatic, then I paused. Was having fun an appropriate thing to say about going to church? But she was already upstairs, so I guessed it didn't matter anyway.

I poured my own coffee, gratefully savoring that first sip. Then poured another cup and took it upstairs.

I'd left an unopened toothbrush, a disposable razor, and fresh towels on the counter for Clark, and by the time I returned, he was shaving. The door to the bathroom was open, and he had a towel around his waist and that was all.

Setting the mugs down, I quickly turned away. His shirt was ruined and he'd need another. I scrounged in my closet, remembering a T-shirt I'd once ordered where they'd accidentally sent the wrong size. I'd never gotten around to returning it, and it might fit Clark. *Ah. There it is.*

"This might fit you," I said curtly, handing it to Clark. "And I need to redress your wound."

He'd just finished shaving and rinsed the remaining suds from his face. I gathered the things I needed and motioned for him to sit on the lid of the toilet.

We didn't speak as I removed the old gauze and tape. I winced in sympathy as the tape removed some hair, though Clark didn't so much as twitch.

The wound looked better and wasn't inflamed, which was a good thing. I used some antibiotic ointment this time before rebandaging, hoping that would keep infection at bay.

"All done," I said, putting the supplies away again.

"*A To-Do list*?" Clark read from the shirt. He glanced up. "You're kidding, right?"

"It's all I had that might fit."

"*Rule Middle Earth, Rebuild the Death Star, Open the Ark of the Covenant* . . . what kind of list is this?"

I shifted from one foot to another, impatient to leave the room so Clark could get dressed. "It's a villain's to-do list," I explained. "They sent the wrong size."

"I don't even know what some of this stuff means," he said, looking back at the shirt. "What the hell is a Pikachu? And why would I want to steal dinosaur embryos?"

I raised an eyebrow. "Really? I'll give you a minute for that one."

Clark frowned and I waited. His face cleared. "Oh. Got it." He chuckled. "I'm honored," he said with a wry smile. "I get to wear one of your precious fandom T-shirts."

Pulling it over his head, he had to do some maneuvering with his injured shoulder, and I had to stop myself from trying to help. It fit tighter than the shirts he usually wore—not that I was going to complain. At least he was covered.

I exited the bathroom, not needing to see him put his jeans on, and waited until he came out, fully dressed.

"What's your plan?" I asked, handing him his cup of coffee. I didn't want to talk about "us" anymore. There was no "us" anyway.

"To find out what the hell this is," he said. Reaching into his back pocket, he pulled out an identical talisman to the one that had been in the Jaguar.

The shock on my face must've been apparent, because he said, "What? What's wrong?"

"That." I pointed. "Where did you get it?"

"Pickpocket slipped it on me yesterday," he said. "Right before my . . . disagreement."

"There was one in the car," I explained. "Right before the accident."

He raised one dark eyebrow. "I'm going to go out on a limb and say that this isn't a coincidence."

"The chances of that would be highly unlikely. But I fail to see the significance of a Roman numeral two."

Clark looked at me strangely. "Roman numeral? It's not a two. It's a Gemini."

I took the talisman from him. "Gemini? You mean the zodiac symbol."

"Yeah."

"That hadn't occurred to me," I said, somewhat chagrined. "But then again, I don't believe in horoscopes or that your personality is influenced by how the stars are aligned in the sky the day you were born."

"Let's set aside the validity of astrology as a science for the time being—"

"It is *not* a science," I scoffed. "You'd have better odds of knowing the future with one of those cootie catchers than a horoscope."

"*Anyway,*" he said, giving me a look, "both you, Coop, and me got a Gemini sign right before someone tried to kill us. I want to know why."

"When were you born?" I asked.

"May tenth," he said. "Taurus, not Gemini. You?"

"Although I don't subscribe to the theory, I was born under the sign of . . ." I took a breath and rolled my eyes. ". . . Virgo."

Clark snorted. "Seriously? The Virgin? And you say you don't believe in that stuff?"

"Coincidence is far more likely," I retorted. "And besides, I'm obviously not a virgin any longer."

Something crossed Clark's face, almost like a wince, but I blinked and it was gone.

"What about Coop?" he asked. "Not a Gemini either?"

"His birthday is January third, which puts him under the Capricorn sign." I handed the metal symbol back to him. He took it without comment, staring at it in his palm.

There was a knock on my door. "I'm leaving now," Mia hollered.

"Okay, bye," I called back.

A moment later, I heard the front door open and close.

"We can go downstairs now," I said, anxious to be in a room with Clark that did *not* include the bed we'd slept in last night. Not waiting to see if he followed, I headed for the kitchen.

Everything Clark had done and said reverberated in the back of my mind, and I didn't know what to do about it. I didn't want to rock the boat I was in. Change was awful—and painful. I was right when I'd told him it was too late.

I'd rinsed my mug and put it in the dishwasher by the time Clark came in. "So how do you plan on figuring out what that means or who sent it?" I asked.

"I know of a place to start," he said, finishing his coffee. "It's just not going to be pleasant."

That didn't sound good. "What do you mean?"

"Remember that place I took you when you got shot?"

Vague images of a hospital-like surgery room, then a recovery room. "Dr. Jay," I said. "You said he owed you a favor."

"He did. Which he paid. He works for PFG Security, not that they advertise. At least, not in the Yellow Pages."

I didn't get the Yellow Pages reference, but grasped the gist. "Why would you go to them? They didn't seem very helpful the first time around."

"Zane has lots of contacts in very high places. Someone who has a beef with the president, me, and Coop has to have talked to somebody. I'd like to know who it is before he tries again. Zane's the best, and quickest, bet."

"How do you know Zane?"

He hesitated, "Let's just say that when I left the service, I wasn't in a Good Place." He used air quotes for *Good Place*.

That wasn't an idiom I was familiar with. I shook my head, confused. "What do you mean? What place were you trying to get to?"

"I don't mean an actual location—"

"But you said place," I interrupted.

"I know, but I meant . . . mentally."

"Oh." I didn't know what else to say.

"That mission I told you about," he said, leaning back against the counter, "was my last. I got out. But I was . . . messed up. I had no job, so I was approached by PFG. I worked for them for a few years."

"What did you do for Zane?" The firm's name was "security," so I assumed he'd been a bodyguard or consultant or something.

"Paid assassin."

I stared at him. "I'm sorry, I must have misheard you. I thought you said 'assassin'?"

"That's right." He crossed his arms over his chest, his gaze narrowing as he watched my reaction.

Clark had killed people before. I knew that. But I'd also thought he'd done it in the name of duty. He'd been dealing in information when I'd first met him. Dangerous information, yes, but still things that were beneficial to the country. For him to suddenly tell me that he'd killed people for money . . . I had to sit down. Luckily, the kitchen table was there, and I yanked out a chair to collapse into.

"You mean . . . you're a bad guy?" I asked. It seemed unreal. "But . . . you saved me. Rescued me."

Clark was suddenly there, crouching down in front of me. "I don't do it anymore," he said. "And I wish now I never had. But . . . I was dead inside back then. I'm not trying to excuse it or make it sound like it was okay. It wasn't—"

"Then what are you trying to make it sound like?" I interrupted, failing to keep the anger from my voice. "Why would you do that?"

His lips thinned. "I've never told anyone about this part of my past," he said. "I don't know why I thought maybe you . . . Never mind." He stood and grabbed his jacket, shrugging into it. "I'd better go."

I jumped to my feet and planted myself squarely in front of him. "No way. Not alone."

"Don't be stupid, Mack. Step aside."

Clark hadn't called me *Mack* in a while. I wasn't fond of the nickname, and the way his voice had sounded when he'd called me *baby* this morning flitted through my head. I pushed the random thoughts away.

"Don't *ever* insult my intelligence," I said, poking him in the chest with a finger. "And I mean it. You're not going without me."

"And how do you propose to make me take you along?" The mask was back in place, hiding the vulnerability he'd let me see earlier. I felt a pang of regret for not tempering my reaction better. I'd just been so shocked.

"I'm your partner. You showed up *here* when you were hurt. You owe it to me to let me come along." I didn't know how far that would get me, so I added, "Besides, you think this Zane is just going to tell you what you want to know? Won't he want something in return?"

Clark studied me, his expression unreadable. "Yes," he said at last.

"And what do you have to trade?"

"I used to do a job for Zane. I can do it again."

Horrified, I shook my head. "No. Absolutely not. No way."

"I don't have any other choice," he bit out. "I don't want to just sit around being a walking target." He paused, reaching out to drape my long ponytail on my shoulder. "Or risk you being caught in the cross fire."

"I already am." I reached into my basket of newfound idioms. "A dime a dozen." Wait, that didn't sound right.

Clark frowned. "What?"

"A penny saved is a penny earned?" I tried. No, that wasn't right either. "Something about money." It was so frustrating when things didn't come out of my mouth right.

"In for a penny, in for a pound?" Clark said.

"Yes! That's the one." What were we talking about again? "Yes, so I'm coming with you. Two heads are better than one." I smiled smugly. I knew I'd gotten that one right. "We'll figure something out." I held my breath. I couldn't let him go without me. What if someone took another shot at him? Next time he might not be so lucky.

"Fine," he said, snapping out the word. "But you have to do what I say, understood? These people don't fuck around."

I was already nodding. "Got it."

He let out a sigh and scrubbed a hand over his face, muttering, "I know I'm gonna regret this."

Choosing to ignore his less-than-complimentary prediction, I put on my jacket and grabbed my backpack and keys. "We're taking my car, though," I said. "I'm not riding on the back of the organ donor again."

He held out his hand. "Deal. But I'm driving."

I hesitated, but the look in his eye said he wasn't going to budge on this point, so I handed them over. "Be careful," I warned him. "She's my baby."

"She's a car," he said. "Not a person."

"That's your opinion. And don't say that where she can hear you."

He rolled his eyes but didn't disparage my Mustang further as we went outside and I locked the door behind me. Mia had retrieved my car from Jackson's, thank goodness, though I'd tried not to think too deeply about her barely sixteen-year-old-self driving it.

Clark got in and immediately banged his knees on the steering column. He cursed and I winced.

"Be careful," I said again.

"How do you even drive this?" he groused, moving the seat back a good foot. "Can you see over the steering wheel?"

"Of course I can," I retorted, then added, "Mostly."

His lips twitched, but he didn't complain any more as he finished adjusting the seat and mirrors. Then we were off. To my surprise, he swung into a fast-food drive-thru.

"What are you doing?" I asked.

"Eating. Aren't you hungry?"

I was already shaking my head. "No. Absolutely not. You will *not* be eating in my car."

"You can't be serious."

"I never joke, especially about my car. I refuse to have fossilized french fries atrophying between the seats, or sticky Coke residue coating the cup holders. No. No food."

Clark heaved a sigh of long-suffering and pulled into a parking spot.

"I don't go inside fast-food restaurants either," I added.

He rested his forehead against the top of the steering wheel. An odd thing to do, but maybe his shoulder was hurting him.

"I'm going to regret asking this, but why?" His voice was muffled from the way he was sitting.

"Because of the noxious odor of oil frying," I said. "It permeates everything. Sit inside there for fifteen minutes and we'll both smell like we pulled an eight-hour shift. It ruins my appetite."

"So why don't you tell me where is an acceptable venue for you to eat this morning?"

"I thought you were in a big hurry to get to PFG?" I asked. "Why are you worried about eating?"

"Soldier rules," he said, lifting his head. "Never skip an opportunity to eat or sleep, because you don't know when you'll get the next chance for either. Plus, both of us were hurt yesterday. We need the nutrition. I can't go in anywhere and you won't let us eat in the car. What's your solution?"

I opened my mouth, then shut it again. He was right. We couldn't take the chance of someone recognizing him by going into an actual restaurant. So as much as I hated it, I gritted my teeth and said, "Fine. We can eat in the car. But *don't* spill anything."

"I'm not a toddler," he retorted, backing out of the space.

In the interest of keeping the peace, I refrained from pointing out that his temper was coming close to tantrum stage.

He ordered for us through the fuzzy speaker. The worker's tinny voice came back, repeating everything, then asked, "Do you want fries with that?"

I said nothing, just glared. Clark glanced my way. "Uh, no thanks. Not this time." He gave me a totally fake, thin-lipped smile. "Happy?" he asked.

I thought it was rhetorical, so I didn't reply with more than a harrumph.

"How are you feeling?" he asked. He inched the car forward in line.

I wasn't sure if he meant physically or emotionally, but the former was easiest to answer. "Sore. I popped a couple of ibuprofen to take the edge off. My wrist is really tender and swollen."

"And Coop?" The name seemed forced, as was the light tone with which he said it.

"Should be released today," I said, glancing away. An awkward silence fell.

"Where's your ring?" he asked.

"I . . . uh . . . I didn't want to risk losing it," I lied. The truth was, my conscience wouldn't let me wear it. "It's expensive."

The harried worker at the drive-thru window passed us two bags and two large drinks. Clark pulled away as I dug through the bags. I grimaced. I could already tell the smell was overtaking the leather aroma of the interior. Yuck.

I insisted he pull over and not drive while eating, which he did after much huffing and rolling of his eyes. Only then did I hand him his burgers. He devoured one then the other in short order, then went to put his hands on the steering wheel . . . and stopped.

I was holding a napkin an inch from his nose.

"Wipe your greasy paws," I demanded.

I popped open the glove box while he did as he was told, then handed him a wet wipe. "Now use this."

"Has anyone ever told you that you might be just a few fries short of a Happy Meal?" he asked.

"To quote Sheldon, 'I'm not crazy. My mom had me tested.'"

That startled a short laugh from him, then I finally allowed him to drive the car again while I unwrapped my food. I ate daintily, leaning over the paper bag in case anything dripped from my turkey-club wrap.

I made him pull off at a gas station to dispose of the trash as soon as I'd finished. I didn't want the smell in my car any longer than absolutely necessary. I also ran inside and bought a new air freshener, which I hung from the rearview mirror.

Clark watched me without comment. I inhaled deeply.

"Mmmm. Much better," I said happily.

"You know, this all could've been avoided if you'd just cooked this morning," he said, pulling back onto the highway.

I glanced at him. His profile was sharply outlined against the sunshine on display outside his window. He'd put on sunglasses, hiding his eyes, and his hair was mussed from running his fingers through it. Not for the first time did I wonder how in the world I ever had bought the lie that he "worked in HR." He no more looked like he worked in HR than I was a runway model.

"Sunday is grocery-shopping day," I said. "The only thing I had to cook was grilled cheese and pizza rolls."

"Breakfast of champions," he deadpanned.

Neither of us spoke about the arguments we'd had, but my guilt ate at me as he drove, until I couldn't hold my silence.

"Clark, I want to say that I'm sorry."

"For what?" His voice was flat. Not exactly rolling out the welcome mat for my apology.

"You told me something very personal, and I reacted . . . badly." To put it mildly.

"You reacted like a normal person," he said. "I shouldn't have been so hard on you."

"But I'm *not* a normal person."

"Don't say that." He spoke so harshly that I was momentarily silenced. "I've told you before," he continued, "you're better than normal. You're . . . one of a kind."

"So are factory rejects." I didn't say it in a bad way. It was a fact.

"You're not a fucking reject," he snapped. "You're like one of those eggs."

"A what?"

"You know." He waved his hand in the air. "The ridiculously expensive eggs made in Russia or whatever."

"Fabergé?"

"Yeah. Those. You're like one of those."

I was at a loss as to how to respond, other than "Thank you, Clark. That's an . . . original compliment." I frowned. "It was a compliment, right?"

He rolled his eyes. "No. Comparing you to priceless, one-of-a-kind works of art was an insult."

I considered. "Sarcasm?"

He shot me a look.

Yep. Sarcasm.

We arrived at PFG a short while later. Clark pulled up to an intercom in front of a formidable black gate.

The intercom burst into life as Clark rolled down the window. The sun had disappeared now and clouds were rolling in.

"State your name and business," the disembodied voice said.

"You know my name, and my business is private. I'll discuss it with Zane, and him only."

There was a length of silence that was just starting to make me uncomfortable when the voice returned.

"Stay on the path. Do not deviate. Any deviation will be seen as a provocation and met with lethal force."

Okay, then.

"They aren't exactly welcoming you with open arms," I said as the gate began to swing ponderously open. "I feel like we're about to land on Bespin."

"A *Star Wars* reference," Clark said. "I got that one."

"Then you know that Vader could be waiting for us," I said.

"What's waiting for us is way worse than Vader," he replied, which didn't make me feel one bit better.

CH 9

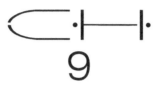

I was conscious this time, and could appreciate the imposing three-story building that loomed in front of us. Made of stone, it had two-story columns that spanned the sprawling front facade. Cars with dark-tinted windows appeared in front and behind us as Clark drove.

"Yeah, this isn't creepy at all," I muttered.

"These aren't people to fuck with," he replied. "I wouldn't be here if I knew of anyone else who might know what I need to know."

"How did you get out?" I asked. "I can't imagine they'd just let you retire with a nice pen as a farewell gift."

He snorted a laugh. "Yeah, the retirement plans here aren't worth writing home about."

"So how did you leave?"

"Remind me and I'll tell you sometime," he said, pulling to a halt in front of the behemoth of a headquarters.

Our doors were opened simultaneously as the engine died. I glanced at Clark, but he was getting out of the car. I followed his example.

Four serious-looking men with serious-looking weapons surrounded us. A fifth man, unarmed, stepped forward. He was massive and bald, immediately making me think of The Rock, and I shrank backward from his intimidating scowl.

"Ease up, Terry," Clark said, sliding an arm around my waist and pulling me protectively closer to him. "You're scaring my girl."

"It's Slade, not Terry," not-Terry said. Clark laughed.

"You make them call you that? Seriously? Someone's overcompensating . . ." His singsong rejoinder only made not-Terry look pissed off and scarier.

"What do you want, Slattery? You know you're not welcome here."

Clark's smirk disappeared. "I said I'd speak to Zane. Not his flunkies. I have something he wants."

I almost turned to look at Clark but stopped myself in time. Of course. This was his bluff. Get us in to see Zane with the promise of something, then figure out what that something was later.

Not-Terry's jaw worked for a minute, then he motioned curtly to the guards. "Fine," he bit out. "Follow me."

Clark kept me close by his side as we walked, and I felt eyes boring a hole into my back. We were led through a massive wooden door at least twelve feet tall. I had the impression we were entering a facility not unlike NORAD, especially when I glimpsed the discreet sensors built inside the frame.

The foyer was elegant without being ostentatious. A ceramic-tiled floor led to a curved staircase, and a chandelier hung high above us. Everything was done in shades of grays—pale-dove gray all the way to gunmetal-steel gray. It was a clean, modern look, and definitely masculine.

Two of the guards melted away, leaving us with two remaining and . . . Slade. One of them covered us with his weapon while the other did a patdown. He removed two handguns from Clark as well as a knife from his ankle that I had no idea he carried.

The patdown of me was pretty quick and efficient. I nervously pushed my glasses back up my nose as the guard stepped back. "She's clean," he said.

Slade glanced at me with a sneer. "Not your usual type," he said to Clark. "You sure it's even a girl?"

The comment was surprisingly catty coming from a man, not to mention a man of his size, but before I could respond, Clark did. Snarling, he leaped at him, but the guards were quick, grabbing his arms and holding him back. Slade gave a low laugh.

"Now who's overcompensating?" he sneered.

"You sound like a Mean Girl," I snapped at the guy. "Are you going to start a hashtag now? Though I have to admit, your boobs are bigger than mine."

His smirk disappeared as Clark snorted, freeing himself from the guards. "No offense, Terry, but you're definitely not my type."

He was scowling now and I didn't want to push our luck, so I shoved my elbow into Clark's side. He responded by slinging his arm over my shoulders.

"You were taking us to Zane," he said, gesturing toward the stairs.

Slade looked like he'd like to take us somewhere, all right, and we probably wouldn't like it one little bit. But instead, he headed up the winding staircase. Clark had me go in front of him, the guards following us.

I was scared the deeper we went into the fortress. The farther we were in, the farther we'd have to go to get out. I only hoped we wouldn't be fighting our way out.

The hallway was thickly carpeted, swallowing our steps as we walked. The decor was different on this level, with ornate wood paneling on the walls and crown molding. Elegant and tasteful, the rooms I glimpsed as we passed were understated, yet obviously expensive.

We stopped in front of a set of double doors. Slade knocked and waited. A man's voice answered.

"Come in."

I thought perhaps we were about to meet the pope or someone of equal religious import, judging by the reverent way Slade opened the doors. So, I was a little disappointed that it was just another man, only this time he was sitting behind a desk and didn't appear to have a weapon.

He rose when we walked in, and his gaze landed on Clark. Rounding his desk, he approached us until we stood mere feet away, then stopped.

Shorter than Slade, he was well dressed in a three-piece suit and tie. His shoes were polished to a high gleam, and his hair looked like something out of a fashion magazine. He was olive-skinned, and one of the most attractive men I'd ever seen, but his eyes were cold and calculating as he sized us up.

Giving me a once-over, he dismissed me and turned his attention to Clark. "Slattery," he said, "I didn't think you'd be gracing us with your presence anytime soon, especially not with your current level of . . . notoriety. Can you give me one good reason why I shouldn't kill you right now and save the taxpayers' money on a trial?"

I sucked in a breath in alarm, my head going through scenarios to try to get us out of there alive . . . and coming up empty.

"Since when have you been concerned about the taxpayers, Zane?" Clark scoffed. "Don't tell me you're a Republican now."

My eyebrows climbed to my hairline. Antagonizing the already-angry man didn't seem like the smartest way to go, though perhaps the quickest, judging by the guards' itchy trigger fingers.

Zane didn't reply, and it felt as though the whole room had taken a breath and was holding it, then he suddenly grinned.

"Holy shit, Slattery. I should've known only you would have the balls to pull a job like that, then stick around. Though I have to say, I'm surprised that you missed. Losing your touch in your old age?" He laughed, then moved forward to clap a hand to Clark's injured shoulder. "Good to see you again. God, how long has it been?"

This must've signaled something to Slade, because he made a gesture with his hand, and he plus the two guards melted into the hallway, closing the doors behind them and leaving us alone with Zane.

I let out my breath, but didn't relax. We were still in the lion's den.

"Sit down," Zane said, gesturing to a sofa close to the windows. He took an armchair opposite. "So tell me," he continued once we were all settled, "what brings you here, and who is your lovely friend? And what's this about something I need?"

"This is China," Clark said. "She's my partner."

I scrutinized Clark. He was a shade paler than he had been before, though he acted fine. I wondered if the pain of his wound was getting to him.

"It's a pleasure to meet you, China," Zane said, turning on the charm. "Clark, you've certainly increased the caliber of your companions."

Clark just responded with a thin-lipped smile. "I need your help," he said. "And you need mine."

"Of course, absolutely," Zane said. "You may not have left under the best circumstances, but we don't hold grudges."

I wasn't a human lie detector by any stretch of the imagination, but even I wanted to guffaw at that whopper.

"What do you need?"

"Information." He pulled the Gemini talisman out of his pocket. "On this." He handed it over. "We found two of those yesterday, right before someone tried to punch our ticket out of here. No other message or motive. Does it ring a bell?"

Zane frowned as he examined the metal symbol. "It's certainly been a long time, but yes, I remember." He glanced back up at Clark. "I don't think you were privy to all the particulars of Operation Gemini."

"Never heard of it."

"I don't know the finer points. I thought it happened around the time of your last mission, before you came to work for me."

Clark stiffened at the mention of his last mission. "So you can't help me?"

"I can give you a name," Zane said. "Someone who should know and be able to help you."

"Who?"

"Ah," Zane said, steepling his fingers underneath his chin. "Information is an expensive commodity, Slattery."

"Which is why I didn't come empty-handed," Clark said.

"So I see," Zane said. "I've been trying to find just the right person for a job I need done." His gaze swung to mine. "And here you are." He smiled and it sent a chill down my spine.

"She's not an assassin," Clark said. "And she's not what I meant."

"I don't care what you meant. I know exactly who she is," Zane replied. "One of the top cybersecurity hackers in the world, and you bring her right in the front door. The only thing you missed is gift wrap."

"Would you believe she's a med student that I sweet-talked?" Clark said. "It's been a little lonely on the road."

Zane's friendly pretense fell away. "Stop bullshitting me. I knew you'd be coming here before you did. And I've known about her for longer. So, if you want something from me, you'll do what I say. When you came here, you gave up your choices."

"I walked out of here once," Clark said. "I can do it again."

"Maybe. But *she* won't."

As if orchestrated, the doors opened again and we were surrounded. Two men yanked me up from the chair and began dragging me toward the door. I fought them, twisting to see Clark fighting as well, though doing a much better job than I was.

But as good a fighter as Clark was, he was outmatched six to one. There was a flurry of fists, and they had Clark's arms pinned behind him. Not-Terry landed a punishing blow to Clark's jaw, and I screamed, terrified.

"Let him go! You asshole!" I struggled, dragging my feet, but they treated me like a sack of potatoes.

"Hurt her and you die," Clark hissed through blood staining his mouth.

"I'll be sure to take that under advisement. In the meantime, I believe a bit of payback is in order."

Before I could see what they were going to do to him, I was dragged through the doorway and down the hallway. Literally. Because I was fighting to get back to Clark. It was like trying to move a brick wall. We halted when they dragged me into an elevator, and I decided fighting any further was useless. All it was doing was draining my energy.

No one said anything as the elevator moved. I was in the middle, surrounded by armed men. I didn't even reach shoulder height of any of them. Neil Diamond's "Sweet Caroline" played over the elevator's speaker. The lights changed above the doors, signaling we were on level BB. A ding sounded and the doors slid open.

I walked on my own power down the concrete hallway that looked like a leftover bunker from the Cold War. We came to what could only be termed a cell, and they pushed me inside, closing a pocket door made of one-way glass to lock me in.

Well.

They hadn't taken my phone, but there was no signal available and—surprise, surprise—no complimentary Wi-Fi. A lone twin-size cot was in the room, along with a modern-looking sink and toilet. I'd been inside another prison cell before, though it had been in China, and a shiver of dread snaked down my spine. I'd been badly beaten the last time I'd been a captive. It was something I tried not to think about.

I had several useful apps on my phone. One of them was handy for accessing networks when a password wasn't just left on the bedside table for you. I scanned for available networks and started the program working. It took some time—and I was sure PFG security wasn't going to be like hacking into a coffee shop—but it hadn't failed me yet.

The door swooshed open and Clark was shoved inside. I jumped to my feet as he collapsed to his knees. The door closed again, but I barely noticed, falling to my knees by Clark.

"Oh my God, are you all right?" An idiotic question, in retrospect, as he obviously wasn't all right. But it's what fell out of my mouth.

"Ouch," he mumbled, his eyes fluttering open. "The floor is hard."

I helped him up and over to the bed. That's when I noticed the shirt I'd given him had a darker, wet spot on his shoulder. I touched it lightly, and my fingers came away red with blood.

"Oh no. They opened your wound." Distraught, I didn't know what to do. I had no medical supplies here.

"Least of our worries." He grimaced. "Zane holds a grudge. Apparently."

"Lie down," I said, going to the sink. I took off my long-sleeve shirt and wet it. "You need to rest." When I returned, he was still sitting up. A bruise was darkening his jaw, and his blood was drying above his lips. I pushed lightly and he fell back on the bed.

"If you insist," he deadpanned.

I carefully cleaned the blood from his face. His eyes were closed again, and I winced at the cuts to his face and lips. Even with the marks and bruising, he was still beautiful.

"Zane really doesn't like you," I said, dabbing at a spot of blood on his neck.

"Yeah, well, I kind of have that effect on people."

"Are you going to tell me now how you got out? Because, obviously, Zane isn't over it." I settled next to him on the cot.

"I'd love to say I suddenly grew a conscience, but that's not a hundred percent true," he said. "I just got sick of working for someone else. Decided I was done with PFG and Zane. Problem was, I took a couple very lucrative clients on my way out."

I paused in cleaning him up. "You have clients that just want people killed?"

His eyes cracked open. "No. I stopped that line of work. They're people who need information, usually on other people."

Relieved, I went back to work. "Sounds like business, then. He shouldn't have taken it so personally."

"The accounts were worth over a hundred million."

My jaw dropped. "In dollars?"

He gave me a look that said I'd just said something stupid. "No, in chickens. Of course in dollars."

I'd had no idea Clark had that kind of money. I'd never put a great deal of thought into it, either, though I knew he lived in that gorgeous log home in the backwoods outside of Raleigh.

"Okay, then. I can see why he might still carry a grudge," I allowed. "But beating on you was uncalled for and childish."

Clark huffed a laugh. "I'll make sure to tell him that next time."

"There won't be a next time," I said. I was angry. Pissed off, to be accurate. Clark was important to me, and within the span of a day, he'd been shot and now beaten up. For someone who'd saved me so many times, this time he was the one who needed saving.

"You've got mad ninja skills that I'm just now hearing about?" he asked as I pulled my phone from my pocket.

"Something like that," I replied, only half paying attention. My little app had done its work. I was inside the network. "Try to rest," I told him, smoothing his hair back from his forehead. It was soft and silky between my fingers. His eyes fluttered closed at my touch.

My heart twisted inside. Clark had no one, it seemed. He reminded me . . . of me. I'd used my routine and schedule to help keep a barrier around myself for years. So many people who'd come into my life when I was younger had hurt me. My self-imposed isolation had been an act of self-defense. As for Clark, his last mission must have messed him up so badly, it had killed him inside for a while.

I worked on my phone for a few minutes, gratified to find that Zane wasn't as smart as he thought he was. All kinds of things connected to Wi-Fi now, ubiquitously called the Internet of Things. And the vast majority of them were unsecured.

"Clark?" I asked, once I'd finished what I needed to do.

"Mmmm?"

"Something happened on your last mission. Something really bad. I know you—at least I think I do, and you wouldn't just start . . . doing what you did . . . without an impetus strong enough to overcome who you really are." I needed to know. Or perhaps he needed to tell me.

His eyes opened again and he looked steadily at me.

"What was it?" I was shooting in the dark here, but I wanted to understand. Because the two sides of the equation didn't correlate. Not unless everything I knew and felt about Clark was somehow flawed, and that I'd been duped by my own naïveté.

I waited, mindlessly combing my fingers slowly through his hair, and wondered if I was right.

"It was my brother."

My fingers froze. He was gazing at me, his blue eyes clear and unblinking.

"My younger brother," he continued. "He'd joined the Army the same as I had, followed in my footsteps, turning Special Forces. We were together on the mission. We worked together a lot. Knew each other's moves and how we each thought.

"When things went to shit that night, the team got separated. I was in communication with command but had lost radio contact with the members of the team, including my brother. Command told me to get out. I had the flash drive with what we needed. But I refused to leave the team. CO told me they'd made it out, that I was the last one, and I believed him. So I bugged out."

"What happened?"

"They'd lied to me," he said. "They told me whatever I wanted to hear so I'd get the drive to them. It wasn't until I was back that I found out only three other guys besides me made it out. The rest had been killed."

"Including your brother."

"Yes."

Well. That explained . . . so very much.

"What was his name?" I asked.

The Adam's apple in Clark's throat moved as he swallowed before answering. "Rob. His name was Rob."

I slotted my fingers through his. "I'm sorry for your loss, Clark. You punished yourself, didn't you. That was what working for PFG was all about."

He glanced away, staring up at the ceiling. "I was angry. At myself. At the Army. I'd given them my loyalty and put my life on the line so many times. And they lied to me. They couldn't even retrieve his body for a burial. He was just . . . gone."

I didn't have the right words to say to him, so I held his hand and hoped talking about it helped him. He'd left PFG, so at some point, he had moved on. But it was clear the pain was still there.

"I've never told anyone before," he said.

Startled, my gaze flew to his. "Why not?"

He shrugged. "Never had anyone to tell. No one to give a shit enough to hear my sorry-ass sad story."

This was important. It took a lot for me to share personal things, so I understood that his telling me—and only me—was a Very Big Deal.

"I'm glad you told me." I said the words with as much sincerity as I could imbue them with, since I lacked the skills of prose to convey how much it meant that he had confided his deepest pain with me.

"I thought, if I'm going to have any shot of us being more . . . then you should know what I am. The good, the bad, and the ugly."

The words . . . *us being more* . . hung in the air between us.

"Clark—"

The door swished open and I jumped to my feet, standing protectively in front of the bed. Zane walked in.

"Hiding behind a woman now, are we?" he asked with a sneer. "How progressive of you, Clark."

I could hear Clark moving to stand. "She's my friend. An unknown concept to you."

"What do you want?" I asked.

"I believe we were in the middle of negotiations," Zane replied. "I have a job I need done. You need a name."

"China's not going to do a job for you," Clark scoffed. "She's not for sale."

"China," Zane said, addressing me, "you've seen that there is no love lost between Clark and me, so I will have no qualms about using him for target practice, should you refuse."

There was no doubt in my mind that he was absolutely serious. "What's the job?"

"An easy one, for you. A database hack, changing some information, and removing a couple of names."

I was sure there was a catch. "What database?"

"The FBI's Terrorist Screening database."

And there it was. "And how do I know you'll keep your word if I do this?"

"You don't. But then again, you don't have much choice."

He was right and we all knew it. I wasn't about to let Zane punish Clark further or hurt him in any way.

"He goes where I go," I demanded, taking Clark's hand. "I'm not letting him out of my sight."

"Agreed."

"And he gets medical treatment," I added. "From Dr. Jay."

Zane rolled his eyes. "You're not in much of a position to make demands, but fine. I'll have him patched up. Now let's go. We're in a bit of a time crunch."

The two guards who'd accompanied Zane escorted us out of the cell. I walked slowly, not wanting to let them rush Clark, who I knew had to be hurting even though his face remained stoic.

"Doctor first," I said to Zane's back.

"Doctor during," he tossed back. "Like I said, we have a deadline. And I'm done negotiating."

We were led to stairs and climbed to the floor above us, which was again decorated in the style of the foyer, with tiled floors, muted gray walls, and indirect lighting. Zane used a key card to open a door, and we followed him into an oversize office.

A line of six workstations were set up in one area, while a long conference table was in another. There were a couple of couches arranged perpendicular to each other. Windows lined one wall, and there was a man working behind a metal-and-glass desk that stood alone. He glanced up from his monitor when we entered.

"How are we doing on time?" Zane asked him.

"Two hours from touchdown." He glanced at me and Clark, but didn't seem surprised to see strangers there, not even bruised and bloodied strangers.

"Get ahold of the doctor and send him up here," Zane said. "And set this one up on a computer." He gestured toward me.

The man scurried to do Zane's bidding, and before long I was ensconced at one of the workstations while Clark was sitting on a couch, being examined by the same tall doctor who'd attended me.

"China, this is Rey. Rey, China," Zane introduced the man to me. "He'll tell you what we need you to do and monitor you to make sure it gets done without you doing anything you shouldn't. If you *do* step out of line, he'll be the one to inform me, who'll inform that guard over there." He pointed to the one by Clark. "He'll make life most unpleasant for Slattery."

Not exactly the motivational speeches I was used to. "Fear does not inspire loyalty," I said.

"Maybe not," he said with a shrug. "But fear gets results, which is all I'm interested in." He walked away.

I turned to Rey. "So why the timetable?"

"Because the guy whose name is in that database is going to land at JFK in two hours. His father is paying us to get his name off that list before he lands."

"Wouldn't it have been better for him not to fly here before confirmation that his name has been removed?" I asked.

"It would," he sighed. "But he's a Saudi big shot and used to people catering to his every whim. He thought this would give us greater impetus to get the job done."

"He's not wrong about that," I mumbled. "What's the name?"

Rey handed me a piece of paper with a name, birth date, and country of citizenship on it. "That's the one."

It wasn't a name I recognized, which was a good thing. We'd kept our own list at Vigilance, and my near-eidetic memory helped when going through data. I hoped it really was just one of those things where the guy was a harmless, rich idiot.

"Time?" I asked. Rey glanced at his watch.

"One hour, fifty minutes until touchdown."

One of my favorite things to scoff at on television was shows where a character throws out the words "So I hacked in to" fill-in-the-blank, as if it were as easy as making a telephone call. *Bones* was a favorite target of mine, as much as I could relate to Dr. Brennan. Angela—starving artist turned computer maven—was forever tossing off the "So I hacked in to" phrase.

The truth was, hacking was a tedious process that was akin to standing on a busy street, outside a locked door, with surveillance cameras filming you, and trying key after key until one worked. The Internet wasn't a private place, and the more prime the target, the more defense measures were in place to watch for intruders, deter them, and hunt them down.

It was an art form that took intuition, cleverness, subterfuge, and sheer audacity. I'd learned how to do it out of curiosity, and I had a talent for it. But I didn't make a habit of it. For one, my conscience wouldn't allow me to break in to secure networks just to see if I could. And second, I didn't want to constantly be looking over my shoulder for that one time I made a mistake—because mistakes were inevitable.

After a while I glanced over at Clark, who had his shirt off, and Dr. Jay was sewing up the wound in his arm and had hooked up an IV. But Clark was watching me with single-minded focus. The expression on his face said he was not fazed by what was going on around him, but was . . . guarding me. It was the best description I could come up with.

"Thirty minutes," Rey said. He'd settled into the chair next to me, essentially watching over my shoulder. It irritated me. I hated being watched when I worked. At least he wasn't asking questions. That would have been worse.

I'd gotten into the network and had found the server hosting the database, but still needed to crack the security on the database to edit the tables. My fingers flew over the keys as I concentrated.

"Ticktock, ticktock." The voice at my ear made me stiffen. "You're not as good as I thought you'd be." Zane was leaning over me, braced on the back of my chair.

"It's the FBI," I retorted. "I'm going as fast as I can."

"Here's some added incentive," he said, then straightened and nodded at the guards.

One of them shouldered the rifle he was holding and removed a handgun from its holster at his hip. He racked the slide, then held the muzzle to the back of Clark's head.

"Seven minutes before I redecorate with your boyfriend's brains."

CH 10

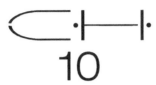

Fear and frustrated rage made my hands shake, but I didn't doubt for an instant that Zane would do it. Clark's life was quite literally in my hands.

Pushing aside my emotions, I concentrated on the work. The database the FBI was using wasn't proprietary, and there had been a security vulnerability published just last week about this particular product and version. If the database hadn't yet been patched, I could exploit that hole. A query against the database gave me the information I needed, and I breathed a sigh of relief. I'd caught a break.

A database isn't like a spreadsheet, but like a maze of tables that are all interconnected, referring back to one another. Deleting one record from one table would do nothing except compromise the data and alert administrators that someone had tampered with it. A restore from backup would undo everything I did. I had to figure out the map of the database and structure my query to modify and delete the specific data, not leaving anything corrupted, and I had . . . I glanced at the clock on the computer monitor . . . two minutes left in which to do it.

I dropped into my zone, blocking out all sound around me and seeing only the words on the screen. My fingers flew over the keyboard, querying the structure and tables of the database, then memorizing the results it returned. Thank God whoever had designed the thing hadn't gotten fancy with table names.

Over a dozen tables would need to be modified to delete this particular name from existence, and the query I wrote was more than ten lines long by the time I sent the command to execute. I waited, barely breathing, counting the seconds inside my head.

One . . . two . . . three . . . four . . .

The blinking cursor returned. QUERY COMPLETE. TWELVE ROWS MODIFIED.

I let out my breath in a huff. "Done," I said loudly, then turned around in my chair to Zane. "It's done."

He smiled. "Right down to the wire. Impressive."

"Call off the gun," I demanded.

He took longer than I wanted before nodding at the guard holding Clark at gunpoint. The guard unchambered the round, then put the weapon back in his holster.

The anger I'd kept compartmentalized while I worked now broke free. I stood and got in Zane's face.

"You're a real asshole," I hissed. "Someone like you should be careful of the enemies you make. They might come back to bite you in the ass."

He had the audacity to laugh. "You mean like you? You're about as threatening as a Chihuahua." Then he *patted my head.*

I gasped in outrage and jerked away. My fists were clenched in impotent rage. I hated Zane with every breath I took.

Everyone was watching us. Rey, Dr. Jay, the two guards, and Clark, who looked like he wanted to tear Zane limb from limb.

Zane's cell phone rang. Completely unfazed by my anger, he pulled his phone from his pocket and glanced at the screen. "It's my wife," he said. "Gotta take it. You know how it is." He winked and smiled, casually turning away as he answered. "Hey, babe, what do you need? I'm a little busy—"

She interrupted him and I couldn't make out what she was saying, but she was obviously upset.

"Slow down, start again," Zane said. "What's going on?" He listened. "No . . . no, I didn't change anything."

Turning away, I headed toward Clark. The doctor was removing the IV from his arm, and Clark pulled his shirt back on, grimacing slightly. I sat next to him on the couch.

"Will he be okay?" I asked the doctor, who nodded.

"You did a good job getting the slug out and cleaning the wound," he said. "I sewed him up and gave him an antibiotic in case of infection. He also has a couple cracked ribs, I believe, but they'll heal on their own. The rest is just abrasions and contusions."

"Good." I smiled when Clark glanced at me.

"What did you do?" Zane asked, his voice tight with anger. He'd walked over and now stood a few feet away, still with his cell at his ear.

"What are you talking about?" I asked, barely summoning enough interest in his plight to bother responding.

"My wife can't leave our house," he said.

"Why would she want to leave?" I asked, frowning. "You live in a luxury mansion just built last year, with all the bells and whistles."

Zane tapped a button on his cell, putting his wife on speaker. "Tell me what's happening, honey."

"It's been going on for a couple of hours," she said, her voice tinny from the speaker. "At first, I thought it was just a problem in the wiring, but now . . . now it's forty degrees in here, and I-I'm locked in.

"The lights won't come on, but the televisions won't turn off," she continued. "They're all blasting the same channel. The hot tub is boiling, and I'm afraid to go in the kitchen. The appliances are all on and I can't turn them off."

"Oh yeah," I said, "you've got one of those smart houses, right? Everything's hooked up to a central system that you use voice control for, right?" I leaned forward, asking conspiratorially, "I don't suppose your wife knows Mandarin Chinese, does she? I bet that would help."

Zane's face turned purple in mottled rage.

"Wait, I found a door unlocked," his wife said, sounding relieved. "Oh thank God, it's the garage. I'll be able to drive out of here, Zane."

Zane's face went from red to white in an instant. "No, wait—"

"Zane, the cars! They're all running! And I can't . . ." There was a rattle and thumping sound. "I can't get out of the garage now. The door locked behind me." Panic threaded her voice. "Zane? Can you hear me? I'm locked in the garage. All three cars are running. What do I do?"

"*Oooh*, that sounds bad," I said casually. "Those remote auto-starts are so handy, right? But carbon monoxide poisoning can be a real danger. Three cars running with exhaust inside an enclosed space for two hours? I bet that air is already heavily contaminated." I shook my head in mock sadness.

"Zane?" His wife's voice was panicked.

Quick as a flash, he raised his arm to hit me, and just as quickly, Clark caught it before he could land a blow.

"Try that again and I'll break your arm," Clark said.

The guards looked unsure as to what to do, while Rey and Dr. Jay just watched. As I'd told Zane before, fear didn't inspire loyalty. They weren't going to put their lives on the line for him, that was obvious. And it seemed as though they didn't particularly care very much as to what the outcome of this standoff would be. They merely watched with interest.

"How does it feel?" I asked Zane. "To know someone you love is in danger? That their life is in someone else's hands? Someone who doesn't give a damn what happens to them?"

"I didn't kill him," he said. "He's alive and well, right next to you. I kept my word."

"Yay, you," I deadpanned. "Give me the name. Give me the name and I'll consider giving you your house back. Otherwise, well, carbon monoxide isn't a bad way to go. You just . . . fall asleep. Tell your wife she may want to remain standing as long as possible."

"Zane? I can't hear what's going on. Can you fix this? Help me."

"If my wife dies, I'll kill you."

"If you kill us, your wife is still dead," I said, my voice hard. "Give me the name."

His jaw worked as though he was chewing on the words. He glared at me, unblinking. But I wasn't fazed and stared back. This was a bad man, an evil man, with no conscience. I wasn't surprised he was taking longer than he should to contemplate his decision, and I felt a brief pang of sympathy for his wife, married to a man like that.

She began to cough and that spurred Zane. "Danvers," he spit out. "Mark Danvers. He was in charge of Operation Gemini. Now let my wife go."

"I'll let your wife go once we are beyond the front gate," I said. "I'm not about to give up our only leverage just so you can have us shot on the way out."

"How do I know you'll let her go?"

"You don't," I said, echoing his earlier derisive response. "But then again, you don't have much choice." His wife coughed again. "I'd suggest making a decision quickly. It doesn't sound like she has much time left."

"Let them go," he told the guards, then to us he said, "Get out and don't come back."

I got up in his face. "Gladly," I hissed. "And remember, you made an enemy today. We'll call this a draw, but if you ever come near me or Clark again, I'll take this fucking place apart piece by piece."

Clark relieved the guards of their rifles, handing me one, as well as the handgun. "It's been real," he said to Zane. "And I hope you learned your lesson."

"What's that?" Zane called out as we headed out the door.

"Never piss off a Chihuahua."

◆ ◆ ◆

Clark drove while I took care of Zane's wife, turning off the cars and remotely opening all the garage doors. I watched on their surveillance camera as she stumbled outside and took a few deep breaths. Other than shaken, she looked fine. I disconnected from their system.

"Would you really have done it?" Clark asked. He was watching the road. It was dark by now and my stomach growled. The fast food had been a long time ago.

"Done what?" I had a dozen missed calls, and the texts were piling in.

"Let her die."

I glanced up from my phone in surprise. Of all people to question my motives and conscience, I hadn't expected it from Clark.

"No, I don't think so," I answered truthfully. "I'd like to think I wouldn't have. At the time, I was . . . angry. Enraged. Furious."

He snorted. "Yeah. I got that. Remind me never to pat you on the head."

I smiled and shook my head. "It wasn't that. I mean, not *just* that. When they held a gun to your head, and he treated you like a punching bag, so casual with your life . . . I wanted revenge. I wanted to make him feel the same helpless fury and despair that I had felt."

He didn't say anything and I squirmed a little in my seat.

"It's not a pretty part of me," I said. "Frankly, I didn't know I could be so . . . angry and . . . and—"

"Ruthless?" Clark finished.

I nodded. "Yeah. I guess that's the word."

"You don't work for the Gap, sweetheart. This business ain't for the fainthearted."

I wasn't sure how I felt about my actions, but I did know that we were both alive and out of PFG. My cell rang as I was scrolling. Jackson.

"Hey," I answered, "did they let you out of the hospital?"

"I've been out for hours. Where the hell are you? I've been worried sick. So is Mia."

Oh noooo . . .

"Um, I know, and I'm sorry. I didn't have a signal where I was so I couldn't call you."

"Where were you?"

Really didn't want to go there. "I'm on my way home. I'll tell you all about it then."

"Come to my place instead."

I glanced at Clark. "Um, I will, I just . . . need to go by my house first and see Mia. I hate that she was worried."

"Fine, but then come. I have information about the assassination attempt."

"Okay. See you soon." I ended the call and turned to Clark. "Jackson says he has information about the shooter."

"Did he say what it was?"

"Not yet. Said he'd tell me tonight."

"You're going over there?"

"Of course. I haven't seen him since we woke up in the hospital. I'm worried about him." And that wasn't all. I needed his arms around me, needed the normalcy Jackson now represented. Clark had turned my world upside down in two days. I craved my routine.

"Yeah, yeah. I'm sure you are. That makes sense."

His words were common enough and easily said, but his hands had tightened on the wheel. I felt like there was tension between us, though I didn't know why.

"Are you angry?" I asked. "Or hurting?" The doctor had patched him up and given him the antibiotic, but no pain medication that I could see. Not even ibuprofen. "You can have another one of my pain pills tonight."

"I'm fine," he said, glancing at me. "You can keep your pain meds."

I nodded and left it at that.

Mia was waiting for me, and boy, was she in a snit.

"You could've left a note," she said, crossing her arms over her chest and blocking the door into the house. "I've been worried sick."

"I have an excuse," I said. Clark stepped from behind me into the light, a rifle slung over each shoulder and the handgun tucked into the front waistband of his jeans. I jerked my thumb. "Him."

Clark gave a thin-lipped smile and waggled his fingers at her. "Hiya, Mia."

Mia's eyes narrowed. "Asshat," she greeted him. "You're causing trouble for Aunt Chi again, aren't you."

"Don't be rude," I admonished her. "Let us in. I'm starving."

Reluctantly, she moved aside, eyeing Clark with the look of someone watching a misbehaving toddler.

"I made dinner," she said, heading into the kitchen. "Just in case you got home in time."

I sniffed appreciatively, my mouth watering. "Mmm, spaghetti and meatballs?"

"Your favorite," she said, taking down another plate and setting it alongside the other two already on the table.

"Technically, not true," I said. "But of the Italian dishes that you've attempted, it's definitely the best."

"What's your favorite, then?" Clark asked.

"Oh boy," Mia muttered. Clark glanced at her.

"I can't answer that," I said.

"Why not?"

"Don't ask."

Mia's hissed comment came at the same time as Clark's follow-up question, and I gave her a questioning look before answering Clark.

"Favorite food implies there's one meal or dish that I prefer above all others and would always choose to have if that choice was possible. But not only would that be unhealthy, it's discriminatory against all other foods. Not to mention that I've only eaten a fraction of a fraction of all possible combinations of nutrients in the world, so the sampling size is scientifically too small for there to be a preferred item."

Clark's lips had a twist to them, and his blue eyes had a softness I wasn't accustomed to seeing.

"Um, but I guess if I were to go with the conventional answer to the question . . . I'd say pizza."

Clark's smile widened. "Nice job."

Mia was looking at me, too, brows raised, spaghetti noodles dripping from her ladle. "Okay, then," she said. "Let's eat."

The three of us sat down to laden plates and dug in. I was on my third meatball when Mia asked, "So, are you two a thing now?"

I looked at her as if she'd just told me the meatballs were store-bought. Clark promptly began choking. I pounded on his back and shot her a dirty look. She just sucked up more noodles, oblivious. Or pretending to be oblivious.

"I'm engaged to Jackson," I said sternly to her. "Clark and I are partners. And friends. That's all."

Clark said nothing, just took another sip of his wine. A very long sip.

"I'm just a teenager," Mia said calmly. "So I don't know much. But I think that it would be better to face the hard questions *before* the wedding rather than after. Maybe you two need to have a talk. Or some alone time." She popped up her phone. "I'm going to stay with Megan tonight. I'll check you two tomorrow." With one last slurp of her noodles, she jumped up and pecked her lips to my cheek. "Leave the dishes. I'll do them in the morning." She winked at me and left.

It happened so fast, I was left staring at the closed door in open-mouthed shock. Had she just suggested . . .

"I'm not a genius like you," Clark said drily, "but I think Mia just tried to insinuate we should have sex."

I turned to him. "We are *not* going to do that. I-I'm supposed to be going over to Jackson's."

"Right. I almost forgot." Getting up, he took our empty plates to the sink and began rinsing them.

"We are two relatively young people with healthy libidos," I said. "It's only natural that we would have a certain . . . physical attraction. Plus, we've been put into life-threatening situations several times, which can heighten and accentuate . . . feelings. Making them feel more urgent and real than they actually are."

Clark didn't respond. He just kept rinsing, then began putting the dishes in the dishwasher and storing the leftovers in Tupperware.

"We're just acting out millennia of fight-or-flight tendencies as well as the natural reaction of gratitude that someone feels when another person puts their life on the line to help them. It's the highest form of . . . of . . . affection . . . and . . . and . . . friendship . . ." I ran out of words.

Clark finished and turned toward me, leaning back against the counter. His gaze was dark and his mouth unsmiling.

"I'm not going to argue with you," he said at last. "I want you to be happy. I'm just not sure if you'd be happier with someone else instead of Jackson."

I shrugged helplessly. "That's sweet of you, but there is no one else. Jackson is the man in my life."

"There's me."

I froze, staring at him. This was the first time he'd actually offered me something. "What are you saying?"

There was a hard knock on the front door, then I heard the lock clicking, and it opened. Jackson walked in. He came in about ten feet until he got a good look in the kitchen, and he stopped.

"You've got to be fucking kidding me," he ground out.

Oh shit.

"Jackson!" I jumped to my feet and rushed to him. "It's so good to see you." I threw my arms around his neck and hugged him hard. He didn't hug me back.

"Why is Clark in your house?" Jackson's question was asked with deceptive calmness.

"Um, it's kind of a long story," I said carefully, gazing up at him. He still hadn't put his arms around me. I felt awkward, so I took a step backward.

Jackson's gaze landed on Clark. "What the fuck are you doing here? How much of your shit have you gotten China involved in now?"

"Jackson—"

"No, it's okay," Clark interrupted. "He's right. I've gotten you way too involved in things that are dangerous. I should never have come." He grabbed his jacket, and my stomach fell to my shoes.

"No, no! Wait!" I grabbed his arm, latching on to him. "You can't go."

"Let him," Jackson said. "He's poison, China."

I turned on him. "He is *not* poison," I hissed. "He's been framed, and I'm not about to let him leave when I—when *we*—are in a position to help him."

"I am not helping him," he sneered. "He's wanted by every law-enforcement agency we have."

"They're wrong," I insisted. "He's not guilty. And he's my partner. I can help him and so can you. If you refuse to help me, then . . . then I guess we have a problem."

Jackson looked at me, his jaw tight and his eyes flashing anger.

"Is that an ultimatum?" he asked.

I hesitated. Ultimatums were bad. Every reality show I'd ever watched said that. "Umm . . ."

"Because it sounds like one," he said.

"It's a call to do the right thing," I said, lifting my chin. "We've always maintained that we were on the side of what's right. Are you going to put restrictions on that now, just because it's Clark?"

"How long have you been helping him?"

I shrugged. "A couple of days."

"Why haven't you said anything to me?"

I was at a loss for that one, because if I answered with the truth, I'd be throwing Clark under the bus.

"I asked her not to," Clark interjected. Jackson's gaze swung to him.

"Why not?"

"Because I knew you'd freak the fuck out, just like you're doing," Clark retorted. "And I trust you about as much as you trust me."

"I know who you really are and what you've done," Jackson said. "I've not told China because I didn't want to ruin what little innocence she has left by knowing the truth about you."

"I know," I interrupted. Jackson glanced at me. "He told me," I said. "He told me everything." At least I hoped it was everything.

"Really. And how do you feel about your 'partner' who used to be a paid assassin?"

I swallowed. "Um, well, it was unexpected, but sometimes people do things they wouldn't normally do when they've undergone a period of extreme stress . . . or . . . or grief."

"So you're defending him?" Jackson's tone was a mix of anger and incredulity.

"I'm not defending him," I said. "I'm saying that I understand. Plus, that was then and this is now. It's not like he was an assassin just last week. He's in trouble and so are you, and I think they're tied together."

"Why would you think that?"

"Because of this." I pulled the Gemini talisman out of my pocket. "Look familiar? Someone left it for Clark, too, right before they tried to kill him. And I bet if I look deeper into those deaths I told you about"—I was looking at Clark now—"I'll find something similar." I turned back to Jackson. "It's not the number two, it's a Gemini sign. Gemini was the name of an operation. I don't know why this is important or who's doing it, but someone obviously has a vendetta. And if we work together, we may find out who it is and can stop him before he kills someone else."

Jackson's jaw worked for a moment, then he said, "That's what I wanted to tell you. That symbol was found spray-painted on the wall where the sniper shot at the president."

We all took a moment to process that.

"Okay, then. We need to find Mark Danvers and William Buckton," I said. "Buckton is probably next on whatever list this guy is using. He's the one with the security firm."

"Speaking of which," Clark added, "why would you get a Gemini, Coop? When have you ever worked for the military?"

"I was never in the military," Jackson retorted. "A Google search will tell you everything you need to know about me. For all I know, it could be some nutjob who decided something Cysnet created or was involved in is worth killing over. I don't think we can classify whoever's doing this as someone who's sane."

"We can try to find Danvers while we go see Buckton," I said. "We need to find out what he knows."

"Can't we just call?" Jackson asked.

"I did," I said. "He's out of the country at the moment, expected back in Omaha on Wednesday."

"Buckton could be the shooter *or* the target, for all we know," Clark added. "We need to see him face-to-face, ask him some questions."

"We can leave tomorrow," I said.

"If you're set on this, then I'll call and get my plane ready." Jackson reached for his cell.

"We can't take your plane," Clark scoffed. "Those require flight plans and lists of passengers. I'm still wanted."

"There's an easy way to take care of that," Jackson threatened.

"Just try it, geek boy."

"What are you? Twelve?"

I interrupted their argument. "Knock it off. I thought you two had buried the hatchet. This is ridiculous."

"Is it?" Jackson asked. "I'm your fiancé and am just now finding out you've been helping him for two days?"

"Maybe if you didn't go so crazy when it came to Clark and me, I would've told you sooner," I shot back. "And, yes, *you're* my fiancé, not him, so how about a little trust?"

My Hypocrite Alarm was sounding loud and clear, but I ignored it. I wasn't wrong. Jackson hadn't even let me explain before jumping to bad conclusions.

"Fine," he said at last. "But you're not going alone with him. We'll all go."

"That's all I wanted," I said. "Go home and pack. You can pick us up in the morning."

"I don't think so," he said. "I'll go pack, but I'll be back tonight."

I sighed. "Whatever. That's fine."

"Think I'm going to seduce your girlfriend the moment you're gone?" Clark sneered.

Jackson shot him a look of pure loathing. "I think you'd try. She may be oblivious to your obsession with her, but I'm not."

"Jackson—" I warned.

He cut me off with a hard kiss to my lips. "I'll be back. And don't think I didn't notice that he's wearing your clothes." Then he was out the door and gone.

CH 11

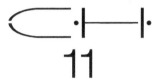

I heaved a sigh of relief when Jackson left. I honestly didn't know if I had it in me to drive nineteen hours to Nebraska from Raleigh with just them and me.

Wait a second . . .

"Mia," I said to myself, grabbing my phone from my pocket. I shot her a text.

Spontaneous trip to NE tomorrow. Come home and pack.

Her response was quick and to the point. Srsly?! Omw.

Clark was standing in the kitchen. He'd gotten a towel and was taking apart the weapons he'd acquired. Cleaning them, I guessed. The tension felt very thick, though I wasn't always the best judge of that.

"I really hate it when you antagonize Jackson," I said.

"I think it's a mutual antipathy," he replied.

"Yes, but it takes two to tango." Those idioms really came in handy in everyday conversation. "I'd appreciate it if you could be the bigger man."

"I am the bigger man."

I rolled my eyes. "I didn't mean literally—for once. I meant—"

"I know what you meant," he interrupted, finally glancing up at me. "Fine. I'll attempt not to antagonize him. But it's not as though we're going to be buddies."

"I'm not asking for that. Just a cease-fire, okay? For me? Because I can't take you two fighting."

His lips twitched. "I thought every woman's fantasy was to have two men fighting over her."

"I'm not every woman," I shot back. "And my friends are few. I'd prefer those I do have not despise each another."

There was a flicker of something in his eyes that I couldn't read.

"I understand. I really do. There aren't many in my life I'd label as a friend either. I'll try to get along with Coop."

He didn't mention the conversation we'd been having when Jackson arrived, and I didn't bring it up either. Best to just let that one drop.

"Good," I answered just as the front door opened and Mia came bounding inside.

I explained to Mia that we had to go see someone in Nebraska and that it'd be a good time to visit her parents, too, but that we'd be driving instead of flying due to Clark's current . . . status.

"Road trip!" she exclaimed. "That's awesome!"

I wished I could have felt some of her enthusiasm as she hurried upstairs to pack. Not only did I not want to be stuck in a car with Jackson and Clark, I wasn't exactly looking forward to showing up on my dad's doorstep with them in tow. But there was no way I could take Mia with me and not show my face at home. Jackson had said he wanted to meet my family. Well, he was going to get his wish.

Clark borrowed my keys to take my car, saying he had a "go bag" nearby that he could retrieve since he still couldn't go back to his house. Which left me standing alone in my living room after what felt like a whirlwind had gone through it.

I was at a momentary loss as to what to do. It was Sunday, which meant I needed to do laundry. Since I also had to pack, those two things went well together. There. A plan. I could follow a plan.

Mechanically, I headed upstairs to my bedroom. My lingerie was already in little bags to keep the hooks from the bras catching on the delicate lace of other items. I separated my clothes when I changed, so there was not much to do besides put a load into the washer, which I did.

My luggage was in the office closet, and I retrieved a bag from there. I printed off the winter version of my Seven-to-Ten-Day Trip packing list and began checking things off. It served to keep my mind busy for a while.

I was hanging up my best Victoria's Secret lingerie to air-dry when the boys returned. At the same time. I'd changed into my pajamas and washed my face. I wanted to watch television and eat my Fig Newtons, and I really didn't care what they did.

Plopping myself in the middle of the sofa, I crossed my legs and chewed on my cookies, remote in hand. I watched as Clark hauled in a duffel and backpack. The amount of small arms and ammunition he had with him made me chew a bit slower. In addition to what we'd already taken from PFG, it looked as though he was ready to take on a small army. He'd changed into his typical plain black T-shirt.

Jackson had a small suitcase and a backpack, too, but his contained the tech, in contrast to Clark's guns. I chewed my second cookie as I watched him plug in his laptops to charge. Neither he nor Clark spoke to each other. I flipped channels on the television and finished my cookies, wishing I'd gotten more.

"*Smallville* is on," I said to the room in general. My voice sounded too loud. They both stopped what they were doing and glanced at me. I cleared my throat and pushed my glasses up my nose. "If anyone wants to . . . you know . . . watch, too," I finished.

I hugged my legs to my chest and rested my chin on my knees, focusing on the screen opposite me. I'd done my hostess duty; now it was up to them to behave.

Jackson was the first to respond, coming to sit next to me. He put his arm around my shoulders and pulled me toward him. I rested my head against his shoulder with a sigh.

"How are you feeling?" he asked quietly. His fingers played with the ends of my ponytail.

"Achy," I answered truthfully. "I've been popping ibuprofen all day."

"You should've been resting in bed," he lightly reprimanded me.

"That would've been nice. I'm sorry about the Jag. It was gorgeous." It was a crime for that car to have been totaled before it had even hit a hundred miles.

"I don't care about the car. I'm just glad we're all right." His lips pressed a kiss to my forehead.

We watched for a few minutes in silence. The warmth of his hold was comforting and secure. I took a deep breath and relaxed. After the nonstop stress of the past two days, I felt as though my limbs were made of lead. Exhaustion seemed to ooze from my bones. Even my hair hurt, which was a ridiculous assertion, but still . . . Jackson's hand moved to the back of my neck, lightly massaging, and I nearly groaned at the relief that brought me.

Clark had been sitting at the kitchen table, finishing cleaning and reassembling the weapons. The sound of metal clinking was comforting, in some strange way. My eyes drifted closed. I felt Jackson slide my glasses off, which enabled me to snuggle closer to him. I sighed deeply, my body taking on the consistency of warm clay.

I was in that dreamy place between sleep and awake, where things sound far away and you can't be bothered to move limbs grown heavy with lethargy, when I heard the metal noises stop and only the sound of the television. Then the couch dipped slightly and my bare feet were laid on a denim-clad thigh. A roughened, warm palm curved around my instep and chilly toes.

"What are you doing?" Jackson's voice rumbled in his chest.

"Keeping her feet warm. It's the only part I'm worthy of touching, and it's asexual. So don't get all pissy about it." Clark's voice was just as quiet.

"I wonder why you feel the need to touch her at all. You're just partners, remember?"

Silence.

"I'm not gonna lie to you, Coop." Fingers tightened on my foot and ankle. "I will fight you for her."

"She's marrying *me*."

"But she's not married yet."

More silence.

"Why? Why her? Why now? You were gone. Left. Now you've been back for, what, two days? And decide that she's the one for you? I call bullshit."

"Sometimes you don't know that something's worth fighting for until you're faced with living without it."

A delicate snort. "What, did you read that off a fucking Hallmark card?"

"What's the matter, Coop? If you're so sure you're the one for her, then why are you worried? Don't you think she can decide for herself who she wants?"

"China is . . . special." I felt fingers combing through my ponytail.

"You say that like you think she should be on the short bus."

Jackson's reply was sharp. "You know that's not true. But you and I both know that China can be blinded by her . . . issues."

"You mean, her personality?"

"You're deliberately being obtuse."

"She's not a science experiment, to see if you can make little Einsteins together." It was hard to mistake the undercurrent of anger in his voice. By now I was awake, but dared not move a muscle to give myself away.

"I never said she was. But she and I . . . we're cut from the same cloth. I understand her the way few else would or could. We belong together."

"If you ask me, your issues would be better resolved with a shrink than getting married to China."

"No one asked you."

"Just saying."

"And I could say the same for you."

Another pause. "Then I guess it just comes down to who *she* wants, doesn't it." Clark's hand curled around my toes, warming them.

My eyes were shut and my breaths were slow and deep. I didn't want to think about what I'd just heard. I couldn't process that, for some incredibly unknown reason, these two men had each decided they wanted me. *Me.* China Mack. An awkward, average-looking girl with too many brains and not enough boobs. A girl with more fandom toys in her office than shoes in her closet. Someone who had a schedule for each day of the week and was physically incapable of eating Thai food on any day but Thursday.

The silence lengthened and only the television could be heard. I didn't want to deal with any of that conversation. It made my heart hurt. I loved Jackson fiercely . . . but then what did I feel about Clark? Was Mia right? Did I need to take a good, hard look at our relationship and see if there was more to it than friendship?

My head ached and the lethargy I'd felt earlier crept back into my bones. The pain medication was doing its job, and I welcomed sleep with open arms.

◆ ◆ ◆

I woke up the next morning with no recollection of how I'd gotten to my bed or of anything during the night. I must've slept like the dead, though I still felt as if I could sleep for another six hours. The headache I'd gone to bed with was still there, a dull throbbing that said it was going to stick around all day. Awesome.

"Brought you some coffee," Mia said, pushing open my bedroom door. She carried two mugs and shoved the door closed with her foot. "Thought you might need it."

I sat up and reached for my glasses, sliding them on, and the world came into focus. I took the coffee she handed me.

"What time is it?"

"Early o'clock," she said, taking a sip from her own mug. "Clark is anxious to get going."

"Where's Jackson?"

"Packing the car. Lance brought 'round the Beemer for him to use. Roomier than your car."

I glanced at the pillow next to me. It had an indentation.

"Jackson slept in here last night with you," Mia said, answering my unspoken question. "Clark slept in the office." She took another sip. "I'm thinking this trip might be a little awkward, especially considering the mutual freeze-out they were doing this morning. Thought I was going to have to heat up the coffee again, it's so chilly."

A euphemism. I recognized it and let it pass.

"I . . . heard them talking last night," I said haltingly. "I think they thought I was asleep."

Mia's eyes widened and she leaned forward. "*Ooh,* this sounds good. So what did they say?"

I briefly recounted the conversation. Her eyes grew rounder as I spoke, and the coffee seemed to be forgotten in her hand.

"So . . . what do I do?" I asked her.

"I have no idea," she said. "I'm not you. But marriage is a big deal, and you shouldn't rush into it if you have any doubts that Jackson's not the right man for you."

"How do I know? What if I make the wrong decision?"

She shrugged. "I don't know."

I took a long gulp of my coffee and changed the subject. "Are you packed?"

"Just waiting for my laundry to finish drying."

"Did you e-mail your teachers that you'll be gone?" I asked.

She nodded. "A couple of them sent my assignments already."

I wasn't worried about Mia keeping up with her schoolwork. She was a math whiz and had no trouble keeping her grades up. If anything, some of her classes weren't challenging enough and bored her.

"I should get in the shower," I said, finishing my coffee. Setting it aside, I stood up, and immediately a wave of dizziness washed over me. I swayed and grabbed onto the bedside table.

"Aunt Chi!" Mia sprang up, dropping her cup, and latched on to my arm. "Are you okay?"

My vision had darkened but was clearing already. "Yeah, I'm fine. Just stood up too fast. Got a little light-headed." I patted her twice. I'd gotten better with random affectionate touching since she'd moved in. I still had to remind myself to do it, but at least I thought about it more often.

"Are you sure?" She sounded terribly anxious, which was terribly sweet.

"I'm fine. Promise. I just need a nice, hot shower."

Mia still looked a little unconvinced, but took our mugs from the room. I was glad she'd finished hers before dropping it. Coffee would've stained my duvet.

A shower did help me feel better, and when I was done getting dressed and drying my hair, I felt more energetic. I hesitated for only a moment before slipping on my engagement ring. As far as I was concerned, last night's overheard conversation had never happened.

I finished packing and hauled my suitcase down the hall, running into Clark as he stepped out of the office.

I gasped in surprise, then immediately thought of everything I said I *wasn't* going to think about. My face flushed and I had no idea what to say. His blue eyes gazed unblinkingly down at me, his dark brows like arched wings, and a lock of his hair brushing his forehead. I was even more strongly reminded of the Man of Steel as he loomed over me—his navy-blue T-shirt stretched over the muscles in his shoulders and biceps.

"Let me get that for you." He leaned over me, bringing our faces way too close, as I stood, frozen. His fingers brushed mine as he took the suitcase from my lax grip. "After you."

"Uh, yeah. Thanks." I hurried down the stairs, only to meet Jackson as he came in from outside.

"'Morning," he said, brushing a kiss to my lips. "How'd you sleep?"

"Okay, I guess. I don't remember much."

"You fell asleep on the couch," he said. "I carried you upstairs and put you to bed. I don't think you moved a muscle all night."

"Oh. Well, thanks for taking care of me," I said.

He smiled and pulled me in for a hug. "Of course. It's what love and marriage is about. Good and bad, richer and poorer, in sickness and in health."

"Here's her suitcase," Clark said from behind me. "Might want to stick that in the car, Coop. I believe carrying heavy things is in the fine print of those vows."

Jackson's jaw grew tight as Clark thrust the suitcase at him. My phone buzzed in my pocket and I gratefully grabbed it, slipping away from the two men to answer. The number wasn't one I recognized.

"Glad you're still alive," the man on the phone said.

I frowned, moving farther into the kitchen so the sound of Jackson and Clark arguing was lessened. "Who is this?"

"Your new boss, remember?" Ah, yes. The scary guy, Kade Dennon. "That was a hell of a car wreck."

"Was it you?" I asked, suddenly suspicious. "Did you sabotage the car?"

He snorted. "Please. If *I* wanted you dead, I wouldn't be so sloppy. And you wouldn't be talking to me because you'd be dead." He paused. "I take it you've found Slattery by now?"

I didn't answer.

"Thought so. I'm hoping you have a really good reason that you haven't turned him over to me."

"He didn't do it," I said. "He's being framed. The same person that sabotaged our car also took a shot at him. And it's the same person who shot the president."

"And what do you have to prove this?" he asked.

"Right now, just the same message left at each scene," I said. "A Gemini talisman, possibly a reference to an Operation Gemini. We're following up now on who would know what that could be."

"This guy doesn't seem very competent," Kade commented. "He's oh for three."

"Not quite," I said. "Two men are dead under suspicious circumstances."

"A vendetta, then," he said, his voice flat.

"I'm not a psychiatrist," I said, "so I'm not qualified to render that opinion . . . though it would seem a logical conclusion. Perhaps you could speak with the president and see if he can shed any light on what Operation Gemini was?"

"Hold on a second, now, I'm giving the orders around here." The words weren't very friendly, but he said them easily, which meant I had zero clue as to whether he was serious, angry, or joking. Since assuming he was serious was the best choice, I went with that.

"My apologies," I said. "I meant no dis—"

"Got it," he interrupted me. "I'll check back in with you in a couple of days. I'm not thrilled that some nutjob with an ax to grind is out there taking potshots at people. In the meantime, don't die."

"Yes, sir." He ended the call almost before the words were out of my mouth. I guess he wasn't into social norms, which was fine by me. I didn't know why he was letting me pursue this investigation—I wasn't law enforcement, by any stretch—I was just glad that he was. It would be a lot harder to prove Clark's innocence if he was behind bars.

I found Mia in the kitchen, packing snacks for the trip.

"Hungry?" she asked.

My stomach rolled at the mere mention of food, and I shook my head. "No, thanks. Are you almost ready? I think the guys are."

She nodded. "Yep. I particularly enjoyed watching Jackson fit my Hello Kitty suitcases into the trunk."

I grinned at the mental image. "Did you call Oslo and let him know we were coming?" I asked.

She grimaced. "Dad wasn't home, so I talked to Heather." Heather was her stepmom.

"You need to stop freezing her out," I said. "Heather loves you, and being a stepmom has got to be really hard."

But Mia was already shaking her head. "It's fine. We're polite and get along okay. It's not as though we have to be best friends or super close."

"But there's also no reason why you can't," I persisted. "I mean, if I'd had a stepmom, that would've been nice."

She stopped packing the snack bag and looked at me. "Really? Because, think about it. As hard as losing your mom was, what if you'd had a stepmom and been close to her. Then something happened to her, too." She shook her head and went back to packing. "It's better to just keep your distance."

I frowned as realization dawned. "You're afraid if you let yourself get close to Heather that she'll leave like your real mom did?"

"I don't want to talk about it, Aunt Chi."

"But surely you know you can't predict someone's future behavior based on an entirely different person's past actions—"

"I said"—she zipped the bag closed—"I don't want to talk about it." Slinging the bag over her shoulder, she passed by me. "See you in the car."

Okay, well, that hadn't gone well. So much for taking up a career as a therapist. And now Mia was angry with me.

I leaned over the counter, bracing my arms flat out, and rested my forehead on the chilly granite. I felt much older than twenty-four. My body ached, my head hurt, I was still tired, and I was really, *really* sick of people.

"Hey, you okay?" Clark's hand slid over my back to my shoulder, squeezing slightly.

I shrugged, still facedown. "I'm tired," I said. "And I don't want to do any of this. I just want to go to work and do my job and come home to my usual routine. I don't want to be responsible for saving anyone. That's not what I ever wanted."

"Well, that's too bad." The hard edge to his words made me straighten.

"Excuse me?"

"I said, that's too bad," he repeated. "Your opportunity to change paths passed a while ago. Maybe you told yourself that you didn't have a choice. Maybe that made things easier. But with your exceptional ability and talent comes responsibility. Now, if you want to crawl into a hole and pretend you're just like everyone else, don't let me stop you. But enough of the whiny, poor-me, sob routine."

I stared at him, openmouthed. "Whiny, poor-me, sob routine?" I repeated.

"Yeah," he said. "You're not a kid, Mack. You're a big fucking deal with a lot at stake. You may not like it, but nothing's going to change unless you go at this head-on, fix the problem, and decide your own course. For sure, crying in the kitchen sink isn't going to do a damn thing."

"I was *not* crying," I retorted, stung. "I don't cry."

He opened the refrigerator and snagged a bottle of water. "Maybe not, but you sure whine a lot."

"I-I . . ." I was speechless. He'd utterly stumped me and left me standing there feeling embarrassed and red-faced. Had I been indulging too much in my own discomfort when people's lives were at stake?

Clark had taken a long drink while I stammered. He watched me until I gave up trying to say something, then he took a step closer and I had to tip my head back. "Make a decision, Mack," he said, his voice softer. "You're either in or out, but half-ass is only going to get you or someone else killed." He reached out, taking the length of my ponytail in his hand and laying it gently over my shoulder. "You may not want to hear it, and I know this is hard for you, but you're made of all the right stuff. You'll figure it out." With a crooked half smile, he turned and walked away.

Okay, then.

He was right; I *had* been whining. I'd been whining about Jackson. I'd been whining about Clark. I'd been whining about my job. That wasn't the person I wanted to be. No, I wasn't happy right now, but the only way to get to the end of this job was straight through the middle of the mess I was currently in.

Starting with a road trip.

CH 12

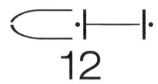

Somehow, Jackson had played Tetris with the luggage, managing to get it all into the trunk, despite Clark's weapons, which were alongside Mia's Hello Kitty suitcases.

"Why two suitcases?" he'd asked Mia. "We won't be gone long."

"One's for my clothes and one's for my makeup," she'd said with a toss of her blond hair. "I call shotgun."

Which was how Mia ended up in the front with Jackson, and me in the back with Clark. I had my laptop open, searching for anything I could find on Mark Danvers . . . which was precisely nothing.

"How can there be nothing on this guy?" I muttered, frustrated.

"No luck?" Clark asked.

I shook my head. "It's like he doesn't exist."

"If he was in the military, then his records will be in Saint Louis," Jackson said. "The National Personnel Records Center is there."

"We'll be driving right by there," Clark added. "Between the three of us, we should be able to con our way in and find what we need."

"I can help, too," Mia said. We all looked at her. "What? You never know."

"It's about twelve hours or so to Saint Louis," Jackson said. "We can stay the night there, go to the center in the morning."

"Maybe," I echoed, unconvinced.

The ride was twelve hours and felt twice that. After only four hours, I was ready to ride on the roof. Outside.

"Let's play Twenty Questions," Mia suggested somewhere in West Virginia.

I perked up at the mention of a game. I loved games and puzzles. "Okay."

"I'll go first," she said.

We stared at each other.

"Well?" she asked, at last.

"Well, what? I'm waiting for you to ask a question," I said.

"But I said I was going first."

"I know. I was letting you ask the first question."

"No, I meant that I was going to *answer* questions first. You have to guess."

"But that's not what you *said*—"

"Is it a person?" Clark interrupted, shutting us both up.

Mia turned away in a huff. "Yes."

My eyes couldn't roll hard enough. "Are they alive?"

"Yes."

"Female?"

"Yes."

"Famous?"

"Yes."

Jackson was getting into it now. "Actress?"

"No."

"Singer?"

"No."

"TV personality?"

"No."

We all fell silent for a moment, then I tried. "She's a political figure."

"No."

"Is she famous for doing something?"

"Yes."

"Is she a famous athlete?"

"No, and that's ten questions."

"Okay, so she's famous for doing something, but nothing athletic or in entertainment," Jackson mused.

"And not in politics either," I added.

"What does that leave?"

"Wait a second," Clark said. "You said this was a person. Is this a living, breathing person?"

I snorted. "I think that's the definition, Clark."

"Not necessarily," he said. "Personhood has been conferred on the oddest things nowadays. So, Mia, is it a living, breathing female person?"

Mia grinned. "No."

Jackson and I erupted into objections at the same time, arguing over each other. "That's against the rules."

"Person implies life. You should've said no."

"If we're going to argue about what constitutes a person, then we might as well throw in female and male as well, if the answers are arbitrary—"

"I know what it is." Clark's voice was louder than ours.

"You do not," I said. He cut his eyes to mine and winked.

"Is it Siri?" he asked.

Mia grinned. "It is."

I slumped back in the seat, sullen. "I don't want to play anymore."

"Ah, you sore loser," Clark chided. "C'mon. I'll go easy on you."

"I'm hungry," I said, changing the subject. That brought up a whole other argument about lunch. I don't know which one of us would've starved if we hadn't found a stretch of highway with a McDonald's, a Taco Bell, and a Burger King.

Mia fell asleep after lunch, softly snoring in the front seat. I was out of range of any signal for my laptop, so I'd put it away. The sun was setting and I stared out the window at the purple clouds. We'd switched shifts and Clark was now driving, with Jackson and me in the back seat.

"C'mere," Jackson said softly, tugging at me. I gratefully slid down to rest my head on his lap. "Rest for a while."

The lull of the wheels against the road was rhythmic, and I dozed.

I was in a cell. Dank and cold. I was hurting everywhere and shivering. They'd be back any minute to hurt me more. Tears and blood dripped down my face, but I was too frozen with fear and pain to wipe my cheeks.

No one was coming to save me. I was going to die a terrible death here. Alone.

The door opened and I cringed, curling tighter into myself on the cement floor. I braced myself for more kicks, but instead, I felt arms lifting me and a familiar voice.

"If you leave, then what?"

It wasn't Clark. It was Jackson, and we were standing on the edge of a cliff, wind whipping our hair and clothes. He was gazing at me, looking much calmer than I felt. Waves crashed below, and I didn't know which one of us was going to fall.

My eyes popped open. The car had stopped. Jackson had rested his head against the back of the seat and fallen asleep. It was fully dark outside. I was breathing fast and sweating, the panic from my nightmare receding slightly.

Clark twisted in the front seat and caught my eye. "Wake up, sunshine. We're here."

Here turned out to be a motel that I was sure rented rooms by the hour. Jackson got out of the car, took one look, and said, "No."

"Oh, I'm sorry, Your Highness," Clark sneered. "Does this not meet with your exalted standards?"

"If you mean standards such as sheets that aren't stained and a neighborhood where my car won't be stripped by morning, then yes." Jackson was matter-of-fact, not rising to Clark's bait.

"We need someplace anonymous," Clark retorted.

"We can achieve that without catching hepatitis." He held out his hand for the keys. Clark glanced at me and I shrugged.

"Give him a chance," I said. Clark scowled, but handed the keys to Jackson.

"Thank God," Mia muttered under her breath. She shot me a look and made a face that told me exactly what she thought of the motel.

Ten minutes later we were handing keys to the valet at the Hilton downtown. Jackson waved off the bellman, saying, "That's okay. He's got it." The "he" in this case being Clark, and the "it" being all of the luggage. Clark shot Jackson a glare as we passed by him on our way inside to the lobby.

"You need to have a credit card," I said to Jackson. "Even if we pay cash, they'll want a credit card on file."

"Don't worry," he assured me, stepping up to the counter.

There was a tall young man working the desk. He looked as fresh and lively as if it were nine in the morning instead of nine at night.

"Good evening. May I help you, sir?"

Jackson smiled. "I'd like to book your Presidential Suite, please, and an adjoining room."

The clerk looked taken aback, but quickly gathered his wits. "Of course, sir. I'll just need your credit card and identification."

Jackson folded his arms on the high counter and leaned closer. "Hey, Liam," he said, reading the clerk's name badge. "Do you know who I am?"

Liam paused, taking a good look. He frowned, and I could practically see the mental wheels turning, then his face cleared and he smiled.

"Mr. Cooper," he said. "Wow. What an honor. Really. I've followed your work for years. I'm so sorry I didn't recognize you. It was just unexpected, you see, and—"

"Not a problem," Jackson interrupted. "But I don't want to use my credit card. I'd rather pay cash. My fiancée and I"—he nodded in my direction—"are looking for a little downtime, and I don't want the media camping out here. I'm sure you don't either, right?" Jackson grimaced, as if they could both agree on what a nuisance the presence of paparazzi would be.

"Absolutely. Understood," Liam said, setting to work on the computer. "It'll just take me a few minutes. What name shall I use for the reservation?" He glanced up at Jackson expectantly.

"How about . . . Bruce Wayne?" Jackson winked at me and I grinned appreciatively.

"Bruce Wayne it is," Liam agreed. A few minutes later, he was handing over the keys to the Presidential Suite, and additional keys for the adjoining room. "Enjoy your stay, sir."

Mia and Clark were waiting alone by the elevators. She was quite impressed with the suite, inspecting all seven hundred square feet of it before going into the room next door with her things.

"You're sure your name isn't anywhere on this?" Clark asked again.

"I'm sure," Jackson replied, filling a glass with ice and opening the minibar. He pulled out a bottle of bourbon and poured two fingers' worth. "I would have preferred the Four Seasons, but it's higher profile. So the Hilton it was."

"Gotta say, Coop. I would've preferred separate beds." Clark plopped on the sofa and propped his feet up on the coffee table.

Jackson raised an eyebrow. "Excuse me?"

"It's not appropriate," Clark said, "is it? For a single, grown man to share a hotel room with an impressionable teenage girl? Unless, of course, you're going to be the gentleman and let the ladies have this bedroom while we take the other."

Jackson looked as if the bourbon he was sipping was laced with lemon. His eyes cut to mine.

"I trust Clark," I said, "but it does look bad. And I don't want to make Mia feel uncomfortable." I shrugged helplessly. "It's nothing personal."

"Fine," Jackson bit out. "I'll just go help Mia move her luggage in here."

He passed by Clark and I heard him mutter, "Nice cockblock, asshole."

To which Clark shot back, "Payback's a bitch."

That headache I'd had earlier was back with a vengeance.

Mia was enchanted with the suite and ordered so much food from room service that we ran out of places to sit the trays. She fell asleep on the sofa, with *Pretty Little Liars* playing on TV, and the desiccated remains of her burger and fries left on the table in front of her.

I'd done more research but had come up empty-handed. Clark and Jackson had set aside their differences to coordinate the best plan of attack tomorrow for infiltrating the records place. I'd left them arguing at the dining table and opted for a hot bath, hoping that would help me feel better.

I was leaning back, eyes closed, water nearly to my chin, when there was a knock on the door.

"Yeah?"

"It's me," Jackson said.

I heaved an internal sigh. So much for some alone time. "Come in."

Jackson closed the door behind him and sat down on the edge of the tub. He rested a hand on my bent knee, his thumb lightly caressing my wet skin.

"I put Mia to bed," he said. "I don't think she even stirred."

"Yeah, she was out pretty hard. I think the drive wore her out." I didn't have a lot to say, so I fell quiet.

"Sorry we can't be together tonight," he said after a pause. "Obviously, I didn't think this through." He picked up a washcloth, soaked it, and squeezed the warm water out of it. Rivulets ran down my thigh and my eyes slipped closed.

"It doesn't matter," I sighed. "I'm too tired for sex anyway."

"Hey."

I opened my eyes at his tone.

"I'm not just talking about sex," he said. "I miss you. You slept like a log last night. We haven't gotten to have a . . . private . . . moment since the accident."

There was an edge to his voice that I guessed was named *Clark*.

"This wasn't exactly my plan," I said, rubbing my temples. The bath hadn't helped my headache much.

"No, but you sure did jump right back in to Clark's mess when he turned up."

I opened my eyes. "And nearly got killed in your car." There might have been an edge to my voice, too. He was silent. "What are you not telling me?"

"What do you mean?"

Anger flashed through me and I stood up, holding on to his shoulder for balance as I stepped out of the tub and snatched up a towel.

"I'm not an idiot," I snapped, wrapping the towel around me. "It's not some coincidence that you and Clark have been targets. You say you don't know what the Gemini means, haven't heard of an Operation Gemini. That you've never worked for the military. I'm supposed to believe that, but it doesn't make sense."

"So you think I'm lying to you?" he asked.

"Are you?"

"I've told you everything that you need to know."

That didn't help my temper. "That's not an answer, Jackson. If anything, it's an admission. I just don't know what you're admitting to."

"Can't you just trust me?" he asked, getting to his feet. "You trust whatever Clark tells you, but me you regard with suspicion. Why?"

That made me pause . . . because he was right. "I-I don't know," I said at last. "Maybe it's because you say you love me, and he doesn't. It's hard for me to believe you. No one . . ." I paused and took a breath. "No one has ever loved me like you say you do, not even the people who are supposed to, like parents and brothers." It was hard to put into words, but I knew as soon as I said it that it was at the core of my doubts.

He stepped closer to me. "I *do* love you," he said, his hands lightly grasping my upper arms. "I want to spend the rest of my life with you. What do I have to do to convince you of that? I feel like you're punishing me for wanting to commit to you."

"I'm not punishing you," I said. "It's just that things have moved so fast. And now this thing hanging over us, when I don't even know what it is—"

"And Clark," he interrupted.

I spun away. "I am so sick of hearing you complain about him," I snapped. "You treat me like a dog with a bone when he's around."

"Because he's in love with you, China. And he's not going to stop until he's stolen you away from me."

I whirled, openmouthed. "*Stolen me away?*" I said, then wished I'd kept my voice lower. It echoed inside my aching head like a megaphone. "I'm not a chess piece, Jackson, going to the player with the cleverest strategy. And I don't know where you get the idea that he's in love with me, but you're wrong. For some reason, yes, he thinks there's something romantic between us. But I'm engaged to *you*. Do you think I'm just going to eenie, meenie, miney, moe this kind of thing?"

"What I know is that you think I'm lying to you, and you've yet to shut down Clark," he said. There was a sadness in his eyes that hurt to see. "It makes me wonder if it's because you feel something for him, too."

"Are you accusing me of being unfaithful?" I asked, my conscience twitching. "Because I haven't been. I mean . . . we kissed. Twice. But that's all. I swear." My stomach rolled, and for a moment I thought I was going to be sick. I swallowed heavily.

Jackson stared at me. "Do you want to run that by me again?" His voice was dangerously quiet.

"I didn't mean for it to happen," I said. "It just . . . did. And I'm sorry. I really am. I'm not that person, and I don't want to be that person."

"What do you expect me to do with this information?" he asked.

"I-I don't know."

"Can you tell me it won't happen again?"

It was my turn for silence. "I don't think I can guarantee future behavior with one hundred percent accuracy," I said at last. "That's not realistic. Or logical."

"I disagree," he said. "If you felt nothing for Clark, you'd have no problem answering that question."

I rubbed my aching head as more silence fell. "So what now?"

Jackson's face was unreadable. "Maybe we should take some time. I don't want you marrying me because it's the path of least resistance. I want you marrying me because you feel the same way about me as I do you. And I definitely don't want you marrying me if you're in love with another man."

He moved past me, exiting the bathroom and closing the door softly behind him. I felt the door close as if he'd slammed it. My vision was blurring, though I didn't know if it was from tears or because my head hurt so damn much.

My knees weakened and I sat heavily on the floor. I rested my forehead on my bent knees. I'd done this wrong, said the wrong things. I hadn't wanted to break up, had I? I didn't want to lose Jackson, but fixing it seemed beyond my mental capabilities at the moment.

No one was around. No one could see. So I didn't bother wiping away the tears I never cried.

I didn't know how long I sat there. Eventually, I lay down on the tile and curled my knees to my chest. I was too mentally and physically exhausted to take myself into the bedroom. I figured Mia would wake me in the morning when she had to step over me to get to the toilet.

I closed my eyes and tried, for once, not to think.

◆ ◆ ◆

I woke when hands jostled me. I mumbled something and tried to brush them away.

"What the hell are you doing, Mack?" Clark said. "You're lying on the damn floor."

I mumbled something else as my hair fell into my eyes. He was moving me and made a grunting sound as he sat down, hauling me up into his lap the way you'd hold a baby.

"You're freezing," he said. Reaching up behind him, he grabbed a towel from the rack and wrapped it around me.

I curled closer into him, grateful for the warmth. "Mmmm."

We sat like that for a while, and I gradually came more awake. I didn't move. My head was silent and my heart ached. I felt the rise and fall of Clark's chest as he breathed and held me.

"What happened?" he asked at last. His voice was a soft breath against my hair.

I didn't say anything. I just breathed. He waited.

"Jackson . . . he was . . . really upset. He . . . he broke up with me. He-he thinks that I . . . that I'm in love with . . . with you."

Clark didn't say anything. He breathed and I closed my eyes, feeling the rise and fall. Memorizing the intervals.

"And what do *you* think?" he asked at last, a breath of sound.

I took my time responding. "I think . . . that you're competitive. And lonely. And going through a personal crisis that has nothing to do with me." I paused. "And . . . everything to do with me."

The silence was thick enough to cut and serve on plates with forks and napkins.

"I can't stop thinking about you." His voice was a raw whisper. "When I was away, I dreamed of you. I . . . missed you. And I've never missed anyone."

The words cut through my skin right down to the bone. I knew I needed to say something. "What do you want from me, Clark?" I whispered.

He tightened his hold on me. "You. I just want you."

I twisted so I could see his eyes. "But . . . why?"

His fingers combed through my hair. "Why? You're smart, strong, beautiful." His hand caressed my cheek and cupped my jaw. "You're fragile, special, and sexy as hell. Why wouldn't I want you?"

"How do I know this is real?" I whispered. His blue eyes seemed to engulf me. "How can I trust you?"

His thumb brushed my jaw. "You would've killed for me. And I would've died for you. You tell me what that means."

I couldn't look away from his eyes. I could feel his knees braced against my back. His arm cradling my head. The light from over the tub filtered through us, throwing his face into shadows.

I felt . . . on edge. With Jackson, I felt secure and safe. The future was easily predicted and safe. I could write out our future as though someone were whispering it into my ear.

But with Clark . . . nothing was predictable. That was both terrifying . . . and exciting.

"I can't do this," I said. "I don't know what to do, what to say. I . . . feel guilty about Jackson being upset. Yet, right now . . . I feel . . . safe."

Clark's face softened ever so slightly. "That's because you are."

He looked beautiful in the low light. Of course, he always looked beautiful. It hurt to look at him, he was so perfect. I stared at him, entranced. He stroked my cheek and jaw, looking as mesmerized as I was . . . which was crazy. I was ordinary and Clark was . . . unique.

"We don't fit," I said.

He frowned. "What are you talking about?"

"You're beautiful. Picture-perfect. I'm short and wear glasses."

"You're *petite*, and I love your glasses." He placed a kiss on the tip of my nose. "And who cares about that superficial shit anyway? We fit like two puzzle pieces. You and Jackson, you're the same puzzle piece. But you and me . . . we make something new together."

It was an interesting way to put it, and I could see his point.

"Jackson's lying, you know," I said. "About Operation Gemini. He knows what it is or knows something, but he won't tell me."

Clark's hold tightened on me. "Yeah. I know."

"Why won't he?" It hurt to know Jackson was keeping something from me, and I couldn't fathom his reasons.

Clark's fingers drifted through my hair. "I don't know. The only thing I can think of is that he's protecting someone or something."

We fell quiet. I hesitated, then reached up, tentatively touching my fingers to his cheek. The skin was smooth, then had the texture of light sandpaper where the bristles from his five-o'clock shadow grew. I traced the path again, then brushed the line of his jaw with the back of my hand. My fingers traced his neck to his nape, then into the soft, inky-black hair. His eyes drifted closed at my touch.

Once I'd started touching him, I didn't particularly want to stop. I traced the texture of his eyebrows, soothed the fine lines across his brow, and ran my fingers through his hair. He opened his eyes, watching me. His gaze caught me and I stared into his eyes. For the first time, it seemed as though he had no guard up. Everything he felt . . . I could see it there in his eyes. Loneliness, heartbreak, hope, fear.

"I'm afraid, too," I whispered.

He turned his face slightly, kissing my fingertips that lingered by his cheek.

"You need some sleep," he said, his voice rough. "And not on the floor. C'mon. I'll take you to your bed."

I was loath to leave his arms, but it turned out that I didn't have to. He stood, still holding me, and I wrapped my arms around his neck.

"That was impressive," I said, smiling a little. "Is this where I *ooh* and *aah* over how strong you are?"

His lips twisted and he gave a one-shouldered shrug. "Hey, if you feel the urge, I'm not gonna stop you."

I laughed lightly, tightening my hold and resting my head against his shoulder. He'd made me feel better. I knew that nothing was fixed, but he'd made me smile and laugh. That was something I'd desperately needed, and I hadn't even realized it.

The bedroom was dark; light from the bathroom lit the way to the bed where Mia was a still lump under the covers. A light snoring reached my ears as Clark lay me on the bed. Mia. Her eyes were covered with her FUCK OFF eye mask.

Clark pulled the blankets up over me, but I stopped him. "I can't sleep in a towel," I whispered. "I need my pajamas."

I felt rather than saw him roll his eyes.

"Fine. Where are they?" he whispered back.

"The bathroom."

"The bathroom? Why didn't you put them on while you were in there?"

"Because you were carrying me out," I whispered, shrugging. "It was a gallant, romantic gesture. I didn't think it would be appropriate to stop you."

Clark shook his head.

"What?"

"Nothing. Hold on."

He went back to the bathroom, got my pajamas, and returned. Mia was still snoring as he handed them to me.

"Good night," he said, pressing a kiss to the top of my head. I watched him leave the room, then squirmed into my pajamas and slipped under the covers. Mia still slept. Eventually, I did, too.

CH. 13

"That'll never work."

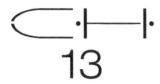

Jackson, Clark, and I were gathered around the dining table, remnants of breakfast scattered on the surface, going over what Clark and Jackson had come up with for getting into the personnel center.

Mia was the one throwing the current objection. She was in full teenage fashion-model mode, dressed in skinny jeans, boots, a flowing dusky pink top, and a scarf. Her long blond hair was perfectly straight, falling to the small of her back. She had a coffee cup in one hand and her phone in the other.

Both Jackson and Clark looked at her, then at each other.

"Why would you say that?" Jackson asked.

"I realize that you two are super smart and all," she said, "but Clark's not going to get within a mile of that place without getting picked up. And Jackson is too recognizable. I think Aunt Chi and I should go."

"Neither of you has military ID," Clark said.

"And you have to have an appointment," Jackson said.

My headache was back and I rubbed my eyes behind my glasses as I listened to them talk. Even though I'd eventually gotten to sleep, I felt as though I hadn't slept a wink. And seeing Jackson this morning had sent my stomach rolling with nausea again.

"I thought you were a computer whiz," Mia said, taking a sip of her coffee. "Can't you hack in to their system and put us in? And make sure you make us authorized representatives."

"Looks like you did something other than watch TV last night," Clark remarked.

She shrugged. "They have a website. It's not rocket science."

"She's right," I said. "Mia and I are more forgettable than either of you. We don't want to arouse suspicion. A grieving widow and daughter arouse more sympathy anyway."

"I don't know if I'm comfortable with that," Jackson said.

"He has a point," Clark chimed in. "If this Mark Danvers's records are flagged, it'll show in the system. They could be watching for anyone who'd submit inquiries—"

"It doesn't matter," I snapped, interrupting him. "It has to be done. We're the best to do it. We're just wasting time arguing."

Everyone looked at me.

"I-I'm sorry," I stammered. "I guess I'm just not feeling well this morning." That and my ex-fiancé was barely speaking to me. We hadn't mentioned last night, and I hadn't been able to eat anything this morning. My stomach was in knots.

"You're too young to be a widow," Jackson said after a moment, glancing away from me. "You'll have to be a cousin or something."

I nodded, eyes on the table. I felt like the worst sort of person. Guilt ate at me . . . and shame. I'd broken Jackson's trust and had feelings for another man. I just didn't understand what kind of feelings. I loved Jackson, but Clark was important to me. And he'd been right. I'd been willing to kill for him. Was that love? If so, was it the kind of romantic love you built a relationship on? Or was it the kind of platonic love you had for a best friend?

The questions spinning inside my head made me feel even more unbalanced than I already did. More than anything, I wished I could be alone for a while. I needed time to recharge.

"Let's go, Aunt Chi," Mia said. Unexpectedly, she took my hand and squeezed it. I'd given her the Reader's Digest Condensed version of last night earlier this morning. She hadn't said much at the time.

"Yeah," I agreed, standing. "No time like the present." I tightened my ponytail and pushed my glasses up my nose. "Just give me a minute." I had some ibuprofen in the bathroom. Maybe they'd help my headache.

I'd swallowed the pills and was just starting to open the door when I heard Mia say my name. I paused, listening.

". . . seen Aunt Chi so upset," she was saying.

"What are you talking about?" Jackson asked. "She's fine."

"Then you obviously don't know her as well as you think." Mia's retort was scathing, and she continued. "You're both assholes. You, rushing her into marriage and then punishing her when it scares her out of her mind. And you, swooping in and putting her in a bad situation from start to finish. You both are expecting her to adapt to how *you* want your relationship with her to be, and *neither* of you has bothered to ask what she wants! And here she's going out of her way to help you both, putting *herself* in danger, and I think both of you should take a long walk off a short cliff," she finished in a loud whisper.

Mia was defending me. It gave me the unexpected urge to go hug her. Instead, I cleared my throat as I opened the door, and grabbed my backpack.

"Okay, let's go," I said.

Mia tossed her hair, shot one last disdainful look at Jackson and Clark, then followed me out the door.

The center was about twenty minutes away, and I plugged the address into Google Maps as we set out. I hadn't been able to stand Siri's voice, so I'd hacked my phone and turned her into Jarvis, who was much more pleasant to listen to.

"I heard you talking to them," I said, glancing at Mia, who suddenly found her fingernails riveting.

"I'm sorry for butting in," she said. "I know it's not my business. I just . . . can't stand to see you treated like . . . like how they're treating you. You don't deserve that."

"I'm not sure I agree," I said. "I did break a major relationship pact when I kissed Clark."

"Okay, first of all, Clark kissed you," she said, "not the other way around. Secondly, it was just a kiss. Jackson's making a big deal out of nothing."

"I don't know what measurement to use," I said. "Are there gradations for this sort of thing?"

"Depends on the person, I guess," Mia replied. "I think he's being ridiculous and selfish."

We were both quiet as Jarvis told me where to turn.

"I don't know what I'm going to do," I said at last. "I can't bear the thought of losing Jackson, but Clark . . ." My voice trailed off.

"It'll all work out," Mia said, patting me lightly on the arm. "It always does."

Her sweetly innocent belief in fate made me smile. That and her staunch defense of me. It wasn't something that happened to me very often.

The morning was busy at the records center, and we had to wait awhile once we'd checked in. The woman at the desk had scrutinized the list of appointments.

"That's strange," she murmured. "I thought there were only a dozen requests today."

"We're lucky thirteen," I said too brightly. Mia elbowed me as the woman glanced up, frowning.

"Mmm," she said, looking at us over the top of the sheet she held. "Have a seat."

The plastic chairs were as uncomfortable as they looked, and I squirmed. I ached in weird places from sleeping on the floor the night before, and I would've given up the title to my Mustang for relief from the headache in my skull.

We waited for thirty-nine minutes and fifty seconds before our name was called. A man who couldn't have been older than I was led us down a hallway and into an office. He motioned us to sit opposite him as he lowered himself into the chair behind the desk. It was on wheels and squeaked when he sat down. His nameplate said *Johnson.*

"I see you're here on a request for Mark Danvers," he said, glancing through some paperwork on a clipboard. He was African American, wore wire-frame glasses and a khaki Army uniform with short sleeves. He was tall—taller than Clark, even—and I wondered if he had to have his pants special-ordered.

"Yes," I replied. He glanced up and I swallowed. "Sir. I mean, yes, sir. We are."

He glanced back at the clipboard, then set it down. Bracing his elbows on the desk, Johnson folded his hands and looked at us.

"What's your interest in him again?" he asked.

"I-I . . . I mean . . . we—"

"It's painful," Mia interrupted, "and hard to talk about." Her big blue eyes glistened with tears.

Johnson looked uncomfortable, but he persisted. "Try."

"He . . . he's my father," she said, as a tear caught on her lashes. "My mother passed away six months ago and . . . on . . . on her-her—" She paused to take a deep breath. Her voice steadied even as twin rivulets of tears slid down her cheeks. "On her death . . . bed, she told me the identity of my father."

I knew she was lying and was still sucked in to her story. Impulsively, I reached for her hand and gave it a squeeze the way she had mine earlier this morning.

Johnson cleared his throat and scrambled inside his desk, coming up with a crumpled and ancient box of tissues. He handed it over to me, and I held it as Mia took a tissue and delicately dabbed at her eyes.

"I see," he said, looking as though he'd rather be anywhere else. "This is . . . highly irregular." He glanced at me. "And you are?"

"She's my aunt," Mia said. "And my legal guardian, since my mom—" Tears started falling again.

"That's okay," Johnson said quickly. "I understand." He shuffled some random papers on his desk while Mia dabbed with another tissue. "I, uh, I'll tell you what." He glanced past us out the open door, then lowered his voice and leaned forward.

"I'm not supposed to do this, but I grew up with a single mom, and well, I can relate to wanting to find your father." He placed a thick file on the desk in a significant move. "Mark Danvers's file is classified. I'm afraid I can't let you see it." He picked up an empty coffee mug sitting on the corner of his desk. "So I'll let you discuss that while I get a refill."

He got up and walked to the door with the mug, then paused. "I may be a few minutes. I think I'll have to brew a fresh pot." Then he was gone, his polished shoes making a tapping sound down the hallway.

Mia was up and out of her seat in a flash, rounding the desk and flipping open the folder.

"What are you doing?" I hissed. "He said we can't look at it and he'll be back soon."

She didn't even look up. "Code, Aunt Chi. He's giving us an opportunity to break the rules. Don't waste any time. Get over here." She was flipping pages and snapping photos of each page as quickly as she could.

Realization struck and I jumped up, rounding the desk to take half the stack. Then I started snapping my own photos.

We'd just finished and replaced the folder when we heard Johnson's slow, ponderous footsteps. Rounding the desk, we plopped into our chairs as he was walking around the corner.

Mia popped up. "I guess I'll just have to find a different way to contact my father," she said, holding out her hand.

Johnson shook it. "I'm sorry we couldn't be of any help today, miss."

Mia nodded sadly. "It's okay. Thank you." She hooked her arm through mine, and we were back to the car lickety-split.

I was out of breath by the time we'd locked ourselves inside. The adrenaline was wearing off and I rested my head against the headrest. I closed my eyes, willing the nausea to go away. I'd felt queasy all morning, and it only seemed to be getting worse.

"Are you okay?" Mia asked.

"Mmm, yeah, just give me a sec," I muttered.

"Do you want me to drive?"

That actually wasn't a bad idea. "Yeah. I'm going to lie down in the back seat, I think."

"Are you sick?" She sounded terribly anxious.

"Probably just a virus or something," I said. I managed, with some difficulty, to get out of the car and into the back seat, gratefully stretching out on the seat. I vaguely heard her close the doors, start the car, and get Google Maps programmed.

I dozed on the way back, my mind too clouded to think clearly. I'd never felt like this before. Each bump in the road was like a knife through my skull.

"Aunt Chi, wake up. Please wake up."

I heard her and slitted my eyes. We were stopped and Mia was leaning over me in the open car door. Her face was white.

"Am sorry," I slurred, pushing myself upward with a massive effort. "Tired." It took way too long for me to turn to get my feet on the ground, and I had to hold on to Mia and the car to stand upright. When I did, darkness flooded my vision as pain spiked in my head.

"Mia—" I gasped. My knees wouldn't obey. They gave out and I clutched at Mia as I fell.

"Aunt Chi!" Her scream was pierced with a sob. She tried to hold me up, but I couldn't help her. "Help me! Somebody!" The panicked terror in her voice made me feel terrible for worrying her, but there was nothing I could do.

◆ ◆ ◆

I drifted in and out of consciousness. I heard Mia screaming for help, felt the cold asphalt of the parking lot, but it was as though it was happening to someone else. I heard sirens in the distance.

Then I lost some time.

When I woke again, I was moving. Correction. I was in a vehicle that was moving.

I blinked. Slowly. The light was bright. There was something on my face, and I tried to lift my arm to take it off.

"Nah, nah, don't be doin' that," someone said.

I blinked again. A man was sitting next to me. Very busy doing . . . stuff. Stuff with me, but I couldn't really tell.

"That mask helps you breathe now, and that's important." He smiled. His teeth blazing white in his dark face. It was a friendly face. "You're okay, so don't worry. We're gonna take real good care of ya."

I closed my eyes. And I lost some more time.

Flashes of faces as I was moved again. The mask was still on my face, and now there was something in my arm, too. I saw Jackson and Clark as I was moved again, then lights passing in a ceiling.

When I opened my eyes again, I felt more aware than I had the times before. I looked around, recognizing a hospital room. A nurse was messing with an IV machine by my bed. She glanced at me and smiled when she saw I was awake.

"Good morning, China," she said. "I'm glad to see you're awake."

"Wh-where am I?" I said, my voice sounding like gravel. My mouth was so dry, it felt like sandpaper.

"You're in Barnes-Jewish Hospital," she said. "Your niece brought you here a short while ago. Let me get the doctor."

She disappeared out the door before I could ask any questions.

I stared at the wall in front of me. I wasn't lying flat, just reclined at an angle. As I glanced around, I realized I wasn't in a regular hospital room. I was in the ICU.

My fingers clutched at the bed as fear spiked. What was wrong with me? What had happened? I remembered being at the records center, and we'd taken photos, and gone to the car. I hadn't been feeling well. Mia had driven back. After that . . . nothing.

Where was Mia? Why wasn't she here? Was she okay? Had Clark and Jackson taken care of her?

There was a nurse's call button next to my bed, and I punched it. I needed answers.

About thirty seconds later the door opened and a doctor walked in, followed by the same nurse. Behind them came Mia and Jackson.

"Aunt Chi," Mia said, her eyes red and swollen. "You're awake. I'm so glad." She looked awful. Pasty white and her nose was pink.

Jackson's expression was drawn as he walked to the opposite side of the bed. His lips curved in a smile that didn't reach his eyes. He took my hand in his, which scared me more than anything else.

"Hi, China," the doctor said. "I'm Dr. Morris. I'm a neurosurgeon here at the hospital. Do you remember what happened before you were brought in?"

"Um, kind of," I said. "I was with Mia and I didn't feel well. She drove back and I was lying in the back seat. That's really the last I remember."

He smiled kindly. "What about before that? You said you weren't feeling well. What symptoms were you experiencing?"

"I-I guess I'd had a bad headache for a few days," I said. "I was tired. I felt a little nauseated, but I thought it was just because of Ja—" I cut myself off.

"Do you remember the car accident you were in a few days ago?" he asked.

I thought. Car accident? Had I been in an accident? I didn't remember anything, but something about the look on his face said I had been. I tried to remember. Car . . . wreck . . . the deer.

"Yeah," I said, glad I wasn't crazy. "I hit a deer."

He smiled again as though I'd given the correct answer in a pop quiz. "You did. You also hit your head, China. Are you familiar with what a subdural hematoma is?"

The fear in my gut solidified into pure anguish. I knew exactly what that was. Bleeding. On my brain. I swallowed.

"Is . . . is that what I have?"

The doctor nodded. "You do. Between the brain and the skull, you're bleeding. And it's putting pressure on the brain. We performed an MRI to confirm this. Yours is slow bleeding, which is why it's taken a few days before the symptoms have gotten so severe."

"So what can be done?" I asked.

"With your particular hematoma, we can perform a burr hole trephination, which is the least invasive. Basically, we drill a hole where the hematoma is and suction out the blood, then repair the artery. It's a common procedure and I've done many of them. But at the moment, the accumulated blood is putting too much pressure on the brain, which is why you're experiencing the symptoms you have. Memory problems and difficulty in coordination are also manifesting."

I stared at him, trying to take it all in. My brain. My brain was bleeding.

"We need your consent," he continued. "And it is of some urgency. We'd like to get you into surgery within the next couple of hours.

"I do need to inform you of some complications that may occur," he continued. "The most common complication after surgery is infection. Other risks include seizures, stroke, bleeding on the brain, coma, and brain damage."

I couldn't breathe. The air was too thick and it was stuffing my lungs. I couldn't see farther than a couple of feet in front of me, so all I could make out was the doctor's face and Jackson's.

"Brain damage?" I echoed. I suddenly realized I had a death grip on Jackson's hand. "What kind of brain damage?"

"There could be memory problems, coordination problems, speech impairments," he said. "I'm not going to lie to you and say it's not a risk. And as with any surgery, there's also a risk of death. But I've yet to have someone die on me, and I don't plan on starting with you."

The doctor patted my shoulder, and his kind face was very serious. "I know it's a lot to take in. We have a little bit of time for you to talk it over."

"We don't have to do this here," Jackson interrupted. "I can get her into any hospital in the country. The Mayo Clinic, Johns Hopkins, you name it. The best neurology department in the country is Mayo. We can be there in a few hours."

Dr. Morris was already shaking his head. "I'm sorry, young man, but the pressure changes of an airline flight would be dangerous for China."

"Then I'll have them flown here," Jackson argued. "Money is no object. I'll pay whatever it takes."

"That's not the issue—"

"They'll come," he persisted. "Everyone has a price. I'm more than capable of meeting it. Just give me a name."

"Jackson, stop." I tugged on his hand until he looked at me. "You can't fix this. Not this time."

His lips thinned and his jaw was set in bands of steel. The color in his cheeks was vivid against the paleness of his skin.

I glanced back at the doctor and swallowed hard. "I consent." He patted my hand.

"I'll be back shortly. If you have any questions in the meantime, just buzz for the nurse and she'll come find me."

He left, the door easing closed behind him, and I was left trying to wrap my head (ha!) around the fact that my brain was bleeding and they wanted to drill a hole in my skull.

"I need my glasses, please."

"Here you go." Mia hurried forward, pulling my glasses from her purse. Her hand shook as she handed them to me, which, conversely, steadied me.

"C'mere," I said, grasping her fingers and sliding over in the bed.

She carefully climbed up and nestled beside me. I wrapped my non-IV arm around her.

"You took care of me," I said. "Thank you."

"I was so scared," she whispered, sniffling.

"I know. I'm sorry, sweetie." I pressed a kiss to the top of her blond head.

"Where's Clark?" I asked.

"Jackson wouldn't let him come," Mia answered. I looked at Jackson.

"I didn't want someone to recognize him," he said, thin-lipped. "Him getting arrested would pretty much make all of this for nothing."

The twist in my gut hurt more than I'd expected, but I just nodded. "Yeah, of course. You're right."

"I'll give you two a few minutes," Jackson said, letting go of my hand. He gave me a meaningful look and left.

I squeezed Mia tighter. She smelled like the shampoo she always used. She insisted it was best for "volumizing," not that I knew how that applied to hair.

"I need you to call your dad," I told her. "Can you do that? Tell him what's going on?"

She nodded against my shoulder. "I can do that."

We lay there like that for a few minutes. It felt good just to hold her. She was like the sister I'd never had. When she'd moved in six months ago, I never would have thought she'd become such an integral part of my life. I suppose it just showed how nothing is planned, no matter how much you think the future is mapped out.

"Are you all right?" I asked softly. I knew she was physically well, but the circumstances and her actions weren't normal. I didn't put much stock in psychology, and as a science, I hated it, but if there was anything I could do to help Mia, I would.

"No," she whispered. "I'm scared. And you're so calm. I should be like you. But I . . . I c-can't . . ." She began to cry.

My heart broke inside at the sound of her crying. Nothing had ever affected me that way before. Usually, tears just made me uncomfortable. But with Mia . . . She'd fixed my hair and makeup. Teased me about my literal world view and language. We'd bonded over Hogwarts Houses. She wasn't an overly emotional girl, so to hear her cry over me tore at my heart like claws.

"Please don't cry," I said. "I'm going to be fine. It-it's a common procedure, he said. They have to tell you all the possible side effects so you don't sue them. Like those commercials on TV that list so many possible side effects, you think it's better to just deal with heartburn rather than possible incontinence."

Mia's laugh was muffled against my shoulder. "I don't think this is quite the same as heartburn," she said, "but I appreciate your effort to reassure me."

I squeezed her again. "You know . . . you know that I love you, right?"

"Of course I do. And I love you." She stretched up and kissed my cheek. "Do you want me to tell Clark to come in?" she whispered. "He's outside, sitting in the car."

The question made tears come to my eyes. I didn't feel normal. My emotions were weird and my thoughts were scattered. I couldn't answer, so I just nodded.

"Okay."

She climbed carefully out of the bed. "I'll send in Jackson, okay?"

I nodded again.

She caught my hand and we squeezed. Her eyes were as bright with tears as mine felt. I was so proud of her. She was such a good girl. Beautiful and caring and smart. So many things that I wasn't. But I didn't have the words to tell her, so I hoped what I couldn't say showed in my eyes.

"I'll see you later, Aunt Chi," she said, her voice resolute.

"Yes," I said. "I will. I'll see you later."

She left the room and a moment later, Jackson entered.

"I've had three other neurosurgeons review your charts and scans," he said. "They all agree with Dr. Morris." He paused, adding reluctantly, "Two of them knew of him and recommended him."

I nodded. Jackson had been working the problem. Logical. Exactly what I would do in his position. I expected nothing less. He was used to getting his way. Money plus his name was a powerful incentive for 99 percent of all things.

But he was very pale and was fidgeting, something I'd never seen him do.

"He seemed very . . . competent," I said, at a loss as to what else to say.

Jackson didn't say anything. He took my hand in his, threading our fingers together. He wasn't looking at me, though, gazing at our hands instead.

"I'm sure I'll be okay," I said, though I wasn't sure at all. I felt the need to reassure him. Jackson was usually so confident and decisive. It was strange to see him looking so rattled.

"I shouldn't have said what I did last night," he said at last. "You were . . . being honest with me, telling me something that you thought I should know, even though you didn't have to. And I reacted like a jealous asshole."

That took me by surprise. Jackson wasn't someone who behaved out of his emotions rather than logic. It was something we usually had in common, though I hadn't felt much like myself the past couple of days, and I felt even weirder.

"Yeah, you were," I said. "But . . . I don't want to lose you."

Jackson's expression was serious as he looked at me. "I don't want to lose you either, China. What we have is too rare, and too special, for me to give up on you because you're not fitting into my timetable."

Tears flooded my eyes. "I'm scared," I whispered.

He gathered me in his arms, touching me so carefully, I could've been made of glass. "I'm scared, too, but you're going to be all right," he soothed. "No matter what happens, I'm not going anywhere. I promise."

It made me feel better. Jackson was the rock I could count on and hold on to. Like the father who'd been conspicuously absent in that duty ever since my mom had died. I squeezed Jackson as hard as I could, trying to convey how thankful I was.

When he stood, I saw tears in his eyes as well. "I love you," he said. "And I'll be waiting for you afterward."

I couldn't speak, my throat was too full, so I just nodded.

The door opened then and another doctor came in. He was in scrubs, with a stethoscope around his neck and one of those little surgical caps on his head. He wore glasses, and his shoes were covered with surgical booties.

My hold on Jackson's hand was a death grip. This was it. They were taking me in to surgery.

To my surprise, though, the doctor removed his hat and glasses as he approached the bed, and I recognized him.

"Clark! You made it." Relief flooded me. Even though it was dangerous for him, he'd come.

"I'll wait outside," Jackson said. He pressed a kiss to my knuckles, gave Clark a curt nod, and left the room.

"I wasn't about to let someone drill a hole in your head without seeing you first," he said. "I knew you hated hospitals, but this isn't something that can be fixed with a Band-Aid."

My smile was weak, as was his.

"How are you feeling?" he asked.

His eyes focused on mine, seeing too much. "I'm terrified," I whispered, trying not to cry. "Th-they said I might have brain . . . damage." I nearly couldn't get the word out. "Clark, what if something happens to my brain? It's who I am. It's what I do. It's *everything*. What if I turn into a vegetable? What if I'm not smart anymore? What if—"

"Hold on, stop right there," he interrupted me. "The chance of that happening is really low. You're worrying and stressing over something that isn't going to happen. I promise. It would take more than a hole in your head to make you not smart."

"But that's who I am," I said again.

"No, it's not." His expression was resolute. "You're more than your intellect. The woman I know is scary smart, yeah. But you're also kind, compassionate, and giving. You're funny, too literal, and need some serious advice on pajamas. You're a million things that, taken separately, aren't anything special, but when you put them all together, they make you *you*, and you *are* special." He paused. "Especially to me."

It was an incredibly sweet thing to say, and I didn't take it for granted that Clark had been the one to say it. I was still scared—I was having brain surgery, after all—but he made me feel better.

He cleared his throat. "I'd get all sappy on you and start spouting declarations of devotion and shit, but that's not really my style. So I'll do this. Come out of this, be well, and I'll watch one episode of *Star Trek*."

I sat up a little straighter. "The original series?"

His eyes closed as if it pained him to answer. "Yeah. The Spock and Kirk one."

I grinned. I couldn't help it. "Awesome. And if I come out of this a vegetable?"

"I'll make you watch an entire season of *Baywatch*."

I grimaced. "You drive a hard bargain."

Clark shrugged. "A bet isn't a bet unless it's worth winning."

"One episode versus an entire season isn't really fair," I argued.

"The man has pointy ears," he shot back.

"Pointy ears versus bouncy boobs." I raised an eyebrow, waiting. Finally, he capitulated.

"Okay, a season for a season, but I reserve the right to make fun of it."

"Ditto."

"Shake on it."

He took my hand and pressed it lightly. The teasing light went out of his eyes, and I could see the strain and worry in them. His thumb lightly caressed the top of my hand. There were a lot of unsaid things in his eyes, but for once, I could read what he held back. Like last night, I could see his soul in his eyes.

The door opened and Dr. Morris walked in along with two nurses. Clark glanced at them, then moved closer to me.

"You're going to be just fine, baby," he whispered, then pressed his lips to mine. "I'll catch you on the flip side."

Before I could reply, he nodded at the nurses and was out the door and gone.

"Okay, Miss China," Dr. Morris said with a smile. "We've come to prep you for surgery, and we have some paperwork for you to look over and sign. The anesthesiologist will be by to discuss his part with you. The nurses here are going to get started, and we'll have you in the OR shortly. Do you have any questions?"

"No. I'm okay," I said, swallowing hard. My gut was churning with fear.

Dr. Morris patted my arm. "It'll be all right. I assure you. I've done many of these surgeries. We're going to give you something now that'll help take the edge off your nerves, okay?"

"That sounds really great." Anything that eased the fear gripping me would be welcome.

"Okay, then," he said. "Let's get started."

CH 14

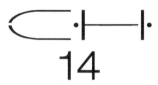

Mia paced the hospital hallway, chewing her nails. Which sucked because she'd just had them done. At thirty-five bucks a pop, it was an expensive habit. One that Aunt Chi had watched in consternation one afternoon.

"She cuts your regular nails, then puts on fake acrylic ones, then spends the better part of an hour using a drill to file them down," she'd said. "Wouldn't it be easier, and cheaper, to just grow your own nails?"

"Yes, but they're always breaking on me," Mia had explained.

Aunt Chi hadn't argued further on the merits of the procedure, just watched with such attention that Mia had no doubt that if suddenly called upon for an emergency manicure, her aunt would be able to do as good a job, if not a better one, than the woman sitting across from them.

They'd become so close over the past few months, Mia couldn't imagine her life without her aunt. She'd always felt a kinship with China, like they connected in a way that was instinctive. She hadn't had that with anyone else. Flying down to barge in on her aunt had been a spur-of-the-moment thing, but it had been the right decision. If the surgery didn't go well—

No. She stopped in her tracks. She couldn't think like that. When she did, she couldn't breathe.

Dropping into a chair, she sniffed back tears and pulled out her cell. She needed to call her dad and let him know what was going on.

The phone rang three times before he answered.

"Hey, honey," Oslo said. "How's the trip going? Everything okay?"

"Um, no, Dad, it's not." It took a few minutes to explain what had happened, but eventually he got the important part. They were in St. Louis. China was in the hospital. She was having emergency brain surgery.

"I'll call your grandpa and Bill," he said. "We'll head out soon. We should be there by morning."

"See you then." Mia ended the call.

"Your dad?" Jackson asked, sitting down beside her.

She nodded. "He's going to come down with Uncle Bill and Grandpa."

"I called Grams," Jackson said. "Sent my plane to pick her up and bring her."

"That was nice of you," she said glumly, plucking at the edge of her blouse. "She'll like having Grams here."

"Are you okay?" he asked.

"I'm better than my aunt," she replied, then looked up at him. "It's your fault, you know. She was in your car. This guy is after *you*. Not her. You're the reason she's in there, the reason they're *drilling* into her *brain*." The bitterness in her voice was apparent.

Jackson took a moment to reply. "I know. No one knows better than I do that she wouldn't be in here if it wasn't for me."

"Then why are you lying to her?" Mia persisted. "Why don't you just tell her what you know about this whole thing? What if you're putting her in more danger by withholding information from her?"

"It's not something I can just blurt out, Mia. And I'd hope you know that if I'm not talking, maybe there's a good reason as to why." He stood. "I'm going to go check on the flight arrangements." He walked away without another word.

Mia felt bad about being so hard on Jackson, but she was hurting, and too worried about her aunt to care if she'd hurt his feelings.

Getting to her feet, she started pacing again. After she grew tired of the same part of the hallway, she drew closer to the waiting room. At least there were televisions there. Maybe she could distract herself from worrying.

Her gaze landed on Clark, sitting in a dim corner. His elbows were braced on his spread knees, and his hands were linked as he hunched over, staring at the floor.

Mia dropped into the chair next to him. They said nothing for a while, just sat there together.

"My brother is coming," she said after a while. "He's bringing my uncle and grandpa. They should be here by morning."

Clark glanced up, one dark eyebrow cocked as he listened. "Well, this should be an easy situation to explain," he deadpanned. "What'd you tell him?"

Mia shrugged. "Just that there was a car accident and that she's got that subdural thing. That she's in surgery. That's all."

"And I'm guessing no one in your family really knows what China was doing for a living."

"*I* don't even know what she does for a living," Mia replied. "She said it was secret and she couldn't tell me. Just something with computers."

"That's the most people can comprehend of her job anyway," Clark muttered.

"How long is this surgery supposed to take?" she asked.

"About an hour. Then about another hour for the anesthesia to wear off. The doctor said he'd be out to let us know how the surgery went."

"How long has it been?"

"Thirty-seven minutes."

The minutes crawled by. Jackson returned, taking the seat next to Mia.

"Grams is on her way," he said. His eyes were bloodshot and he barely glanced at them.

A pang inside made Mia reach over and take his hand. "I'm sorry about earlier," she said. "I was just . . ." Her voice trailed off.

"I know." He squeezed her hand.

More minutes went by. The hour came and went. Mia started chewing her nails again until Clark reached over and took her other hand.

These were the two men who'd worked their way into her aunt's life and heart. They were both good guys, and it seemed like they each gave her something she needed. Mia didn't know how things would end up. She just wanted Aunt Chi to be happy.

If she ever got out of surgery.

"How long—" she began, but Jackson interrupted.

"Here he comes."

All three of them got to their feet. "How is she?" Mia blurted. Both her hands were crushing Jackson's and Clark's.

Dr. Morris smiled. "Relax, please, she's fine."

Mia released her breath on a gasp, tears welling in her eyes. Her knees gave out and she sat back down.

"China did very well in the surgery, and the artery was repaired. The brain wasn't swollen, so that's good news, and will speed her recovery."

"Can we see her?" Jackson asked.

"Not yet. The anesthesia still needs to wear off, and she'll be moved into the ICU. Right now, she's in recovery. If everything looks good by morning, we can move her into a regular room."

Jackson put his arm around Mia's shoulders. She was crying into her hands.

"What about the complications you mentioned?" Jackson asked. "When will we know about them?"

"We'll perform some tests tomorrow," he answered. "Considering how well the surgery went, I am cautiously optimistic that she won't suffer any serious side effects or complications.

"The nurse will be out once China comes around," he continued. "You can each go in and see her, just for a few minutes. She's on a lot of medication, so she may or may not be lucid. Maybe won't even remember tonight at all, come tomorrow. But I think it'll make you all feel better to see that she's all right."

Mia took a shuddering breath as the doctor's footsteps faded away. She swiped at her wet cheeks. Jackson rubbed her shoulder lightly as he sat back down.

"You okay?" he asked.

She nodded. "It was such a relief. It . . . took me by surprise. I guess I'd been preparing for different news." Her throat thickened again and she had to clear her throat.

Jackson pushed his fingers through his hair, letting out a deep sigh. "I think we all were preparing for different news."

"C'mon," Clark said to Mia, getting to his feet. "I could use a cup of coffee, and so could you."

Mia nodded and rose, then glanced from Clark to Jackson and back again.

Clark rolled his eyes. "Fine. Coop can come, too."

"Gee, thanks for including me in the cool kids' club," Jackson said wryly.

"It's a truce right now, you two," Mia interjected. "Cease-fire."

Which meant all three of them were in the nearly empty cafeteria, sitting at a table, drinking bad hospital coffee. Mia took one sip of her cream-and-sugar-with-some-added-coffee, wrinkled her nose, and set it aside.

Jackson and Clark drank theirs without comment. The minutes crept by until Mia couldn't take the silence anymore.

"So, Clark," she said, "what, um . . . what have you been up to these past few months?"

"I've been around. Doing a few odds and ends, here and there," he answered, taking another drink of his coffee.

"Vague much?" Mia muttered. "Okay, then. Jackson, how about you? Have you told your parents about your engagement to my aunt?"

"They live in Florida and are retired. They live separately, keep a low profile, play bridge and golf, and occasionally remember they have a son. Usually about the time the bills roll in. So, no, I haven't mentioned my life choices to them recently."

"Should I call Dr. Phil?" Clark asked.

"If anyone's got issues that need a shrink, it's you," Jackson retorted.

"Says the control freak to someone he can't control."

"I'm not the one trying to fuck with China's head."

"Enough!" Mia threw out her hands, shutting them both up. "I was just trying to make conversation, okay? Geez, no wonder you two stress her out."

"Who says we stress her out?" Clark asked.

"Anyone with eyes," Mia retorted. "You two are going to have to figure this out. Because she isn't a bone to be fought over. She needs you both, just in different ways. Surely you see that."

Both men were silent.

"Listen," Mia said. "I love my aunt. But you've gotta understand that emotions and going with your gut are foreign concepts to her. She's much more likely to make a pros-and-cons list for each of you and decide based on that."

"There are worse ways," Clark muttered.

"I wouldn't be so quick to advocate that approach," Jackson said. "I don't think you'd like the result."

"You mean the fact that I don't require her to fit into my world, ready to say the vows and start popping out little Einsteins before she's thirty?" Clark bit out. "Have you even asked her what she wants?"

"At least I have something to offer her other than being on the run from my past," Jackson retorted. "A normal life with a family. You wouldn't recognize that if it bit you on the ass. You don't understand her in the slightest, someone of her genius."

"And you do?" Clark shot back. "You treat her like a science project."

"And you treat her like a trophy."

Mia shoved her chair back, the legs scraping against the linoleum floor with a sound that set her teeth on edge. "You're both douches," she said. "If I were her, I'd tell you both to bugger off."

"What are you? British?" Clark called after her.

"I've yet to find an American phrase that has the same level of insult and apathy as that one," she tossed back.

When Mia returned to the waiting room, she found a nurse looking for her.

"Your aunt has woken," she said. "Do you want to see her for a few minutes?"

"Oh yes, please!"

"Just keep in mind, she's going to be very groggy. She probably won't say much. And it's doubtful she'll remember anything tomorrow. Okay?"

"Yeah, that's fine."

Mia followed the nurse through two sets of double doors, one of which required her ID to unlock, then they were in the ICU. They passed curtained-off patient areas, and the smell of disinfectant was strong.

They stopped at a room, and the nurse held the door for Mia to enter ahead of her. Mia took three steps and stopped.

China was barely discernible in the bed. She was hooked up to so many machines, and her head was wrapped in bandages . . . the sight of her was shocking. She was small anyway, but now seemed dwarfed in the bed, and she wasn't moving.

"You don't have to get closer," the nurse said kindly. "I know it's hard seeing her like that, but she's going to be okay. We just need to monitor her and make sure she stays healthy."

"Um, okay. Thanks." Mia cast one last look at the bed, turned, and left. She made it to the waiting room, saw Jackson, and promptly burst into tears.

"Hey, hey, don't cry. It's okay." Jackson put his arms around her and pulled her in for a hug.

Mia cried harder. "I s-saw her," she stammered through her tears. "Sh-she looked s-so . . ."

"It's okay. She's going to be okay," he soothed. "I know it looks bad now, but the doctor said everything went well. In a couple of days, you won't even be able to tell your aunt had brain surgery."

"I know they said that," she said, sniffling. Her tears had slowed to a trickle.

"It's just relief, what you're feeling," Jackson said, giving her another squeeze. "The cathartic release provided by crying is actually very healthy."

Mia's laugh was a little watery. "Now you sound like Aunt Chi."

Jackson smiled. "She must be rubbing off on me."

"All right, maybe you're not a *total* douche," she said.

"High praise, indeed," he said. "Now I'm going to go peek in on her, okay? You stay here. I'll be back."

Mia moved away. "Wait—where's Clark?"

Jackson shrugged. "I'm not his keeper."

◆ ◆ ◆

I'd lost time, but not in the unconscious way of before. Then, I'd sensed time passing. But this was a drug-induced lost time, so it felt very different and unnatural. One second I'd been staring up at the bright lights of the OR, people bustling around me, and the next second I was opening my eyes someplace else, with the realization that it was already over.

"You're in recovery," someone said, then I saw the face as a woman leaned over me. She was wearing scrubs with a print of Hello Kitty on it. That meant something to me, but I couldn't remember what. "Everything went really well. The doctor said he couldn't have planned it any better."

My mouth felt like cotton and everything was fuzzy. I wasn't in any pain, but neither could I summon the energy to move. Blinking required effort.

"You'll be groggy for a while as the anesthesia wears off, but the pain medication will still make you feel sleepy," she continued. "I can get you something to drink shortly. That'll make you feel better, I'm sure."

"M'kay," I mumbled.

I closed my eyes again and listened to the sounds of the nurse working in the room, checking the machines and my vitals. The blood-pressure cuff tightened again, then slowly released. I heard the door open and close as she left.

I drifted in and out of sleep, which felt better than just being unconscious. I thought I heard the door open again and the sound of muffled voices, but they retreated. and silence fell.

A few minutes later, or perhaps it was longer, the door opened and footsteps approached the bed. I cracked my eyes open again and saw someone. As they moved closer to the bed, my vision cleared and I saw Jackson's face.

"Hey, sweetheart," he said, smiling. "How are you feeling?"

"Tired," I rasped. "Sore."

"You'll feel better tomorrow. Right now, you just need to get your rest, okay?"

"Is my brain okay?" I managed. That was what I was worrying about the most.

"Of course it is."

"H-how can you tell?"

"Because I know you wouldn't have it any other way." He smiled and leaned down, pressing his lips to my forehead. "Now rest. Your Grams will be here in the morning."

I smiled at the thought of seeing my grandma. She could always make me feel better. "Thank you. What about Mia? Is she okay?"

"She's fine. I'm going to take her back to the hotel and make her get some sleep."

"That's good." I slowly blinked. "Glad you're taking care of her."

"Don't worry about anything," he said. "Just get some rest."

"Okay." I closed my eyes and then didn't open them for a while. When I did, Jackson was gone.

I felt a little more lucid this time. The visit from Jackson was vague, like a dream, but I remembered he was going to take care of Mia and was bringing Grams to me. Both things eased my mind. Speaking of which . . .

How did I know if I had memory problems? How would I know what I couldn't remember? What about my intellect? Again, how would I know if my brain was damaged if I didn't know what I didn't know?

I stared at the ceiling, anxiety growing inside, until the door opened and someone came in. I assumed it was the nurse and waited until she got closer.

"Clark," I said in surprise. "You shouldn't be here."

"There's a lot of things I shouldn't be," he said, pulling a chair up next to the bed. "I hear you did great."

"I had nothing to do with it," I replied. "The doctor and the nurses are responsible for the results of the surgery. Complimenting me is . . . redundant. Not to mention preemptive. We don't know if I have any complications, most importantly, brain damage."

"Given that little speech, I'm gonna lay odds that your brain is just fine, Mack."

"You can't possibly know that."

He leaned over and folded his arms on the edge of the bed, then rested his chin on them. "I know *you*, and that's all I need."

I smiled. It was a sweet and completely illogical thing to say, yet I didn't mind.

"So it looks like you're going to be watching a season of *Star Trek*," I reminded him.

He winced. "*That* I was hoping you wouldn't remember."

The machine next to me made a slight noise, and I glanced at it.

Clark jerked upright. "What's that? Are you okay?" I could hear the anxiousness in his voice that hadn't been there before.

"Yeah, it's fine," I said. "Pain meds, on a timer." I narrowed my eyes, studying Clark. "You're projecting an attitude of ease, but your reaction to the machine shows that you're much more on edge than it would seem."

Clark didn't respond right away, his eyes on mine. His gaze went to my bandaged head, then slowly moved to the tubes attached to my arm and the machines at my bedside.

"I might be projecting an air of . . . ease, as you put it. But, that doesn't mean I'm taking this lightly."

"Then how are you taking it?" I asked.

He didn't answer, just reached out and took my hand in his. Pressing my palm against his cheek, he closed his eyes and let out a deep breath.

I didn't say anything. His jaw was rough against my skin. He hadn't shaved. They'd all been here for hours, waiting to see if I was okay.

He opened his eyes, his gaze piercing as it met mine. "How am I taking it?" he echoed. "How do you think I'm taking it?" His voice was rough and painful to hear.

The look in his eyes made me hurt in my chest. "I don't know," I said softly. I brushed my thumb across his cheekbone. "This is hard."

"As usual, you have a knack for understatement."

He got to his feet and pushed away the chair. "You need sleep," he said, pressing his lips to the center of my palm. "I'll see you in the morning."

"Wait, Clark," I said. "What if . . . what if something does go wrong with my brain? And I don't know it. Will you tell me?"

"Yeah. I'll tell you."

"Promise?" I didn't want to be wandering around thinking I was the same as before when really it was like *A Beautiful Mind* and everyone knew I was crazy, except me.

"Yes. I promise. Now get some rest." He leaned down and I expected him to kiss my forehead or my cheek, but his lips grazed mine in the lightest of touches. Then he was gone.

I was too tired to dwell on my visitors tonight, and the pain medication was kicking in. Before I could buzz the nurse to ask for more Sprite, I was asleep.

◆ ◆ ◆

Breakfast was the best food I'd ever eaten. Well, actually not. But I was so hungry, I didn't care. The nurses were smiling and didn't mind that I asked for an antibacterial wipe for my hands before I ate.

"How's that oatmeal?" Dr. Morris asked, walking into the room. He was in slacks and a tie, his white coat pristine.

"Best thing ever," I replied.

"Good, I'm glad to hear it. How are you feeling?"

"Okay. A bit of an ache in my head, but it's dulled. Probably from the pain medication."

"True," he said with a smile.

"Other than that, I feel much better than I did yesterday."

"I'm sure you do," he said. "Let's take a look at the site, shall we?"

A nurse assisted in removing the bandages, and he inspected my head.

"Um, how much hair did you have to shave off?" I asked. I didn't consider myself a vain person, but I found I had an uncomfortably high level of anxiety about how much of my hair had been removed to access the injury.

"Only a small patch," the doctor said. "Less than an inch square. You'll be able to cover it with the rest of your hair, once it's healed."

I let out a small sigh of relief, somewhat chagrined that I'd been so worried. If it had been worse, they'd have had to shave half my head. I couldn't imagine that, as much as it struck me how ridiculous I was being about my appearance.

"Everything looks good. No signs of infection. We're going to continue with the antibiotics, of course, but there was no swelling of the brain, so that's very good news."

"Will I recover okay? Or will I have brain . . . damage?"

"It's soon, but from what I've seen so far, you don't seem to be experiencing any of the more serious complications."

Oh thank God.

"You're young and healthy. I don't see any reason why you wouldn't experience a full recovery," he continued. "I'll be back to check on you in a few hours, but I do think you have some visitors wanting to see you, so let's get you moved to the patients' ward."

An hour later, I'd finally been moved to a regular room and out of the ICU. I was anxious to see a friendly face, so when Grams came bursting through the door, I was smiling so hard that my cheeks hurt.

"Grams!"

"Oh my China-girl!" she exclaimed, rushing over to me. Her eyes were watering as she took in my bandages and machines. "What on earth happened to you?"

"Just a car accident," I explained. "Thanks to Dr. Morris, I'm better now. How did you get here?"

"Why, Jackson sent his plane for me," she said, pulling up a chair. "Terribly thoughtful of him, bless his heart." She'd been wearing a matching egg-yolk-yellow crocheted shawl and hat, which she took off. "I was in such a state, but he was all calm and collected. Had everything all arranged to get me to you."

"I'm so glad you could come," I said.

"Don't be silly, girl." She pooh-poohed me. "As if I could stay away, knowing you're in trouble."

The door opened again, and I was shocked to see Oslo and Bill walk in, followed by Mia.

"What are you two doing here?" I blurted.

"Um, sis, you had brain surgery. It's kind of a big deal," Bill said, approaching the bed. He gingerly hugged me. "It's good to see you, Chi."

"Yeah, it's been a while," I said. He was several years older than I was, and at the moment, he looked it. I wondered how much of a toll taking care of Dad and the farm had been on him.

"The doctor says you're going to be okay, little sis," Oslo said, rounding the other side of the bed. He pressed a chaste kiss to my cheek and squeezed my shoulder. He and Oslo hugged Grams, too.

"Yeah, I think so. So far, so good, at least. Where's Dad? Did he come, too?" I hadn't seen my dad since I'd gone home for Christmas two years ago. The thought of him coming to the hospital to see me made me both hopeful and nervous.

Oslo didn't answer. Instead, he glanced at Bill, who shifted from one foot to another.

"Dad couldn't come," Bill said at last. "But he said he'd call once you were feeling better."

The pain those words caused was unexpected, which was ridiculous. I'd gotten over expecting any kind of close relationship with my father years ago.

"Um, yeah, of course," I said. "The surgery went well, so there was really no cause for him to make the trip, especially overnight."

There was a silence after I spoke. Bill and Oslo exchanged another glance, but I didn't know what it meant.

"Harrumph," Grams said, shifting in her chair. Before I could question what that meant, Mia approached the foot of the bed.

"I brought you some fresh clothes," she said. "For when they let you out of here. And some of your own toiletries." She handed me a bag.

"Thanks." I smiled. "I appreciate that. Did you get any sleep?" I opened up the bag, hoping she'd remembered to bring my razor.

"Yeah. Jackson made me."

"Who's Jackson?" Oslo asked.

"He's my fiancé," I answered, pawing through the bag. Yes, she had my razor and my hairbrush. That was going to be a trial, trying to fix my hair—

Grams let out a whoop as Oslo and Bill spoke in unison, with equal amounts of surprise in their voices. "Fiancé?"

I glanced up from the bag. "Um, yeah," I said. "Why are you looking at me like that?"

Grams jumped to her feet and hugged me. "Aw, honey, I'm glad you made your decision. Have you set a date?"

"Um, no, not yet," I replied.

"Wait a second," Bill interrupted. "There is no way in hell that you're getting *married* to some guy that we haven't even met."

"Excuse me?" I couldn't have heard him correctly.

"You're only twenty-four years old," Oslo said, using his Big Brother Voice. "Marriage is a big step, Chi. And I agree with Bill. What if this guy is taking advantage of you?"

"Taking advantage of me?" I was confused. "How could he possibly—"

"You're not . . . used to dating and men and the shitty things they can do," Bill said. "You make decent money, you're too trusting, you're young. Basically, every con artist's dream mark."

Grams laughed outright and Mia snickered. Both Bill and Oslo looked at them askance.

"You should be on our side, Grams," Oslo scolded. "You know how China is. I'd think you of all people would want to help us protect her."

"You're talking about me as if I'm naive and stupid," I said, looking from Oslo to Bill, then back. "Is that what you think of me? That I'd just let some random guy sweep me off my feet and be so . . . so flattered by the attention that I'd agree to marry him?"

By their silence and mutual glances, I knew I was right. Everyone was quiet.

"Wow." I didn't know if I should be angry, or flattered that they'd taken such a protective stance toward me. I was saved from deciding by another visitor. This time, the very man of whom they spoke.

"Jackson," I said. "Perfect timing. Please meet my brothers, Bill and Oslo."

He'd showered and shaved, changed into jeans that I was sure cost more than $500, and a similarly priced designer shirt. Before I'd begun dating Jackson, I'd noticed he dressed well. I just hadn't known the price tag before. I was biased, but I thought he looked every inch the successful technocrat billionaire.

"Nice to meet you," Jackson said, shaking their hands.

Oslo and Bill stared. Oslo found his voice first.

"Um, I don't mean to sound rude—"

"Then don't," Jackson interrupted, leaning down to give Grams a hug. "How was your flight?"

"Wonderful," she said. "That little flight attendant, what was her name?"

"You mean Dana?"

"Yes, that's her. She was so sweet! Why, she made me two mint juleps, and they were perfect. That plane was just lovely. I felt like a queen." She laughed and patted his arm like a flirtatious girl.

"I'm glad I could help," Jackson said, moving to my side. "And how are you, sweetheart?" His eyes were soft and his smile genuine. "You look more awake, that's for sure." His hand cupped my cheek.

"Yes, I'm much better than last night," I said, covering his hand with mine and squeezing. A knot in my stomach eased at seeing him.

He poked at the remains of my breakfast on the tray and made a face. "Ugh. Hospital food. No way is my girl eating that. I'm friends with the head chef at Niche. They have a restaurant that does brunch. Let me have him whip you up something."

I began, "It's okay, you don't have—"

"You mean Brasserie," Oslo interrupted. "I've heard of that place. I thought fancy restaurants only did brunch on Sundays."

Jackson looked at him. "So?"

"Yeah, it's Wednesday," Bill quietly added. I didn't think he'd blinked since Jackson had walked in.

"He won't mind," Jackson said. He kissed my forehead. "I'll be back shortly. Let me give him a quick call." He turned to the room at large. "Everyone's probably hungry, right?"

Mia and Grams agreed, but Bill and Oslo were still staring, jaws slightly agape.

"Okay, then. Brunch for everyone." He smiled and left the room.

Bill and Oslo looked at each other, then at me.

"Was that—?" Bill asked.

"No," Oslo said. "No . . . really?"

"What was that you were saying about her fiancé taking advantage of her?" Mia piped up.

Grams just cackled.

CH. 15

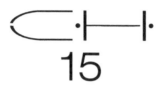

Jackson was as good as his word, a full table setup with real plates, heavy silverware, and dishes such as eggs benedict, quiche, hazelnut waffles, French toast, beignets, the works. The smells in the room made my mouth water.

The chef was really nice, serving me first in the bed while his two assistants served everyone else. Soon, the room was filled with the sounds of cutlery and clinking glass. Bill and Oslo weren't too starstruck to eat, each of them polishing off two full plates of food, with Mia not far behind.

Jackson sat next to me on the bed, making sure I ate. It wasn't necessary. The food was amazing. Dr. Morris even appeared in the middle of brunch, looked around in some amazement, asked me a few questions, then said he'd be back again in a few hours.

By the time brunch was cleared away, I could barely keep my eyes open. A full stomach and all the visitors had worn me out. Jackson fluffed the pillows behind my head and remained behind when Grams shooed everyone else out. The pain medication had beeped into my IV again.

"Thanks for the food," I said, "and for taking care of Mia and Grams. I really 'preciate it."

"That's why I'm here," he said softly, slotting his fingers with mine. "I don't want you to worry about anything. I'll take care of everything, I just need you to get better."

He closed the blinds on the windows, dimming the room, then returned to my side. Pulling up the chair Grams had been using, he sat down.

"My dad didn't come."

"I know."

My eyes started to leak, though I didn't know why. "I shouldn't have expected him to."

"He's your father. Of course you should have. I'm sorry he didn't."

"Yeah. Well." Putting emotions into words was hard when I was healthy. At the moment, trying to put what I was feeling about my dad into cogent sentences was completely beyond me.

Jackson leaned forward, wiping away the wet tracks from my cheeks.

"You're just gonna watch me sleep?" I murmured, my eyes heavy.

"Maybe. Is that okay?"

"Why?"

"Because I can," he said softly. "The thought of losing you . . . I don't ever want to feel like that again. And there wasn't a damn thing I could do about it."

"You helped," I argued. "With Grams and Mia . . ."

"Shh," he said. "Get some rest."

I pried my eyes open one more time. "'kay, but don't stay in that awful chair the whole time. It doesn't look at all ergonomic."

"I'll keep that in mind."

He held my hand until I feel into a deep, dreamless sleep.

◆ ◆ ◆

When next I opened my eyes, Oslo was sitting in the chair, messing with his phone.

"Hey," I said, my voice raspy, "where's Jackson?"

"You mean your billionaire boyfriend that you haven't ever mentioned to your family?" he asked.

"It was all over Twitter," I muttered, adjusting the controls on the bed to sit up. Someone had left a glass of water within reach, and I gratefully swallowed some.

"Yeah. I'm a social-media addict," Oslo said drily. "I . . . Twitter all the time."

"Tweet."

"Whatever. The point is, you haven't breathed a word of this to us. And now you're engaged to him?"

"I was bringing him home to meet everyone," I said. "This just happened first."

"*This?*" he echoed. "This is you nearly dying, China." His voice cracked on *dying*, and I stared at him, wide-eyed. Oslo was the calm, steady, oldest sibling who had taken more care of me than he should've had to after Mom died. Dad had been in such shock, and I'd been so young . . . Oslo had been the one to step up and make sure Bill and I got fed and had clean clothes.

"I'm sorry," I said. "It wasn't something I did intentionally."

"I know, I know," he said, rubbing his forehead. "I'm not mad at you. You were just . . . being you."

As always, I felt that stab of guilt for not being more . . . normal. If I was normal, I'd know the right things to say to make him not look at me as though I was a science experiment he liked but didn't quite understand.

"Do you like Jackson?" I asked, changing the subject.

"He seems nice," Oslo said. "Bill's been giving him the third degree. I don't think he's stopped asking him questions for the past two hours."

"Why?"

He gave me a funny look. "Because despite his money, we're not about to let some playboy toy with you if he's not for real. If he wants to marry you, he's going to have to pass muster."

I didn't know what to say. Oslo and Bill were performing the age-old ritual of hazing my suitor to ensure he was worthy of my affections. Considering how often I'd fended for myself, this was unexpected. But unlike most surprises, this one wasn't unwelcome. It made me feel . . . valued. Which wasn't a feeling I often associated with my testosterone-laden family.

"He's taking everyone to dinner," Oslo continued. "Some fancy restaurant. I think a limo is coming to pick us up." He snorted.

"What's wrong with that?" I asked.

"He's not going to buy our approval," he groused. "He can throw his money around all he wants. At least Grams seems to appreciate it."

I laughed. "Grams thinks he's the cat's meow." My memory still provided idioms on demand, which was a good sign.

Speak of the devil . . . Jackson walked in then. When he saw me sitting up, he smiled.

"You are looking better every time I see you," he said, wrapping me in a gentle hug. He glanced at Oslo. "Thanks for keeping her company."

"She's my sister," Oslo said archly. "Thanks are unnecessary."

"Yes, I see by how often you call and visit China that she's near and dear to your heart." Not even I could miss the edge in Jackson's voice.

"Dating my sister doesn't give you the right to judge our family." Oslo got to his feet, and I recognized the angry line of his jaw.

"Please don't fight," I said. "This really isn't the time or place for all that."

"You're right," Jackson said. "I'm sorry, sweetheart."

"I'm going to find Bill," Oslo said. "I'd like to grab a shower. I'm sure he does, too."

"The car will pick you up from the hotel in an hour," Jackson said. "Grams and Mia are coming, too, of course."

"Of course they are."

There was a bit of a staring contest between them, then Oslo left.

I rested my head against the pillow. "He doesn't like you."

"Nonsense. He's just under a lot of emotional stress because his sister is in the hospital and just underwent brain surgery. We'll all go to dinner tonight, have a pleasant time, and they'll relax."

"I don't know why they're being so weird about this," I said. "It's not as if it's unheard of for a girl to bring home a boyfriend."

"Yes. They just didn't expect it of *you*."

That hurt, but I also knew it was true.

"Chef Rafe is going to bring by your dinner shortly," Jackson said. "I hope you don't mind me taking this opportunity to schmooze with your family."

"No, no, it's fine. I appreciate you doing all of this. You've gone above and beyond."

"You're worth much more," he said with a soft smile. "I have to admit, I carry some animosity toward your brothers for how they've treated you in the past, but I'm willing to put that aside in favor of an amiable relationship that puts you at ease."

"I really want to get out of here," I said. "We have work to do. Have you and Clark found anything out from the file Mia and I got?"

"Clark is working on it," he said. "We've divvied up duties."

There was a knock on the door, and Dr. Morris came in. "And how's my patient doing?" he asked.

"Impatient to leave your care," I said.

He laughed. "Well, let's see what we can do about that." A nurse walked in behind him with fresh bandages.

"I'll check in on you later," Jackson said.

"Okay. Have a good dinner. Don't let Grams have too many mint juleps. She'll start hitting on the waiter."

"Got it."

The doctor examined me after Jackson left. "You're doing very well," he said. "Tomorrow morning we'll do a CT scan and make sure everything is healing as it should. If it is, then you can go home. How's your pain level?"

"Not bad."

"I'll scale back the meds tonight and see how you do. If you're feeling too uncomfortable, just buzz the nurse."

They rebandaged my head, this time with a much smaller patch that didn't wrap all the way around my head. My scalp itched. It had been too long since I'd washed my hair. It was starting to irritate me.

"Can I take a shower or anything?" I asked. That was getting to me, too.

"I don't see why not. We'll give you a shower cap to wear over your hair, and the nurse can help you."

Great. A stranger watching me wash my privates. Awesome.

"Um, okay. Maybe later," I said.

They left, and true to his word, Jackson's chef friend came by later. He left a four-course meal that was way too much for me to eat, but what I *could* eat was incredible.

I was watching reruns of *The Big Bang Theory* and trying not to think about how bored I was when the door opened again.

"Clark!" He looked good. He'd changed clothes, too, but still sported a five-o'clock shadow that made my eyes linger. He'd abandoned his disguise save for a Cardinals baseball hat and the fake glasses. "Thanks for coming."

"I knew everyone would be at dinner. Thought it'd be the best time to come by." He pulled up the chair and settled in, removing his hat and glasses.

"The doctor says I can get out tomorrow," I said. "I can't wait. I've had enough of this place."

"I hear Coop's been pulling gourmet strings today," he said. "Impressing the fam."

"Trying, anyway." I plucked at my blanket. "My brothers came to see me. Not my dad, though."

His eyes were too knowing as he looked at me. I had to glance away. "But he's busy, you know, and I'm fine anyway. So it wasn't a big deal that he didn't come."

"Right."

I absently scratched at my itchy scalp. "Yeah. Anyway. Oslo and Bill are playing the big-brothers role to the hilt, grilling Jackson. As if he's some gold digger out to steal my fortune and virtue."

"What's wrong?" Clark asked.

I tried to follow his question based on what I'd said, but was lost. "Wrong with what? My brothers? I have no idea. Guilt, maybe?"

"No, I mean you keep scratching. Are you all right? Should I get the nurse?"

"Oh. That. No, it's just I need a shower. I feel gross and dirty. But the nurse has to help me and, well, having some stranger see me naked isn't really my thing. I can wait until tomorrow."

"I can help you."

I looked at him and laughed. "You. You're going to help me take a shower."

He shrugged. "I won't look."

I hesitated, but the temptation to be clean was too great. "Okay. There's a shower cap I'm supposed to wear . . ."

Clark found where the nurse had left it, and together, we managed to get my hair into it and cover my bandage.

"Okay, just lean on me," he said. "Falling would be a really bad idea."

He slipped his arm around my back and inside the open back of the gown. My breath hitched at the touch of his skin on mine, but he didn't seem to react, so I didn't say anything.

He supported me as we made the slow journey to the bathroom, IV stand in tow. "Stand here," he said, making me hold on to the handicap bar. There was a folded seat in the shower that he put down. The shower had a hand attachment, and Clark started the water, waiting for the temperature to heat before coming back to me.

"I'm going to sit you in the chair," he said, "and I'll be right outside the door. Just call out if you need me."

"Okay," I said. Cool air hit my skin and I shivered.

"Turn around." He undid the ties behind me, then helped slip my gown off my arms.

My cheeks warmed, but Clark was as businesslike as a nurse, helping me into the seat, arranging the IV to stay out of the way, and giving me soap and the hand wand. Clark took a step toward the door.

"Wait," I said, panicking, "you're just going to leave me? What if I pass out? What if I get dizzy and fall?"

"Listen, there's nothing higher on my bucket list than to watch you take a bath, so if you want me to stay . . ."

That made me laugh . . . and blush. "I guess that wouldn't be very appropriate," I said. "Just . . . can you stay close?"

"I'll be right outside the door." For the first time, I saw his gaze travel from my eyes down my body, then back up. The Adam's apple moved in his throat as he swallowed. "I'm not going to let anything happen to you." He stepped out, leaving the door cracked a couple of inches.

It took me a while, and the warm water felt so good that I just let it run over my shoulders for a few minutes. The soap was what Mia had brought—my nonperfumed, sensitive-skin Dove—and I was again thankful for her being so thoughtful.

Finally, I turned off the water and immediately heard Clark speak. "You okay?"

"Yes. I'm done."

He was instantly back inside and grabbed a towel. "Here you go," he said, handing it to me. He helped me to my feet, and I wrapped the towel around me.

It took some doing, but we managed to get back to the bed, and when he sat me on the edge, I heaved a tired sigh.

"That felt good, but now I'm worn out," I said with a little laugh.

"You'll sleep well and feel good in the morning," he replied.

"I really hate to put on that dirty hospital gown," I said, wrinkling my nose. And that wasn't my OCD talking. No one would like putting a hospital gown back on.

"Then you're in luck. I got you a get-well present."

Bemused, I watched him rummage inside a bag and pull out a bundle of clothing. Unfolding it, he held it up for me to see, and I laughed in delight.

Somehow, he'd found a set of *Star Wars* pajamas, covered in red-and-pink Valentine's hearts, with a photo of Han and Leia from *The Empire Strikes Back* on the chest.

"Where in the world did you get that?" I asked.

"The clearance rack in the kids' section of Kohl's," he replied, unbuttoning the top. "I figured you could probably fit."

Sure enough, he helped me into the pajamas, and they weren't too small. Sometimes being short and skinny had its advantages.

Discarding the wet shower cap, I tried finger-combing my hair, which was a no-go.

"Here," Clark said, holding a brush. "Turn around."

I turned my back to him, crisscrossed my legs, and waited. The tugs on my hair were slow and exceedingly gentle. It felt amazing, and my eyes drifted closed.

"Can I ask you something?" he said after a while.

"Sure." I was clean, in fresh pj's, and my hair was being untangled. Altogether, I was in a much happier place than yesterday.

"Do you remember the other night? In the hotel bathroom?"

I frowned, concentrating. "Um, I think so. I took a bath and Jackson came in." There was more, and I searched my memory for it. "Oh. I told him. About us kissing. And then he was upset. And I was upset. You were there, too. Did I sleep on the floor?" How weird. Why would I have done that? It would've been uncomfortable, not to mention unsanitary.

"The doc mentioned that some of the symptoms you were experiencing might have also affected your personality and reasoning," he said quietly. "The pressure on your brain . . ." His voice trailed off.

I didn't speak. He continued brushing my hair. I was thinking, trying to recall all that had been said between Jackson and me that night as well as what Clark and I had said. It came back to me in bits and pieces. Jackson hadn't mentioned that night.

"I remember," I said at last. My words made the brush pause in its path, then he resumed.

"And?"

I took a deep breath. "And . . . I don't want to lose what you and I have. We're friends, partners, we work well together. Attempting a romantic relationship would be . . . unwise. Especially considering the fact that I am already engaged to marry Jackson."

"Who says we'll be working together much longer?"

My eyes slid shut at those words. It was suddenly painful to breathe. "I had hoped . . . perhaps you'd return to Vigilance once this case was resolved."

"And be your maid of honor? No, thanks."

"Y-you wouldn't want to preserve our friendship? Our partnership?" I paused. "I don't have many friends. And none that are like you."

He stopped brushing and I turned to look up at him.

"Are you asking me to stay?"

"Well, I wouldn't ask you to be my maid of honor," I said. "Besides, that's a role traditionally reserved for females."

"That's not an answer."

I shrugged helplessly. "I don't know what to do, Clark. Tell me the path I can take where I don't lose one of you."

His fingers combed through my hair, laying it over my shoulder. "I don't know, baby. But something's gotta give." Setting down the brush, he turned and left the room.

Pulling the covers up over me, I settled back down in bed. I was tired, but in a good way. Getting up and moving had helped me. The pain in my head wasn't bad, and my tummy was full. So long as I didn't dwell on the tangled relationships among myself, Clark, and Jackson, everything was hunky-dory.

◆ ◆ ◆

Something woke me, and for a moment I was disoriented. The room was dark, but I sensed someone in there with me. As soon as I realized that, I also realized they weren't moving but standing by the bed, staring at me.

Adrenaline poured through me in a cold rush, but before I could react, something moved in the darkness. Another figure was there, and there was a scuffle and grunts. I scooted away on the bed, nearly falling out in my haste to get away, when the door was suddenly flung open, and I saw Oslo flip on the overhead lights.

"Bill!" Relief and anger flooded me. "What the hell are you doing?"

"You know this guy?" Clark asked me. He currently had Bill facedown on the bed, his right arm twisted up behind his back in what looked like a very painful position.

"Hey! Who the hell are you? Let him go." Oslo hurried forward, but stopped at the look Clark shot him.

"Clark, these are my brothers. That's Bill, and that's Oslo." I motioned with my hand. The adrenaline had worn off, but my heart was still racing. "This is Clark. I . . . work with him."

"Nice to meet ya." He let go of Bill. "Next time, try not to stare at your sister while she's sleeping. It's creepy. Somebody—like me—might get the wrong idea. Especially when you two look nothing like her."

Bill rubbed his shoulder and glared at Clark, who merely gave him a thin-lipped smile.

"What kind of work do you do, exactly?" Bill asked him.

"Mack here is in tech," Clark said. "You could say I'm more of a hands-on kind of guy."

"Mack?" This was Oslo.

Clark passed by Oslo, getting well within the observed eighteen inches of personal space to say, "Yeah. Mack."

He picked up his discarded jacket and shrugged it on. That's when I noticed the handgun lodged in the waist of his jeans, wedged against his lower back. "I'll be back later," he said to me. He left without another word.

Bill and Oslo turned to me as one, expressions of confusion and disbelief on their faces.

"That guy . . ." Bill began. "Who is he?"

"He's my partner," I explained. "He's more of the . . . security part of what I do, so he's familiar with . . . you know . . . self-defense and . . . stuff."

"Self-defense and stuff?" Oslo echoed. "He had a gun. He attacked Bill."

"He didn't attack Bill," I said. "He was protecting me. There's a difference."

"Protecting you from what?"

I shrugged. "From . . . everything."

They shared a look that I couldn't interpret, but that wasn't an uncommon occurrence. Then they must have silently agreed to let Oslo do the talking, because he spoke next.

"I think it's time you tell us exactly what you do," he said. "It sounds like you've gotten mixed up with some dangerous people."

I glanced from one big brother to the other and sighed. "I can't. I'm sorry, but I can't."

"What do you mean, you 'can't'?"

"What I do is secret. You don't have clearance for me to tell you."

Oslo shoved a hand through his dirty-blond hair and turned away. Bill stared at me. "Cool. So you, like, work for the government. In some kind of top-secret job."

"That's dangerous," Oslo interjected. "Is this the first time you've gotten hurt?"

Now, I'd been shot, tortured, and beaten, not to mention nearly blown up in a suicide vest, but I wasn't about to tell them that. But apparently I didn't have to, because Oslo cursed.

Bill's expression of admiration changed to concern. "Seriously?" he asked me. "This isn't the first time?"

I shrugged, noncommittal. I scrutinized Bill, thinking about what Clark had said. We looked alike, right? I mean, yeah, they were both on the blond and tall side with brown eyes, but that was just because they took after Dad, whereas I took after Mom.

"So you're traveling with *both* these guys?" Oslo asked. "Jackson, your fiancé, and this . . . Clark . . . your partner?"

"I know it sounds strange—"

"It only sounds strange if you're involved with both of them," he interrupted. "Are you?"

"You sound suspiciously like a paragon of familial virtue trying to weigh judgment against the promiscuous daughter," I said.

"That's not answering my question."

"The answer to the question is none of your business."

"Wow," Bill said. "Way to go, little sis." He raised his hand like he was going to high-five me, but I just looked at him.

"My relationship, or lack thereof, with Jackson and Clark is private. As is my job. And I'm sorry that I can't share any of it with you, but . . . but it's not as if either of you has been exhibiting any interest in my life until now."

That made them both go silent. Neither of them met my eyes.

"Dad didn't even come to see me," I said. My voice broke in the middle of the sentence. I cleared my throat and swallowed. "Don't get me wrong, I'm really glad you two came. But one act of filial loyalty doesn't give you license to question my judgment or decisions."

The door opened again and Clark walked in. I saw him through Bill's and Oslo's eyes. He must've tired of his disguise or decided the lateness of the hour allowed him leeway because he'd discarded it. Dressed in his usual dark jeans and a black long-sleeve Henley overlaid with the black leather jacket, and knowing the gun was at his back, he looked . . . like someone you wouldn't want to mess with. His hair was as black as his shirt, his eyes the blue of a summer sky, but without any of the innocence.

"They still here?" Clark sneered. "That must be a record."

Oslo began, "Who the hell are you to—"

"We're going," Bill interjected, grabbing Oslo by the arm. He yanked him out of the room, throwing a "We'll see you in the morning" over his shoulder to me.

"You scared off my brothers," I said. "And . . . I haven't seen Jackson in hours. What did you do to him?"

"I didn't do anything to Coop," he said. "He did the brother-in-law-to-be thing and took everyone out to a nice dinner. Flew Grams here on the private plane. I can't compete with that."

"Why would you compete?"

"For you."

I rested back against my pillow, looking at him. "Why were you here in my room?"

"Do you honestly think I'm going to leave you alone in this place? Some may call it paranoid. I call it better safe than sorry." He flipped off the lights. "You need rest. Go back to sleep."

"What are you going to do?" I asked, settling back down and rearranging my covers.

"Write the next great American novel, solve world peace, find the cure for cancer." He tucked the covers around me.

"You're staying here, aren't you," I said. It wasn't a question.

"It's comfy here, and I've got nothing better to do." He settled in the chair.

It was too dark to see his face clearly. But the fact that I felt more at ease with Clark in the room was undeniable.

"Don't stay over there," I said. "That chair looks . . . awful. Come here."

Clark hesitated, then stood and approached the bed. I scooted to the side.

"Here," I said. "There's plenty of room." I couldn't explain it, but I wanted him with me. Wanted his warm body right next to me so I could touch him and feel his presence.

Clark toed off his shoes, then climbed gingerly into the bed. "I don't want to hurt you."

"I'm fine." I was more than fine. The sweet spot inside my chest was warm and sending spirals of happy through me.

He lay down beside me and I rearranged us, putting his arm underneath me and resting my head on his chest. I let out a deep sigh, feeling the peace and relaxation down to my toes. The IV was still irritating, but other than that, it was perfect.

"Thanks, Clark," I said. "Thanks for being what I need."

His hand gently cupped my head, and I felt the press of his lips against my forehead. "You're welcome, baby. I'll be anything you want."

CH 16

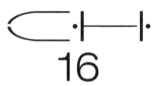

The doctor discharged me the next morning after another CT scan to make sure there was no more swelling or bleeding. I was to follow up with my primary-care physician and stay on the antibiotics to combat any infection, but other than that, I was given a clean bill of health. It was amazing, when I stopped to think about it.

Clark had cleared out and it was Jackson who helped me get ready to leave. Mia had sent more clothes, thank goodness, though Jackson had asked about the pajamas.

"Oh, Clark got them for me," I said. "Nice of him, right?"

"I'd prefer another man doesn't buy you pajamas," he said, frowning.

I looked at him. "They're *Star Wars*. From the kids' section at Kohl's. It's not as if it's a slinky negligee from Victoria's Secret."

"You'd prefer the *Star Wars* ones anyway," he said. "I guess that's why it bothers me. Clark knows you."

"He's my friend," I said. "But I'm marrying *you*, aren't I?" Yes, we'd had the argument in the bathroom, but that was before my life-and-near-death experience.

"I spent last night stealthily watering down your grandma's mint juleps while refereeing Mia and Oslo arguing, and answering Bill's one thousand and one questions about what it's like to be a billionaire. I certainly hope all that wasn't for nothing."

I had to laugh at the image he presented. "Thank you," I said, wrapping my arms around his neck. "Only a man who really loved me would dare to water down Grams's mint julep."

He smiled at my teasing and kissed me. "I brought you this," he said, taking my left hand in his and sliding my engagement ring on. "Thought you might want to wear it."

There was a pang inside that had Clark written all over it, but I ignored the feeling. Marrying Jackson was the right thing to do. It was the logical thing to do. I loved him. He loved me. And he knew me, thought like me—we were on the same wavelength, in the vernacular. I didn't like surprises, I didn't like the unpredictable—neither of which described Jackson.

Clark and I had a connection built on shared mutual experiences, most of which were highly dangerous and emotionally charged. It wasn't unexpected that we'd forged a close friendship. And given his very pleasing physical appearance, it was a perfectly natural reaction to be attracted to him.

"Neither of you has said anything about the file we retrieved from the personnel center," I said, trying to arrange my hair to cover the little bald patch and bandage from where they'd done the surgery. My hair was thick enough to cover it okay, so I fastened it into my normal ponytail. "Did you print it out?"

"We can talk about that later," he said. His gaze skated over mine, which normally wouldn't have struck me as odd, but I'd gotten much better at reading his body language.

"You're keeping something from me." I scrutinized him. "And Clark was here last night, something about 'protecting' me." I crossed my arms over my chest. "What aren't you telling me?"

Jackson just gave me a thin smile. "Let's talk about it on the way, okay? Everyone's waiting on us."

"Everyone" was indeed everyone. Clark was already in the car, and he'd kicked Mia out to ride with Oslo and Bill. I objected at first, but then realized they might not tell me whatever they had to say if she was present.

Once I was ensconced in the back seat, with Clark and Jackson in the front, we left, following Oslo and heading toward Omaha.

"So, what's the big secret?" I asked once we hit the outskirts of the city and the highway stretched before us. "Where's the file?"

Jackson rummaged in his bag and pulled out a file identical in thickness to the one Mia and I had photographed. Mark Danvers's file. He glanced at Clark, who nodded, before he handed it to me, which I thought was strange. Since when did Jackson and Clark have a secret handshake?

"Okay, then," I said, settling back in the seat.

Jackson had piled pillows and blankets all around, ostensibly in case I wanted to take a nap, but in reality it was in case we got in an accident. I flat out refused to wear the bike helmet he'd gotten me to protect my head from further injury. He'd compensated by confiscating half a dozen pillows and two blankets from the hospital, telling them to add it to the bill, even though I said the insurance company wouldn't cover linens.

"Do you guys want to tell me what's in here or what?" I asked, opening the file. "Anything on Operation Gemini?"

"You don't need us to explain things for you, Mack," Clark said. I glanced up and caught his gaze in the rearview mirror. "I heard you're a pretty smart chick."

That made me grin a bit, and I turned my attention to the file. Some sentences—particularly places and times—were blacked out, but enough remained for me to get the general idea of who he was and what he'd done.

Mark Danvers was the kind of Cold War warrior they made movies about. He'd been born nearly sixty years ago and had cut his teeth on Beirut and Libya. Trained in an elite and highly classified branch of the military, he'd crossed over into the CIA, becoming a one-man assassination squad. He'd also planned and executed highly sensitive operations that were under the flag of deniability and disavowal.

"Why would they allow me to see this file?" I asked. "Even surreptitiously. This is . . . classified. He said so, but this . . . I never imagined this." Glancing up at the men in the front seat, I waited for an answer, but Jackson just looked at me. His eyes were hidden behind his sunglasses.

"Keep reading," he said.

Clark didn't respond at all.

Frowning, I returned my attention to the file. Mark's career continued and he proved remarkably adept at transitioning to post–Cold War times. He spoke six languages—wow!—and was a key analyst at the Middle East desk at the CIA through the nineties. He'd managed what looked like a long career.

I'd been studying the file for more than an hour by the time I came to a section on a mission he'd gone on with another agent, posing as husband and wife to infiltrate a Saudi royal family's household. The partnership must've gone well because I saw he'd been paired with the same agent—code-named Raven—on two other occasions. Their last mission together had been about fifteen years ago.

There weren't a lot of photos in the file, but they did have a small black-and-white of Raven. Curious, I looked more closely at it. Then I blinked. And blinked again.

"Oh my God . . ." It couldn't be. I looked up at Jackson, who was watching me. "This . . . this can't be. It's not right. This file is fake. It has to be."

He said nothing. I looked back down at the picture. "It's . . . it's my mom." I looked back up at them. "Isn't it? I mean, it is. That's what you didn't want to tell me. That's what's so important. My mom was this . . . CIA agent."

"I'm sorry," Jackson said. "But you need to see this." He handed me a photograph.

It was a man. And I knew when I saw him that my world had just turned upside down. Again.

"Wh-who is this?" I stammered, my eyes glued to the face I held.

"That . . . is Mark Danvers."

I was looking at a photo of a man with my eyes, my shade of hair, and the same smile that I saw in the mirror when I practiced.

"Sweetheart?"

I glanced up at Jackson.

"Are you all right?"

"Yeah, yeah. I mean, yes, of course I'm all right. This was just very . . . very unexpected. The news that my mom was an agent and that my dad . . . isn't my dad." I paused, thinking. "I guess that explains why he couldn't be bothered to come to the hospital. I'm not even his."

A laugh bubbled up in my throat that I didn't even recognize. I caught them exchanging glances again and forced myself to stop.

"Why don't you lie down?" Jackson suggested. "A nap would be good for you."

Rage boiled up like a match set to tinder. "I don't need a fucking nap," I snapped. "I'm not a child."

The silence in the car was deafening.

"I-I'm sorry," I stammered. "That was rude."

"You're entitled," Clark cut in. "You just found out your mom was a spook and your dad's not your dad."

Suddenly, I couldn't breathe. "I need air. Can we just . . . can we stop? Please? Just . . . stop the car." I jerked at the car handle, but it was locked.

"Don't!" Jackson's voice cut through me, and I stopped.

Clark screeched the car to a halt on the shoulder, and the doors unlocked. I lunged as Jackson grabbed my arm.

"This way." He yanked me to the other side of the car, opposite the traffic.

I threw open the door and stumbled out. It was freezing, and my breath was a white puff of air. Jackson was by my side immediately.

"Be careful, please," he pleaded. "It's slippery."

I barely heard him. All I could think of was trying to breathe. There was nothing in front of me but an ice-encrusted field. Traffic passed by sporadically. We were figuratively in the middle of nowhere.

I didn't know how far I'd walked from the car. I just kept going until I couldn't hear anything anymore. My dad . . . wasn't my dad. And he'd never told me. He'd just . . . hated me. All this time. It explained so much.

"I'm sure he doesn't hate you," Jackson said.

Had I been talking out loud?

"China, please, stop," he said. "Talk to me."

"What do you want me to say?" I asked. My voice sounded strange to my ears. "I don't know what's an appropriate reaction for this."

He grabbed my arm and turned me toward him. "There is no appropriate reaction. However you feel is how you feel. There's no right or wrong."

I stared at him. "Why did you tell me?"

"You'd rather I'd have kept it from you?"

"No, I-I just don't know what to *do* with this information. This . . . man—this *stranger*—is my biological father, and was somehow involved in Operation Gemini—which we *still* don't know the full extent of—and now he's trying to kill everyone who took part in that mission?"

"It would appear so," he said. "And what's more . . . I found phone logs at the personnel center from before and after you went in. They were from inside Vigilance. Someone wanted you to have that file. Maybe someone who's trying to warn you."

Data. Facts. Those I could deal with. The emotions running through me . . . those I couldn't and didn't want to deal with.

"It's cold," Jackson said, taking my hand. "Let's get you back in the car. We can talk some more if you want."

I let him lead me back to the car. Clark was leaning against the side, arms crossed, watching us. Our eyes met but we didn't speak. Jackson put me in the back seat and wrapped a blanket around me. I was shivering and hadn't even noticed.

We got under way again and I stared out the window, my thoughts going a mile a minute. Had Jack and Oslo known? Did Dad even know who my biological father was? Why hadn't he ever told me? I'd always thought his dislike had stemmed from the fact that I survived the wreck that killed my mom, whereas she hadn't. It wasn't logical, but emotions rarely were.

"Did you do any digging on my mom?" I asked Jackson.

"I tried, but there wasn't much I could find," he said. "I'm sorry."

"Was her marriage to my dad just a sham?" I asked. "Part of her cover or something?"

"I don't know, sweetheart."

I felt . . . numb. And I didn't want to think anymore.

"Why are we still bothering to go home?" I asked. "We should just find the other guy, Buckton, and warn him. That's what we were going to do anyway, before . . . everything." *Brain surgery* was now on my permanent list of Things Not To Say Out Loud.

"Stashing you on the farm is a good place to hide you," Clark answered. "You can spend a few days recuperating, have a heart-to-heart with dear old dad, and we can meet Buckton when he returns, and lie in wait for Danvers."

We? Since when were Jackson and Clark buddies? "I don't want to go home. I'm not even related to my dad. I don't belong there." I didn't recognize the feelings I had, and didn't want to put a name to them. I felt as though I was drowning—my own mind felt unrecognizable.

"I wouldn't say that," Clark replied. "Listen, we'll see how it goes. If you want to leave, we'll leave. But you can't just never see your dad again."

I looked at the front seat. Jackson was half-turned, watching me. Clark's gaze flicked to the rearview mirror.

"Do you promise? You won't just leave me?" Jackson and Clark were the only sure things—the only real people—in my life right now. I didn't even know if my brothers were my brothers.

"Promise," Jackson said. "We won't leave you."

"I pinkie swear," Clark chimed in. "It doesn't get any better."

That made me smile. Leave it to Clark to make me smile even under the worst of circumstances.

I settled down in the seat and closed my eyes. For doing nothing but riding in a car and finding out my dad wasn't my dad and my mom was an ex–CIA agent, I was exhausted.

◆ ◆ ◆

The ride went swiftly while I snoozed. When I woke up, we were already in Omaha and heading north. My family's farm was a few miles outside the city, by the river. Butterflies started in my stomach as nerves assailed me. Besides the fact that I hadn't seen my father in months and months, I was now armed with knowledge that made me question my very identity.

The drive down the country road to our old farmhouse was surreal. I'd left here when I was fourteen and never looked back. The fields were barren and coated with a couple of inches of snow. Dead stalks thrust through the frozen carpet at regular intervals. The clouds were heavy and the sky was already growing dark.

We arrived at the house much sooner than I was prepared for. Clark parked and turned off the engine. I didn't move.

"It looks the same," I said quietly. "And yet, not." The house was a two-story farmhouse built in the forties. It had a deep wraparound porch, clapboard shutters, even a storm cellar. But the white paint had faded and chipped. The house looked forlorn and empty, like a grand old lady past her prime and aging less than gracefully.

I looked up at my old window. Second floor, last room on the right. It was dark. As were most of the windows.

"You ready?" Clark asked.

They were both looking at me. Usually, that would make me extremely uncomfortable. Instead, I felt reassured. I wasn't alone, itself an uncommon occurrence.

I nodded. "Yes. I think so."

We got out of the car, and I was trailed by my two rather large, imposing men up the steps of the porch to the front door. I raised my hand to knock, but it swung open.

"Dad," I said reflexively, in spite of myself. "Um, hi."

He was tall and rail thin, the sun having wizened him beyond his years. But his eyes were still sharp, despite the hunch of his shoulders. His hair was still intact, though a lot thinner and a solid silver now rather than the salt and pepper that I remembered. Dad wasn't unfriendly, but he was also the kind of person who made children hurry on past. Instinctively they seemed to know he was more likely to chastise them for playing on his lawn than be charmed by youth's exuberance, and they wouldn't be wrong.

His smile was faint but there as he patted my shoulder. He'd never been one for hugs, and apparently not even brain surgery changed that habit. "The boys said you were comin' to stay a spell, after your surgery. I'm glad to see you."

I realized I was holding my breath, so I let it out. I didn't know what I expected. It wasn't as though there was a sign on my forehead that said Not Really Your Daughter, but it felt as if there were.

"Yeah," I said, "and I brought a couple of people I'd like you to meet." I turned. Jackson and Clark had taken up flanking positions a couple of feet behind me. "This is Jackson Cooper, my fiancé." Jackson stepped forward and shook Dad's hand. "And this is my . . . work colleague, Clark Slattery." Clark took his turn as well.

"Fiancé," Dad echoed, his eyebrows raising slightly. "I guess I should congratulate you, then. Come on in."

The foyer was the same, right down to the old wooden floor creaking under my feet. Dad led us through the hallway to the kitchen. It was warmer in there, as far as temperature went, but not cheerful. The whole house was just too quiet, as if it were holding its breath and waiting for something.

"I just brewed a fresh pot of coffee, if y'all want some," he offered.

"That would be great, thank you," Jackson said.

The three of us took chairs around the table while Dad got mugs and the coffeepot. I could feel Clark's and Jackson's eyes on me, as though waiting to see what I was going to do next. I wished I knew myself.

"Oslo and Mia went on over to Bill's place," Dad said as he poured the coffee. "Said they'd be over later with some dinner for everybody. Heather wanted to see you. She was pretty darn upset, hearing about your surgery."

"More than you were, it would seem." The words were out of my mouth without my planning them first.

He sighed as he lowered himself into a chair, moving more slowly than I remembered. "I knew you'd be upset."

"Your daughter could've died," Jackson said.

"It wasn't as if she was having her tonsils removed," Clark chimed in.

Dad was quiet, looking from one to the other as though measuring their worth. "Oslo said you had a couple fellas lookin' after you. I see they take their job serious."

"China's important," Jackson said. "And she's my future wife. I don't like to see her hurt."

Dad's gaze swung to mine. "I couldn't come because I had an appointment. You see, I've got cancer. Stomach cancer. Nothin' they can do at this point. They still try the chemo. Trying to give me a bit more time, I guess. But I should've come down. You're right.

"I told the boys not to say anything to you," he continued. "I don't want a big fuss. Everybody's got to die at some point. I just know mine's gonna be sooner rather than later."

I stared at him, in shock. His thinning hair and wan appearance made sense now. He'd also been moving more carefully, as though something inside hurt. Because it did.

"Oh, Dad . . . I don't know what to say—" Tears blurred my vision.

"Now, don't go doin' that," he said, awkwardly patting my hand. "Not everyone gets a warning about death coming. I've got time to set my affairs in order."

"Was telling me that you're not my biological father part of putting those affairs in order?" I asked.

"China," Jackson said sharply. He was frowning at me.

"What?" I asked. Had I said something wrong?

"It's a legit question," Clark said, shooting him a look. "She has a right to know."

Dad was quiet, staring into his coffee mug. "Can you and I talk in private?" he asked me.

I nodded at Clark and Jackson, who both rose and left the room.

"I always thought, smart as you were, that you'd figure it out sooner," he said.

"It wasn't something I was ever looking for, so why would I think such a thing?"

He didn't respond right away, and I had the sense that he was lost in memory. "Your mother," he said at last, "she was somethin'. Beautiful. Smart as a whip. When we met, she'd just finished up college and moved back home to teach. I don't know what she saw in me, but we married about six months later.

"Your brothers came along, but we had some trouble," he continued. "Couldn't get pregnant again, though she wanted a girl. It was years later when you surprised us."

"I thought you went on a trip," I said. "And that's when it happened. My name. China."

But he just shook his head. "Your mother went. She was gone for a few months, wanting to be part of a missionary trip over there. When she came back, she was pregnant with you. Not far along, but it was pretty obvious when you were born that you weren't mine."

"She was unfaithful, but you didn't divorce?" I asked.

He looked up from his mug for the first time. "I loved your mother. If she found someone else to give her what I couldn't, I wasn't going to punish her for that or deprive the boys of being with their mom."

Two things were becoming abundantly clear: 1) my dad had loved my mom, and 2) he had no idea she'd been covert CIA. At this point, I thought I could safely assume that my mom had been a sleeper agent, needed only for a particular set of circumstances. I didn't know what those were, but apparently they'd sent her into Mark Danvers's orbit long enough to produce me.

I wasn't about to disillusion Dad about what Mom's real job had been. He'd done enough over the years, raising me after Mom died, all the while knowing I wasn't his.

"I guess that explains why you've never particularly warmed to me," I said.

His eyes were sad when he looked at me. "I'm sorry, China. I tried to provide for you and raise you the way your mom would've wanted. I'm not the most . . . emotional man under the best of circumstances. You were never mine, but you were hers. And I tried my best to honor that."

The truth was painful, but it was also freeing. I'd never known why I'd been treated differently, and, honestly, this was at least a more understandable reason than feeling as though I was blamed for surviving the car crash.

Dad sighed, the lines on his face looked deeper, and I noticed his hand shook slightly with a tremor as he held his mug. I reached out and covered his hand with my own.

"Thank you," I said. "Mom would've been pleased that you took care of me."

"I want you to know," he said, "that I've never mentioned any of this to Bill or Oslo. If you want to tell them or not, that's up to you. But I gave you my name, and I'm not going to take it away just because you found out the truth."

"Okay. Thank you. Why don't you go lie down for a while? You look tired. I know my way around."

His smile was faint. "That obvious, is it? Can't keep going like I used to."

"It's okay. Truly. Go rest."

With one last squeeze of his weathered hand, he rose and left the kitchen.

I stayed at the table, the coffee getting cold, staring out the window. I felt an odd sense of peace—unusual, given the circumstances. Now I needed to figure out what we could do to help my dad.

Footsteps sounded behind me, and I turned to see Jackson had returned. He took the seat next to me.

"Are you all right?" he asked.

"Yeah." I nodded, then told him the story.

"It makes sense," he said. "I take it you didn't say anything about your mom?"

"No. I didn't see a need." I hoped my mom had loved my dad and hadn't just used him as a cover for years. "Is there anything we can do about his condition?"

"I can make some calls, see if we can get him seen by a specialist."

I nodded. "That would be good. I don't know what kind of insurance he has, but I doubt it covers much."

"I'll take care of it," he said. "Clark's getting the luggage from the car."

"Oh?" I scooted my chair back. "I'd better show him where to put it, then." I left the kitchen as Jackson was taking his phone out to begin making calls.

Clark had just stepped inside when I reached the foyer. Flakes were falling outside and had landed on his hair and shoulders. He was carrying my suitcase.

"Where do you want it?" he asked.

"Upstairs. I can take it."

He moved the suitcase beyond my reach. "Nice try. Lead the way."

We went up the creaking stairs and all the way to the end of the hall. My door was shut, as were most that we passed, and it was really cold. Dad must've shut off the vents upstairs to keep the gas bill down.

I opened my door and flipped on the light.

Everything was just as I'd left it, from the aqua-blue bedspread with brown polka dots to the dust-covered trophies on the shelves. There was a poster of Albert Einstein on one wall. The rest were bare.

Clark set down my suitcase, looking around curiously. "What're the trophies for?" he asked.

"Math team, science fairs, that kind of thing."

My gaze was drawn to a photo on my desk. My mom and I, at the circus. I'd been about two at the time, and she'd sat me on the back of this big ceramic lion. She was standing next to me, and someone had taken our picture. We looked happy, both of us smiling. I'd had glasses even then.

"Everything okay with your dad?" he asked.

"Yeah," I said. "It's fine. I just want to do what I can to help him."

"I take it Coop is calling in favors."

I nodded. "He's doing what he can."

Clark turned me around, settling his hands on my shoulders. "How are *you*?"

"I'm fine," I said with a sigh. "I got a nap in the car and my head feels okay. I need to show you to Bill's old room. You can sleep there."

Clark's gaze was too penetrating, and I had to look away. His hands were still on my shoulders, but I didn't feel solid underneath his touch. I felt as fragile as glass.

"Look at me." His voice was a low rasp that went right through me.

"If I do," I whispered, "I'm afraid I'll fall apart."

There was a knock on the door, and I hurriedly moved away from Clark as Jackson poked his head in. "The rest of the family's here," he said.

"Great. I'll be right down."

Jackson gave Clark a look of warning, then closed the door.

"What do you need?" Clark asked. "Just tell me."

"I need . . . I need . . . normal." I looked up at him. "Just . . . normal."

His lips twitched and he reached behind me to my ponytail, tugging it a little tighter. Then he adjusted my glasses, pushing them up on my nose from where they'd slid down.

"Normal," he said. "No problem. Let's go be normal."

CH 17

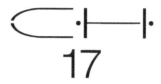

Heather, Oslo's wife, had gone all out for dinner, hauling over two lasagnas, salad, garlic bread—the works. Mia had helped her, she said, which I took to be a good sign. Mia and her stepmom hadn't always had an easy time of it, which was one of the reasons she'd been living with me.

I expected conversation to be stilted and awkward around the table, but to my surprise, it wasn't. Dad sat at the head of the table, and Oslo took the other end. I sat next to Dad.

Plates were passed and filled, and the low hum of conversation filled the dining room. It was a room we'd rarely used except for formal occasions, but it had more chairs than the kitchen table. The clink of silverware was punctuated with compliments to Heather on her cooking skills.

Jackson was exchanging small talk with Dad while Clark teased Mia and charmed Heather. Bill was quiet for the most part, chiming in now and then with Jackson. Oslo seemed to be studying everyone, taking it all in. His eyes softened whenever they landed on Mia, and I thought he was probably glad to have her back home for a while, and seeing her and Heather get along.

"So, have you and Jackson set a date yet?" Heather asked, dishing up a second helping for Bill.

"A date for what?" I added more salad to my plate.

Everyone went quiet. I looked up to find all eyes on me.

"Dum dum dee dum, dum dum dee dum." Clark sang the "Wedding March."

"Oh. Of course. The wedding." My face got hot and I caught Jackson's eye. "Um, no, not yet. We haven't really . . . gotten that far."

"Will I get to be your maid of honor?" Mia piped up.

I smiled at her. "Absolutely."

"Yesssss!"

Everyone laughed at her enthusiasm, and I breathed a sigh of relief. As usual, Mia had saved me from my own awkwardness.

The dishes were cleared away quickly since everyone pitched in and Dad retired early. He looked tired but happy, too, as though being around the whole family for something as simple as dinner had eased his physical pain.

Mia approached me in the kitchen. "Aunt Chi, can I talk to you?"

"Sure," I said. We were alone for the moment as I dried some dishes and put them away. "What's up?"

She seemed nervous as she shifted from one foot to another.

"Is everything okay?" I asked. Surely she hadn't already had a fight with Heather. She'd only been home for a few hours.

"Yes, it's fine. It's just that, I was wondering if you'd still want me around. You know, with you and Jackson getting married. You'll be newlyweds and I'll be a third wheel."

"Don't be silly," I said. "I realize it may look like that from your perspective, but I love having you live with me. At first it took some getting used to, but now I don't know what I'd do without you. Who'd make me eggs in the morning, or curl my hair?"

Her smile looked relieved. "I was hoping you'd say that."

"But what about your parents?" I asked. "Surely they want you to move back home."

"I said I'd come home for the summer," she replied. "I'd hate to switch schools in the middle of a semester anyway." She paused. "I think it's been good to have some space. Heather and I haven't argued at all."

"Jackson said you and Oslo were arguing last night."

She nodded. "He was giving me the third degree about who my friends are, what I've been doing, how my grades are—you name it."

"He just worries about you."

She sighed. "I know. It's just that my inner eight-year-old comes out when I'm with him, and even though I know I'm doing it, I just can't stop."

"It's the curse of being a teenager."

Mia sighed. "You're right. But that means I'll grow out of it, right?"

I grinned at the long-suffering look on her face. "I'm sure you will."

Eventually, everyone left, and it was just Jackson, Clark, and me. We'd moved into the family room, and Clark had built a fire in the fireplace. It was the old-fashioned, real-wood-burning kind, and the sound and smell brought back childhood memories.

"So, what's the plan for tomorrow?" I asked, watching the flames dance.

"Buckton's security firm is in downtown Omaha," Clark said. "We'll go pay him a visit."

"Do you think he'll know anything more than you do?" I asked.

He shrugged. "Maybe not. But at least we can warn him. If he agrees, we'll set a trap. Lie in wait until he shows himself."

"If Mark Danvers is my real father, why would he want to kill me?" It was something that had been bothering me. "Both of you acted as though I wasn't safe in the hospital. But I didn't have anything to do with Operation Gemini."

"Right now we're assuming Danvers is the shooter," Clark said. "But that may be wrong. Whoever is targeting people, they've seen you with me and Coop. Better safe than sorry."

"The sooner we find this guy, the quicker we can get on with our lives," Jackson said.

I turned to look at him. "Were you a part of Operation Gemini, Jackson?" He hesitated. "No more lies. Not from you."

He cast a glance at Clark before returning his gaze to mine. "Yes."

"Tell me."

Jackson sighed as he took a seat on the sofa next to me. Clark sat opposite in a chair. The fire crackled merrily, and I wanted to hold my breath, almost afraid of whatever it was Jackson had been keeping secret.

"It was six . . . seven years ago, something like that," he said. "I'd just sold SocialSpeak and started Cysnet. There was a government contract. Top secret, like so many of them are. A real-time hack on a third-world government, so a team could infiltrate a secure facility."

Clark's body went tense and I glanced from Jackson to him, then back again. Jackson was staring off into the distance as he spoke, as though reliving it.

"There were two teams," he continued. "Though neither of them knew about the other. My job was to disable the security so the teams could enter undetected. But there were two facilities. One team was essentially used as a decoy, to draw attention and any potentially lethal response."

He paused for a moment, seeming to need to collect himself back into the present. "During the mission, something went wrong, and I was told to trip the alarm on the decoy team. I didn't want to. Everything seemed to be going well for both teams to get in and get out. I argued against it because . . . I was afraid men would die. Their blood would be on my hands." He stopped again.

"So what happened?" I asked, though I was afraid I already knew the answer.

"They held a gun to my head. Literally. So . . . I did what I was told. And it all went to hell."

"That was *my* team you sentenced to die," Clark said. "Only four of us made it out." His voice was as cold as the arctic. "I had to leave my brother behind."

"I know," Jackson said, his gaze finally resting on Clark. "I was there, listening as men were killed, as they ran for their lives. The other team was cleared. They achieved the objective and retreated without anyone knowing they were there."

"It was a setup?" I asked, dumbfounded. "They let those men go in there, knowing they were just . . . just Redshirts? Just cannon fodder? And you helped them?"

No one spoke. My questions were rhetorical, but I was reeling. I didn't think I could be surprised anymore by the things people did, and yet . . .

"And Danvers was in charge of this?" I asked. "You know him? You met him? You've met my father?"

Jackson's gaze was steady. "He's the one who held the gun to my head."

"You are such a fucking coward." Clark was seething, his hands tightly fisted. "You killed those men—my brother—the same as if you'd pulled the trigger yourself."

"What would you have done?" Jackson lashed out. "Getting my brains blown out wasn't going to help anyone."

"Is that what you tell yourself so you can sleep at night?"

"Men lost their lives, and that's a tragedy," Jackson said. "But they also knew what they signed up for. They weren't going to fucking Disneyland."

"They signed up for a government that's supposed to have their backs, not treat them like they're disposable—"

Their voices were loud and getting louder. I didn't want them waking or upsetting my dad.

"Both of you, knock it off," I interrupted sharply. "You can duke it out later. Right now, it still makes no sense for Danvers to be the one deciding to off everyone years later. To me, it sounds more likely that one of the four members of the decoy team who escaped found out about it—like Clark just did—and decided on his own revenge."

"Taggert and Williams are both dead," Clark said. "Me and Buckton are all that's left of that team."

"Then it *has* to be Buckton doing this. And if he's been running a security firm, then he still has the skills and equipment to pull this off. He's been 'out of the country,' which could mean that he's just been out of the office performing these hits. You two can't just go waltzing in there when he gets back tomorrow. You could be walking into a trap." My head was starting to hurt again, and I used both hands to rub my temples.

Both men were quiet, thank the heavens. My glasses felt as though they weighed ten pounds, and I pulled them off, rubbing the bridge of my nose where they'd sat.

"You need to rest," Jackson said softly. "It's been a long day."

For once I didn't argue with him. "Okay. I guess we can figure out tomorrow what we'll do." If Buckton was the shooter, I could give that information to Dennon. He could send in the posse to round him up rather than Clark.

Jackson stood and reached for me, but I pulled away. "I need to be by myself tonight," I said. "I need to . . . not think. I'll see you in the morning." Trying to wrap my head around what decisions he'd made . . . it was hard. And playing armchair quarterback was easy, especially in hindsight.

I left them both in the family room and went upstairs. My bedroom was slightly warmer, though I added an additional blanket for the bed and dug out a pair of fuzzy socks to go with my new pajamas. *Victoria's Secret has nothing on me,* I mused, staring at myself in the mirror.

With my hair down, I could see the bandage again. My glasses made me look as nerdy as ever, combined with the kid pajamas and tiger-striped fuzzy socks, I'd be carded buying cigarettes, much less alcohol.

I stood at the window, looking out at the snow. The moon had come out briefly, lighting up the night so that it was as beautiful as a picture. I'd stood at this same window many times when I was younger, wanting a way out of the life I was living. Where no one understood me and I was a freak of nature.

I rested my forehead against the cold glass, past memories floating around me like invisible ghosts. Whereas the future loomed, dark and forbidding. I felt paralyzed—unable to go back to the way things were before, but also unable to move forward. Why hadn't Jackson told me about his part in Operation Gemini—the name of which now made sense. Twins. Twin operations. Only one had been predestined to fail. Clark had barely made it out alive.

There was a tentative knock at the door. "Come in," I said, without bothering to ask who it was. I didn't turn. I knew who'd come.

"You didn't kill Jackson, did you?" I asked.

"Not yet, but the night's still young," Clark quipped.

I felt his presence move behind me and saw his reflection in the glass. "I'm sorry," I said. "About your brother. And for those other men."

"You had nothing to do with it."

"But my father did."

His hands rested on my shoulders. "I don't believe in the daughter paying for the sins of the father."

I leaned back against him, letting his strength help support me. "Do you think I was meant to find that file? Find out the truth?"

"I think it was easier than it should have been. But why? I don't know why."

"Maybe Dennon is having us do his dirty work," I speculated, "leading us to the Danvers file and tracking him down. If the shooter is out for revenge, then the government certainly wouldn't want information about Operation Gemini to come out. If we eliminate Danvers or

Buckton—whoever the guilty party was—no one would know what happened. No one will know those men were deliberately sacrificed."

Clark's hands were squeezing my shoulders too tightly, but I didn't think he realized it. The pain in his eyes was almost too much to bear. I almost regretted voicing the thoughts out loud.

I flinched. "You're hurting me, Clark."

His grip loosened immediately. "Sorry, Mack."

I winced at the nickname, then told myself to stop being stupid. Turning to face him, I caught a glimpse of us in the mirror, and if it hadn't been so demoralizing, I'd have laughed. Me in all my nerd glory, looking like an overgrown twelve-year-old, complete with preteen bedroom. And Clark standing two inches from me, dressed in black, his shirt open at the throat, and looking like a fantasy come to life.

"What?" he asked. "What's the matter? You're upset."

I blinked a few times. "No, I'm just tired." Maybe he'd gotten me the pajamas because that's how he saw me. I wasn't a woman. I was just . . . a girl. A really smart, really young, naive girl who liked to play with toys.

His fingers lifted my chin until I was looking up at him. "Don't lie. And my mind-reading skills aren't so hot, so I'd appreciate the translation."

"Nothing," I insisted. "I'm just . . . feeling a bit sorry for myself, that's all. Everyone's allowed a pity party, now and then."

"Am I invited?" he asked, raising one eyebrow.

I shook my head and looked away, forcing a smile. "Not tonight. *Mack* should go to bed." Pulling back the covers, I sat down on the bed.

Clark was still looking at me funny.

"What?"

"You don't like it when I call you Mack," he said. "You've told me that before."

"No, I haven't," I argued. "Why would I say such a thing? It's my name."

He sat down on the bed, and I had to pull my knees to my chest so he wouldn't sit on my feet.

"You didn't like it," he insisted. "Told me to call you something else."

"When was this?" I was scouring my memory and could recall no conversation where we'd discussed this particular subject.

"When I was carrying you out of the server farm that you blew up in the South China Sea," he said.

Oh. "Well, that explains it," I said. I was suddenly nervous, for some reason. I took off my glasses and set them on the table next to the bed. "Things are little fuzzy about that."

"You weren't at your best."

"Hmm." I couldn't put my feet under the covers because he was sitting on them. I tugged a little, hoping he'd get the hint, but he just sat there.

"Don't you want to know what you wanted me to call you?" he asked. He leaned a little closer, and my nerves shot up again. Maybe it was the way he was talking. As though he was about to tell me a secret.

"I was in pain and barely conscious," I said archly, avoiding his gaze. "I could've told you to call me the queen of England and wouldn't remember."

Clark didn't answer, so I glanced up at him. He was watching me with a look in his blue eyes that made my heart skip a beat.

Reaching out, he took my feet, one at a time, and stretched them across his lap. Then he inched the socks down and peeled them off.

"What are you doing? My toes are cold."

"I'm warming them up," he said, which was true. His hands were large and my feet weren't. He massaged the instep and used his thumbs on the sensitive pad underneath my toes. Slow and gentle, yet firm, he got the blood moving through me until my feet were toasty warm.

By which time, I could hardly breathe. I had no idea feet were such erogenous zones. Or maybe they weren't, and my mind was just in the gutter. But the slow strokes of his thumb, the pressure of his hand curving around my instep—all of it made my heart race as if I'd run a marathon.

"Better?" he asked after a while.

"Yeah," I said in much too high a voice. I sounded strangled. I cleared my throat and tried again. "I mean, yes, they're better, thank you."

He glanced up at me, his lips curved in that wicked way that made me wish I could draw, just to re-create that look.

"I like those on you," he said out of the blue.

"What? You like what?" I normally wasn't this slow.

"Those pajamas."

And suddenly the warm caramel in my veins went cold. I was so stupid. A hot guy massaging my feet and I'd let it go to my head. Clark just had that effect on women. He couldn't help it, and it didn't mean anything.

"Don't make fun," I snapped. "It's not nice."

He frowned, his hands pausing in their work. "I'm not," he said. "I bought them for you. Why would I make fun of you for wearing them?"

Now I felt like an idiot. "I'm sorry, you wouldn't, I didn't mean . . ." I trailed off. I couldn't untangle the feelings Clark created inside me, feelings and desires I had no business having. "It's just sometimes . . ."

"Sometimes what?" he prompted.

"Sometimes I wish I was one of those women who wear silk negligees and baby-doll camisoles to bed. That I was tall and sexy with come-hither eyes and those pouty lips." I shrugged, embarrassed. "I've looked through too many Victoria's Secret catalogs, I guess."

"I get that," he said. "I mean, look at men. If you go by the covers of romance novels, we should all be cut, wear leather, have tattoos, and ride a motorcycle."

I just looked at him strangely. "But . . . you *are* all those things."

He pointed a finger at me. “I do *not* have a tattoo.”

I burst out laughing at his mock seriousness. He smiled, too, as my laughter faded.

“Pouty lips and being tall aren't what make you sexy,” he said after a moment.

“I'm *not* sexy,” I retorted with chagrin. “Look at me.”

“I'm looking,” he said, his smile fading. “But I think you and I see two different things. I see a petite woman with curves in all the right places, whose waist is barely bigger around than my thigh. She's wicked smart and funny, and proven that her loyalty and courage are much larger than her size.”

“Loyalty and courage?” I snorted. “You sure you're not describing a Labrador?”

“And the best thing about those pajamas,” he continued, ignoring me, “is what I know you've got hidden underneath them.”

My desire for self-deprecation went out the window as he scooted closer, putting one of my legs behind him so he was situated squarely between my thighs. The hem of my pajama dress had ridden up, and his hands rested on my bare knees.

“So, what is it tonight?” he asked, his voice that sweet spot between a whisper and a rasp.

I couldn't look away from his eyes as I answered. “A lace string cheekini panty in ginger glaze.”

He leaned forward and I stopped breathing.

“That's what makes you sexy, baby,” he breathed in my ear. His lips grazed my cheek in the lightest of touches, then he was on his feet and turning out my light.

“You're leaving?” I asked, breathless.

“I don't think Jackson would appreciate what would happen if I stayed,” he said. “Good night.” He headed for the door.

“Good night, Clark,” I said as he left.

I flopped down on the bed, breathing hard. Good lord, but that man could melt an ice cube inside of thirty seconds.

My cell buzzed and I glanced at the screen. I knew that number.

"You'd better not have your feet up on my desk," I said by way of greeting.

"You get hurt a lot," Kade Dennon said, ignoring my comment. "But are hard to kill. I like that. You could say I have a bit of a soft spot for tough chicks."

"What a charmer," I mouthed off. "And I'm better, thanks for asking."

"You're walking and talking, so that's what I figured," he shot back. "So how's Clark? Is he dead yet?"

"Of course not. But I am working on clearing him. And me."

"Good to know."

I picked at my sheets, thinking. "You don't really think I'm working to kill the president, do you." Call it a hunch, but I thought if Dennon really thought I was a threat, I wouldn't have been allowed to see the light of day again.

"Nah, but I wasn't sure if you'd need the added incentive to find the real shooter."

"What do you mean, 'added incentive'? To try to clear Clark?"

"Yeah. I wasn't sure if you were the loyal-to-a-fault, stupidly self-sacrificing, save-him-at-any-cost kind of girl. I happen to have experience with that variety. Laudable, and sometimes hot, but also a shitload of trouble."

"He's my friend, and partner," I said, ignoring the comments about my character. "Of course I'd do anything I could to clear his name."

"Exactly. A shitload of trouble. So now you're tracking down members of the team, including Buckton and Danvers."

I wasn't surprised he was keeping tabs. "If Buckton is a suspect, why can't TSA or Customs detain him?" And save us the bother.

"We'd rather handle this on the down low," Dennon replied.

"Because of Operation Gemini," I guessed. So I'd been right. Plus, we were deniable, and expendable. Sounded familiar. "You've never said how President Kirk was involved."

"Nope. I haven't. Man, they weren't kidding when they said you were super smart."

I guessed by his tone rather this his words that he was being sarcastic. Smart-ass.

"Gotta go," he said. "I'll be in touch." He ended the call.

I tossed and turned for a while, with too much stuff going on inside my head. Or maybe I'd just slept too much, but when my phone said it was nearly two in the morning and I was still awake, I decided it was because I hadn't had my two Fig Newtons before bed.

Getting up, I quietly opened my door and peered down the hall. The house was still and dark. Everyone was asleep. I'd put Clark in Bill's room and Jackson in Oslo's. I only had a twin bed, after all, and I didn't think Dad would appreciate his daughter shacking up in his own house, even if it was with her fiancé.

I tiptoed down the stairs, avoiding the third stair from the top because it creaked as though it was alive, and walking on it seemed like a personal affront. Then I wished I'd kept those fuzzy socks on, because my feet were freezing.

The kitchen was only slightly warmer, and the little light above the stove was on, dispelling the darkness somewhat. I didn't know if Dad had any Fig Newtons, but Heather had left some of the chocolate cake she'd made for dessert.

Ice-cold milk and a slice of chocolate cake. Just what the insomnia doctor ordered. I was just pouring the milk when I heard footsteps behind me and turned to see that my dad had come out of his room.

"Thought I heard someone up," he said quietly. "Couldn't sleep?"

I shook my head. "Too much to think about, I guess. Want some?" I motioned to the milk and cake. He raised his eyebrows.

"Well, I hate for you to eat alone," he teased, smiling a little.

"That's mighty big of you," I teased back. I got another glass and plate, and soon we were sitting at the table attacking to two giant slabs of cake.

"Your man seems like a fine choice," he said once we'd finished.

I was leaning back in my chair, regretting those last two bites I'd had. But it had been so good. "He is," I said. "We have a lot in common."

"You enjoy his company?" he asked.

"I do. We get along well. He's dependable, too, and financially sound."

"You sound like you're talkin' about a horse you're thinkin' of buying, not a man you're goin' to marry." He paused to take a swallow of his milk. "You love him, don't ya?"

"Yes, of course I do."

"'Cause that other one looks at you," he said, his eyes narrowing. "And I noticed you look at him, too."

"We're partners, and good friends," I said.

"Which is what a marriage should be," he added. "Is he not . . . dependable or . . . financially sound?"

I blinked. "Yes, I mean . . . I think so."

"Then why ain't you with him?"

I was at a loss as to how to answer. This was a bizarre conversation to have, especially with my dad. He'd never displayed more than a passing interest in my friendships or personal life. Now to be suddenly quizzed about Jackson . . . I wasn't prepared for it. So I answered with what popped into my head.

"I guess . . . I'm not with him because he never asked."

Dad didn't reply; he just looked at me until I had to look away. I was embarrassed now, and unsure how to act. Looking at things from Dad's point of view and his limited time left, I could see how he'd want to know he was leaving me in good hands, that I'd be happy. It was sweet that he'd go outside his own comfort zone to bring up this topic when I knew he had to be as uncomfortable as I was.

"I have something for you," he said, reaching into the pocket of his robe. He set a folded envelope on the table.

"What is it?" I asked, reaching for it. My name was written in faded ink on the outside of the envelope.

"It's a letter," he said, "from your mother."

I glanced up in surprise.

"She wanted you to have it one day, when you were older and realized the truth. Said I should only give it to you then."

I didn't know what to say. *Shock* didn't seem like a strong enough word to convey what I was feeling. My mom had left me a letter, speaking to me from beyond the grave. It was difficult to process. How had she known to write it? Had she been afraid she wouldn't be around when I was older to talk to me herself? Or had it just been easier to say in a letter?

"Dad," I began.

"Shh!"

I shut my mouth, startled. Dad wasn't looking at me anymore. He'd twisted, looking over his shoulder into the darkened hallway beyond the kitchen.

"What—?" I began, but he interrupted me again with a harsh whisper.

"Someone's in the house."

CH. 18

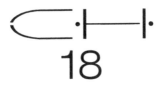

A chill swept over me that had nothing to do with the temperature in the room.

"Maybe it's Jackson," I whispered. "Or Clark."

"Maybe," he said. "You stay here. I'll go check it out." He got silently to his feet and headed for the entryway.

I was frozen for a moment, then stood, too, listening. I heard nothing. Fear for my dad had me exiting the kitchen through the other entry. Our ground floor was built old-style, with lots of separate rooms. There was no such thing as an *open floor plan* in the forties. The formal dining room was behind the kitchen, then you circled through the hallway to the family room and entryway.

It was dark as pitch in the dining room, the only light coming from what was glowing from the moonlit snow outside. Mom's china cabinet reflected bits of light in the cut glass displayed on its shelves. I heard the tick of the clock on the mantel in the family room. I'd never noticed how loud it was.

I couldn't understand why I couldn't hear anything. Dad had heard something, obviously. But where was he?

The carpet was soft under my toes as I took careful steps forward, my eyes peering into the shadows. I thought about flipping on the light, but not only would that tell a possible intruder exactly where I was, it would also blind me for a few precious seconds that might make a difference.

My heart was pounding so loudly, I could hear the blood in my ears. I reached the doorway to the dining room, and beyond that was the blackness of the hallway. I paused again, hearing nothing. Panic made me decide to chance it.

"Dad?" I hissed. My voice seemed much too loud.

I stepped into the hallway, holding my breath . . . but nothing happened. I peered down its length but could discern nothing out of the ordinary.

Letting out a breath of relief, I walked into the family room. Dad had to be in there, though why he hadn't answered me or come back had me worrying. Was he all right?

A hand on my arm nearly made me pee my pants, and I jerked, startled. I looked up, and in the darkness could just discern Clark's features.

"Oh God, Clark," I heaved, my heart racing double time. "You scared me. I thought you were an intruder."

He smiled, which was strange. "You must be China. It's about time we met."

His words made no sense, and I stared at him in confusion, then I realized. His smile was off and his eyes weren't right.

"You're not Clark," I breathed, suddenly realizing what big trouble I was really in.

"'Fraid not," he said briskly. "Though we do sometimes get confused."

"You're Rob," I said. "Clark's brother. But . . . you're supposed to be dead. What are you doing here? Why are you in my house?"

He moved fast, wrapping a hand around the back of my neck and yanking me closer to him. Then I felt the cold press of a gun's muzzle underneath my chin.

"Just here to settle some old scores," he said. "Think I'll leave your body as a warning. Let my brother stew, and spend a few days looking over his shoulder."

My knees were trembling. I had no doubt that he was about to pull that trigger. Would it hurt? Or would I just be here one second . . . then gone the next?

A shotgun came out of nowhere, ramming the butt into the side of Rob's head. It connected with a sickening crack just as I was yanked away. Rob's gun went off, but the bullet didn't hit me.

Rob cursed, rounding on me as he held the side of his head. Blood was dripping down his face, but the hand holding the gun was steady. He leveled it at me . . . and my dad, who held the shotgun.

"I'm going to bet you didn't have time to load that, old man," Rob said. "Or you'd have used it by now."

"You willin' to bet your life on that?" Dad asked, his voice hard.

Rob smiled, and it sent a chill through my bones. "Yes, I am." He fired just as Dad shoved me out of the way. I fell to the ground as all hell broke loose. Dad was lying on top of me, and I could hear footsteps thundering down the stairs.

The front door opened and an icy wind swept through the house.

"I'll go! You help them!"

Clark's voice this time, but I couldn't move. The heavy weight of my father pressed me down against the floor.

"China!" Jackson's voice was frantic as he flipped on the overhead light. He rolled my dad off me, and I sat up.

There was blood. A lot of blood. All over my chest.

"You're hurt," he said. "Where?"

I was frantically feeling around, but nothing hurt. "It's not me." I looked over. "Oh no . . . Dad . . ."

He hadn't moved since Jackson had pulled him off me, and now I could see why. The shot intended for me had hit him instead when he'd shoved me aside. I opened his dressing gown. My breath caught at the bloody wound in his abdomen.

"Oh God," I breathed, horror-struck. "Quick, Jackson, call 9-1-1."

He obeyed, jumping to his feet and running from the room.

"China," Dad said, his voice low and edged with pain.

"Don't try to talk," I said. "You're going to be okay. Jackson's calling an ambulance."

Dad forced a little smile that turned into a grimace of pain. "I don't want that," he said. "A long, drawn-out battle with cancer that'll just sap my strength and my bank account?" He shook his head slightly. "Nah. A quick death, saving you. That's my choice."

The tears were falling hard and fast now, and I swiped my cheeks with the back of my bloodstained hand.

"You shouldn't have done that," I said. "I'm not even yours, remember?"

His eyes were solemn. "I shouldn't have said that," he said. "You were mine . . . in all the ways that mattered. You're my little girl. And I—" Another grimace of pain made him stop.

"Don't talk," I begged him. "The ambulance will be here soon."

"Gotta say this," he managed. "Tell you . . . how sorry I am that we . . . we weren't close."

"It's okay," I assured him. I'd say anything if he'd just stop talking . . . and *where the hell was that ambulance?*

"I love you, China," he said.

I stared at him. Dad had never said those words to me before.

"And I should've told you before now. But I guess . . . better late than never." Another grimace.

"I love you, too, Dad," I whispered, barely able to see through the tears in my eyes.

"You take care of yourself now, you hear? And choose the right fella. That makes all the difference."

I grasped his hand, unable to speak any longer. He held my hand tight, looked at me, and smiled, then another wave of pain washed over him. His grip tightened, then fell slack, and his chest lowered in one long sigh. And that was all. He was gone.

"This can't be happening," I whispered. "Dad?"

"Shhh," Jackson said, crouching down and wrapping his arms around me. "He's gone, sweetheart."

I began to sob. Jackson picked me up and carried me from the room, my tears soaking his shirt. We went into the kitchen, where he sat down with me on his lap and let me cry it out. I didn't stop until I heard the ambulance sirens.

Clark returned while Jackson was handling the EMTs, and the two of us remained in the kitchen. I couldn't bear to see Dad's body as they loaded him into the ambulance. And there were things to do, people to call . . . none of which I could even contemplate doing at the moment.

"I lost him," Clark said, sitting down at the table. "He'd hidden an SUV about a quarter of a mile away. Did you get a good look at him?"

I nodded. "Yeah, Clark. I did."

Something in my voice must've alerted him because he went still. "What? What is it?"

I swallowed, wiping my cheeks again. "It wasn't Buckton. Or Danvers. It was Rob. Your brother."

He stared, the blood draining from his face. "What did you say?"

"It was him, Clark," I insisted, sniffing. "I don't know how, but it was definitely him."

"The ambulance left," Jackson said to me, pulling up another chair. "We'll need to make a statement with the police tomorrow. I found the back-door lock was forced. That's how he got in."

"I-I need to call Oslo. And Bill. They need to know." I couldn't imagine what I was going to say or how I was going to explain. Their dad—my dad—had died protecting me.

"We can call them in the morning," Jackson said. "There's nothing to be gained by calling them now. It'll wait a couple of hours."

He was right. It was after four in the morning by now. The bad news could at least wait until the sun rose.

"You need to try to get some rest," Jackson said. "Let me take you upstairs."

I hesitated. What if Rob came back? But Clark read my mind.

"I'll keep watch," he said, resting his weapon on the kitchen table.

I winced when I saw his face. His expression was stark. It hurt to look in his eyes. He'd just experienced a bad shock, too.

Jackson led me upstairs and I sat down on the bed.

"Stay with me," I said impulsively.

"I wasn't planning on leaving you alone, that's for damn sure," he said. "Let's get those pajamas off you."

I let him pull the bloodstained pajamas off. Then I lay down and scooted so there was room for him. He took me in his arms and pulled the covers over us. Tremors ran through me.

"Are you cold?" he asked. "I can get you more pajamas."

"No. Just hold me." Death had come for me too many times lately. I felt as though I was living on borrowed time.

"You're all right," he assured me. "I've got you."

"It's my fault my dad is dead," I said, resting my head against his chest. "If I'd never come here, he'd still be alive."

"He had cancer," Jackson said. "He wasn't long for this world. His last act was saving your life. There are worse ways to go, sweetheart."

"I'm afraid . . . that Bill and Oslo will blame me."

"That would be an emotional response if they did," Jackson countered. "Not logical. They both struck me as men who aren't particularly given over to their emotions so much as to deny logic."

We lay in silence for a bit, his fingers tracing up and down my bare back. I listened to his heart beat and felt the rise and fall of his chest as he breathed.

"I've almost lost you so many times," he said. "When I heard those gunshots tonight, I was terrified. And when I saw you lying there, and all the blood . . ."

I squeezed him tighter. "I'm here. I'm okay."

"We should go away somewhere," he said. "When this is all over. Get out of Raleigh for a while. Go sit on a beach somewhere. Relax."

The idea of being away from home . . . again . . . for a prolonged length of time did not sound relaxing to me, but I didn't argue.

◆ ◆ ◆

Later that morning I made the hardest phone call I've ever had to make. There was a lot of crying, on everyone's part, and by eight o'clock, the house was full with everyone again.

Heather busied herself making breakfast, which I thought was her way of coping. She was one of those caregiver people. If someone was hurting, food was the best medicine. Not that I could disagree. A couple of her featherlight pancakes made me feel more like myself, even after I swore I wasn't going to be able to eat.

"I'll head into town and start taking care of the funeral details," Oslo said. He sat at the kitchen table, nursing a mug of black coffee. "Dad had already done most of the paperwork, since he was diagnosed, so there won't be a lot to take care of, I don't think."

"I need to go feed the livestock," Bill said, pushing back from the table. "They're probably wondering where their breakfast is."

Neither of them had taken Dad's death horribly, and I wondered if they'd already reconciled themselves to his passing. This was just more sudden and . . . violent. We hadn't told them who the intruder was, just that an armed man had been caught by Dad, who'd shot him, then he'd escaped. Neither Jackson nor Clark mentioned my involvement, and I didn't bring it up either.

It was midmorning by the time we left to go see Buckton at his agency. No one argued against my going—I think they didn't want to let me out of their sight.

Sandwiched between the two of them as we walked into Buckton Security, Inc., I felt smaller and younger than usual. I wished I'd worn something more professional, something that made me feel less vulnerable.

"You okay?" Clark asked me.

His eyes were concealed behind a pair of shades that made him look simultaneously gorgeous and badass.

"Yeah, I just . . . need a vacation." Though a staycation at home would be preferable.

Clark and Jackson both laughed at my emphatic declaration.

"And where would you want to go?" Jackson asked.

"That's right," Clark said. "Moneybags here will make all those dreams come true. You just have to say the word."

"You've got that right," Jackson shot back.

I just sighed.

There was a woman behind the reception desk. She wore one of those trendy suits with a little miniskirt and clunky heels. Her hair was blond and wound up into a messy bun. Young and pretty, she wore glasses, and that was all we had in common.

"We're here to see Bill Buckton," Clark said.

She smiled blandly. "I'm sorry, but he's just returned from a trip. He's not seeing anyone today."

He leaned on the counter and took off his sunglasses. "If you could just tell him that Slattery is here," he said, then smiled. "I promise. He'll want to see me."

The woman took a breath, her eyes glued on Clark, and her pupils were dilated. Hmm.

"I'm sure he wouldn't mind if I just mention it," she said with a smile. "Have a seat."

"Thank you."

We sat on one of the plush couches in the lobby. The place was nice, a three-story building wider than it was tall, and decorated in a classy style that was more masculine than feminine. A lot of taupes, browns, and wood in the decor.

"She doesn't seem very security oriented," I observed under my breath.

"Why do you say that?" Clark asked.

I shot him a look. "A receptionist that can be swayed from her job function by an attractive customer isn't a receptionist who should keep her job."

"He'll see you," she called out to us.

"Let's wait until after the meeting before you fire her," Clark muttered to me.

She led us up to the third floor to a corner office, knocked briefly, and opened the door. Clark entered first.

A man stood in front of the windows, and he turned when he heard us walk in. He was well built and tall and had the kind of face you'd instinctively trust. Salt-and-pepper hair and a complexion that said he spent more time in the sun than out of it. He was dressed casually in slacks and a long-sleeve shirt, though I did notice the holster and handgun at his side.

"Slattery," he said as the receptionist departed. "It's been a long time." He stepped from out behind his desk and shook Clark's hand.

"Hey, Buck, it's good to see you," Clark replied. "These are a couple associates of mine. Cooper and Mack."

We shook hands, too, though I noticed he eyed me a little strangely.

"Let's have a seat," Buck said, gesturing to the sofa and chairs arranged to one side of the expansive office. "And you can tell me what this is about, because I'm sure you're not here just on a social call."

"You'd be right," Clark replied as we all took seats. "I'm here about our last mission together."

"You mean Tripoli," Buck said.

"Yeah."

Buck sighed. "That op went FUBAR so damn quick. We lost some good men."

"I know," Clark said. "But maybe not as many as we think."

"What do you mean?"

"My brother," he said. "Rob. They told me he didn't make it, but . . . I think he did."

"You're kidding me," Buck said, his eyes widening. "But that was . . . six years ago. You're just now finding out he didn't die in there?"

"Not only didn't die . . . but he's alive. And he's here."

Buck's face broke into a wide smile. "That's fantastic news! Where the hell is he? What's he been doing all this time?"

"Yeah, that's the bad news," Clark said. "Taggert's dead. So is Williams. He tried to kill me, but failed. I think he's been killing everyone who left him behind, and you might be next before he comes after me again."

Buck looked shocked as he took in the information. "Are you sure?" he asked at last.

"Rob killed my father last night," I said. "He was trying to kill me."

"Why? What do you have to do with anything?"

"She doesn't," Clark answered. "She's just important. To me."

"Ever heard of a Mark Danvers?" Jackson asked.

Buck's gaze narrowed as it swung to Jackson. "Where'd you hear that name?"

"You know him?" Clark asked.

"Yeah. I did some digging after that mission. He was high up the food chain. Him and some senator on the Armed Forces Committee were tight. From what I could find out, Danvers was the one pulling the strings." He paused, then asked, "Do you know about Operation Gemini?"

"Yeah," Clark said. "We were the decoys."

Buck nodded. "If anybody should be after revenge, it's us. And if I ever come across Danvers, I'll kill the bastard myself."

I decided now wasn't a good time to tell him of my relation.

"Rob's in Omaha," Clark said. "I wanted to warn you."

"Thanks, man," he said. "I appreciate it. And if there's anything I can do for you, just say the word."

He stood, so we all followed suit. "It was nice to meet you," Buck said to me and Jackson. "And good to see you again, Slattery. I hope you're doing all right." He cast a quick glance at me.

"I'm good, thanks," Clark said. "And it's a nice setup you have here. Business is good?"

"Yeah, actually. We operate all over the world." He headed back to the desk, rounding behind it and opening the top drawer. "Hey, listen, let me give you a card, just in case you're ever, you know, looking for work or something."

Glass shattered, and then Buck's head exploded.

CH 19

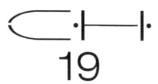

I screamed, then was tackled to the floor.

Buck's body had no head, and it slowly crumpled, landing with a thud on the floor. I was still screaming. I couldn't stop. His head had just . . . disintegrated.

"Oh God oh God oh God . . ." I was curled into a ball. Unable to move.

"Shh, baby, it's okay. You're okay." Clark was the one who'd tackled me.

"B-Buck," I stammered. "He-he's dead. His . . . his head . . ."

"I know, baby," Clark said. His arms were wrapped completely around me. "I know."

Jackson crawled over to us. "You both okay?"

"Yeah," Clark said. "We're good." He looked at me. "We've gotta move. Can you stand?"

What a ridiculous question. Of course I could stand. I'd just seen a man's head explode hours after watching my dad get shot to death, but standing? No problem.

They were both looking at me funny, and I realized I'd babbled all that out loud.

"I'm okay." The shake in my voice belied that, but I struggled to my feet anyway.

"Let's get out of here," Jackson said.

They each had an arm and were half carrying, half herding me toward the door. I put on the brakes, planting my feet on the ground.

"No, we can't! He's still out there. If we walk out of here, he'll shoot us." I couldn't breathe and my knees had folded. Only Jackson's and Clark's hold on my arms kept me upright.

"Look at me." Clark grasped my shoulders and turned me toward him. "Look at me, China!"

His voice broke through my panic.

"You trust me, right? Trust me to keep you safe? Keep you alive?"

I nodded. "Yeah." His eyes were burning into mine. "Yeah. I do."

"Then don't worry. You're going to be fine."

"Okay," I whispered. "Okay. Let's go."

We were downstairs in a flash. The receptionist was nowhere in sight. I just caught a glimpse of people emerging from offices before we were out the door. Jackson and Clark acted as human shields, which I was totally *not okay with*, but I didn't get a say. It wasn't until we were in the car that we saw it.

A Gemini sign had been spray-painted in black on the side of the building.

"Drive," Clark said. Jackson hit the gas.

I slumped in the back seat. My glasses were fogged up from going from the warm into the cold, then back into the warm. I took them off and realized I was crying again. The last time I'd cried so much had been when Rose and the Doctor had been locked into separate universes forever. That had been an ugly cry night.

The drive back to the house was silent.

Everyone had gone by the time we returned. The house was cold and empty. The day was dark and gray with thick, ominous clouds. It was only midday, but it could easily have been closer to twilight.

"What do we do now?" I asked, sitting down in the kitchen. No way could I go into the family room.

"He's obviously going to return here for me," Clark said. "I think you two should bug out before it gets dark. I'll stay here. He'll be back."

"No," I said, shaking my head. "Not going to happen."

"Why not?" Jackson asked.

I looked at him askance. "You'd just leave Clark to face his . . . crazy brother—who wants to kill him—alone?"

"If it means keeping you safe, then yeah."

"You're part of this," I said to Jackson. "He came after you, too. You can't just leave Clark to pay the piper for your sins."

"You think what I did was wrong?"

His question had an edge to it that didn't get by me. "I don't look at things as black and white," I said. "You know that. But leaving Clark to save ourselves . . . I can't do that."

"Yes, you can, and you will," Clark said. "I don't know why Rob is doing what he's doing, but if anyone can talk sense into him, it's me. There's a reason I'm still walking around, a reason he hasn't killed me yet."

"Yes, luck," I retorted. "Who's to say that you're going to be the one to talk him off this psycho cliff? What if he kills you? Then he'll just come after us. What then? And this whole scenario . . . there's something wrong."

"What are you talking about?"

"I mean, Rob just can't come back from the dead and start killing people. He needs basic necessities, ID, transportation, weapons. You can't just get all those things at the corner Walmart." I looked from one to the other. "Someone is helping him. Helping him do the dirty work."

"She's right," Jackson said. "And my best guess would be Danvers."

"Why now? Why wait all this time?"

"We don't know where your brother has been or what he's been doing for six years," I said. "Something must've happened to trigger this. Maybe it was Danvers himself that set Rob on his killing spree."

"But we have no idea where Danvers is or what his motive could be," Clark said.

"We'll have to deal with Danvers later. Right now, Rob is our immediate problem."

"He's not 'our' problem," Clark argued. "He's *my* problem."

Jackson and Clark exchanged a look I couldn't decipher. Then they both stood.

"Time to go," Jackson said, taking a firm grip on my arm.

I tried to yank away. "I said that I wasn't going. If you want to leave, fine. Leave. But I'm not leaving Clark to face his crazy brother alone!"

"Yes, you are," Clark said, taking my other arm. "I appreciate the support, Mack, I really do. But you need to leave now."

They were going to force me, strong-arm me. Make me. Which pissed me off something fierce.

"Don't you *dare* make me go," I threatened, struggling to free myself. We were already nearly to the front door. "I will never forgive either of you if you do this!"

"I'll worry about that later," Jackson said.

"So long as you're alive, you can hate me as much as you want," Clark added.

I started cursing at them and dragging my feet, but I might as well have been a misbehaving toddler, for all the good it did. I was so angry, I could literally feel my blood pressure climbing.

Jackson threw open the door and we all froze.

The barn was about a hundred and fifty yards away from us, and there was a giant flaming Gemini burning on its exterior.

Clark recovered first. "He's here. Get to the car!"

"No!" But I was ignored. Clark picked me up bodily while Jackson ran ahead to open the door. Clark started stuffing me in the front seat.

"I am *not* leaving you!" I gritted out, grabbing fistfuls of his clothing and hanging on for dear life. I managed to get a leg hooked around his waist and clung like a koala bear digging into a tree.

"Look at me," Clark said, grasping my chin and turning my face toward his. "Do you think I could live with myself if something happened to you? Do you?"

His insistence just frustrated me. "And you think I don't feel the same? How can you expect me to just leave you here, maybe to die?" Only one man would walk out of here, I was sure, and I just didn't think Clark had it in him to kill his brother. No matter the justification.

Clark's eyes were filled with an emotion I was too afraid to name. His thumb brushed my cheek, and his gaze roved over my face as if he were memorizing it.

"If you have any faith in me at all, you'll go."

I stared at him, my head trying to form a logical argument. But my emotions were much louder than reason inside.

"There are no atheists in foxholes," I murmured, remembering my idioms.

He frowned. "What? What does God have to do with this?"

"When the stakes are high, all that matters are the things you can't see," I tried to explain. "I have faith in you. I trust you."

His lips did that slow curve into a smile that I knew I'd remember for the rest of my life. I could smell the fire and hear the crackle of burning wood. The cold was biting and the snow a pristine blanket of white. I could feel the warmth of Clark's body as I clung to him, and see the length of his dark lashes framing his beautiful eyes.

"You've got to go," he said, pressing a kiss to my forehead. And before I could protest again, he'd unwrapped me from around him, put me in the car, and slammed the door.

Jackson was behind the wheel, and he wasted no time hitting the locks and the gas. He buckled me in with one hand, and in seconds we were halfway down the drive. I twisted in my seat, but Clark had already disappeared.

I buried my head in my hands. "Oh God, Jackson. What are we going to do?"

"We're going to get some backup," he said. "Even Omaha has cops."

I sat up straight. "You're right! Of course! Why didn't I think of it sooner?" Pulling out my cell phone, I dialed, waiting impatiently as it rang.

"Talk to me," Dennon answered.

"I have your guy, but I need help," I explained as quickly as I could. "And I think he's going to keep going. He'll try for the president again, I'm sure. He's like a hand grenade that someone's pulled the pin on and tossed out."

"That analogy doesn't quite make sense, but I get your drift," he said. "I'll see what I can do and get back to you."

"Get back to me?" I nearly shouted. "This is happening *now*. There's no time for you to 'get back' to me."

"Then stop wasting time by being overly emotional and yelling at me." The line went dead.

It took all my logic and self-control not to throw my phone at the windshield.

Jackson was driving fast and slowed down for a curve. There was something in the road ahead, something small and black. Like a backpack.

"Wait," I said, suddenly realizing what it might be. "Stop—"

The backpack blew up, sending the SUV backward and flipping it. We rolled, the airbags cushioning the initial impact. I lost track of which way was up when we came to a jarring stop.

I was conscious and reached out to Jackson. We were upside down. The windows were gone and the windshield was shattered but still in place. I could feel Jackson's arm.

"Jackson," I half said, half groaned. My body hurt. "Are you okay? Jackson?"

But there was no answer. I couldn't make out his face in the dark, and I began to panic.

"Jackson?" I shook his arm, but he didn't respond.

A crunching sound from outside my window made me jerk in fear. A set of men's boots were walking toward my window, the snow and ice making the crunching noise as he came nearer.

I couldn't breathe and I was shaking. Jackson wasn't okay. Clark was going to die. And whoever was coming for me wasn't someone anxious to help, I was sure.

The feet stopped right outside my window. I waited, barely breathing. Suddenly, he bent down, and once I saw his face, I knew what hopelessness felt like.

Rob smiled. "Leaving so soon?"

◆ ◆ ◆

Clark saw the explosion, and it nearly brought him to his knees. Oh God. China.

He was running before he'd even made the decision to, slipping and sliding on the snow. It seemed to take forever to get as far as Jackson had driven. Past the fields and into where the trees grew tall. Then he saw it . . . and stumbled to a halt.

The SUV was upside down and glass was everywhere. Somehow, the headlights still worked, their beams cutting through the gloom. There was a constant hissing as the hot water from the engine made contact with the snow. But for such a violent scene, it was eerily quiet.

Clark approached as carefully yet as quickly as he could. China was in there, if she hadn't been thrown from the wreckage. He hadn't buckled her in to the seat, so intent had he been on making sure she left quickly.

Crouching down next to the passenger window, he looked inside, using the flashlight on his phone to see.

China's seat was empty. Jackson was still in his, but not moving, just held in place by the seat belt as he hung upside down.

"Looking for something, big bro?"

The voice he hadn't heard in six years was like someone reaching from the grave. Clark stood, bracing himself as he turned, and it was still like a punch to the gut to see Rob standing not ten feet away.

"Rob," he breathed. "I can't believe it's you. After all this time . . ."

"Yeah, I bet you didn't think you'd see me again, that's for damn sure." Rob's voice was hard, and as he stepped farther into the light, Clark saw he had China.

She could barely stand, Rob's arm around her throat holding her upright, and her glasses were gone. Rob held a gun to her temple.

"Toss aside your weapon," he demanded. "I hear her brain is precious, and I'd sure hate to splatter it all over the snow." He tilted his head to the side. "Though I think that'd look real pretty, red against the white? Don't you think?"

Clark swallowed. It was his brother . . . and not his brother. The body was the same, the voice and face the same . . . but that was all. He reached for the gun in the small of his back—

"Slowly, now," Rob said. "I wouldn't want my trigger finger to slip, and I'm feeling a little on edge." His smile was a twisted thing.

Clark slowly pulled out his weapon, then tossed it aside. "Now what?"

"Why, now it's time for that family reunion, brother!" And Rob shot him.

Pain ripped through his knee and Clark fell, his hands burying in the snow. The shock of the wound kept him immobile as he dealt with the pain. Then he was being dragged through the snow all the way to the light in front of the car.

"That should do," Rob said, releasing him. A long red streak marked the snow from Clark's leg, and Rob looked at it for a moment, then seemed to recover himself.

"I bet you're wondering where the hell I've been," Rob said, tucking his gun into a holster at his side. "Or maybe not. Maybe you were glad to put Tripoli behind you." He went back to where China lay crumpled in the snow as he talked.

Grabbing her by the arm, he pulled her over to a tree. He set her upright, then wrapped a bungee cord around her body and hooked it behind the trunk. China's head lolled on her chest.

Rob crouched, the headlights from the car throwing his face into sharp relief. It was only then that Clark saw the thin scar down the side of his face and the way it made his lips somewhat misshapen when he smiled, so it looked all wrong and twisted. Like the Joker but without the symmetry.

"They told me you'd gotten out," Clark said. "They said everyone had gotten out."

"They lied."

"I didn't know that. Not then. And once the mission was over, we thought everyone who didn't make it out was dead. Including you."

"Well, let me enlighten you, brother. I was captured. Not killed. By Gaddafi's men. I'm sure you can imagine what that was like." He was digging in a duffel as he spoke, unearthing a sheathed knife. When he removed the sheath, the silver blade shone.

"They tortured me for five years before I was let go," he continued. "Almost killing me, over and over, then nursing me back to the edge of the land of the living. Then doing it all over again. You can't imagine what it's like, when you're begging to die."

Clark was cold all over, and it wasn't because of the snow. "Rob—" His voice cracked. "God, Rob, I'm so sorry. I would never, *never* have left you there if I'd known—"

"How could you not know?" Rob's shout reverberated through the trees, and Clark winced. "You were my brother," he continued, not shouting, but his voice shook with anger. "You were supposed to have my back. And you *left* me there, in that *shithole*, to *rot*!"

"Rob, if I could have taken your place, I would've," Clark said, trying to keep his voice calm despite the pain racking his body, inside and out. His gaze was following the knife as Rob stood and walked back over to China.

"Well, you're going to," Rob said. "Right now. Because it wasn't just the physical pain. I guess anybody could get through that. It was knowing you'd been *left*. That everyone you counted on to help you make it out alive had turned their backs on you." He waved his hand. "I guess you might say I have abandonment issues." His laugh was chilling.

"Please, Rob, just stop all this," Clark begged. "We can get you help. We can be brothers again. You're the only family I have left. Just you and me."

"Really? I don't think so." Now Rob crouched next to China, and fear spiked in Clark. "I think you've got a major thing for this one." He yanked on China's hair, pulling her head back, and Clark heard her gasp in pain.

"Rob, c'mon. You're better than this. Hurting a woman? A girl? Are you insane?"

Rob seemed to think about that for a moment, and hope flared briefly in Clark, only to come crashing down with his next words. "Yeah, I think I might be. Which is why I can do this." His knife caught the light.

"No!" Clark lurched to his feet, then crashed down again, gritting his teeth against the pain. He couldn't black out.

"Take it easy there, bro," Rob said affably. "I just nicked her carotid. They taught me just how to do it, so you bleed out real slow-like. We'll just sit here and watch her fade away. Nothing you can do about it. That's the real bitch."

Clark stared in horror at China, who was awake and aware. Blood was seeping from her neck in a thin, steady stream, soaking her shirt in garish red.

"No, please," Clark gasped, using his arms to crawl forward. "Please, Rob." He couldn't see, his eyes were blurry, and he had to blink hard. He moved another painful six inches.

"Now this . . . this is sweet revenge," Rob said. He was leaning against a tree, taking in the scene with the same twisted smile. "She'll bleed out, then you'll get to cradle her lifeless body while you slowly die, too." He sniffed an imaginary tear. "Honestly, someone should be filming this for the fucking Oscars or some shit."

Rob didn't impede Clark's painfully slow journey to China. Dirt and snow crusted Clark's hands and under his fingernails, each inch dragging white-hot claws into his injured knee. He was gasping for breath, able to go on through sheer will alone by the time he reached China's side.

"Clark," she said in a hoarse whisper, "I can't move. Why? What happened?"

"Shh, baby. I'm here." He moved as close as he could and unlatched the bungee cord. China fell into his arms. Blood soaked the front of her shirt as she gazed up at him. She wasn't shivering.

"I'm so cold," she said. "I can't feel my legs. Or my hands." She looked up into his eyes. "Am I dying?"

"No, of course not," he assured her. He smiled through the tears dripping down his face. "Would I let you die?"

Her smile was slow. "No. I have faith in you, remember?"

Pain was a knife in his gut, but it wasn't from his knee. China trusted him. And he'd let her down. Even now, he was lying to her. *He* was the reason she was dying.

Her eyes drifted closed and he bent his knees, pulling her closer to his chest. "Don't shut your eyes, baby. Keep them open. Stay awake for me."

"Seriously," Rob said, "I'm getting all choked up, imagining a hiker or farmer stumbling on your frozen, entwined bodies. They're going to make a movie of the week out of this. Definitely."

Hatred and rage unlike anything he'd ever known welled up in Clark, until he shook with wanting to tear his brother apart.

"Don't forget your last words," Rob said. "Anything you want to tell her while she's still conscious enough to hear you? I'd be quick, if I were you. She's kind of small, so I can't think she's got much blood left in her."

"China," Clark whispered in her ear, "can you hear me, baby?" Snot, tears, sweat, and blood mingled on his face, marring her skin. She made a noise and opened her eyes.

"'m cold, Clark," she said, frowning. "Why is it so cold? Why are you crying? What's wrong?"

He forced himself to smile and stop bawling. "Nothing's wrong, baby. I just wanted to tell you . . . h-how much . . . I love you. I thought you should know." His fingers were dirt smeared, but he gently touched her cold cheek anyway. She was so pale.

"That's so nice," she said, smiling. "You love me. I'm glad."

A gunshot rang out and Clark instinctively covered China with his body, waiting for the pain. But nothing happened. Tentatively, he looked up.

Rob stood, an expression of shock on his face, as he looked down at the blooming red stain on his chest. Then he looked to his right.

Jackson stood there, holding Clark's discarded weapon. He was holding his left arm awkwardly against his side, but the hand pointing the gun at Rob was steady.

"You're one sick son of a bitch," Jackson bit out.

Rob fell to the ground and didn't move.

Jackson approached him carefully, removed the gun from Rob's holster, and tossed it aside, then felt for a pulse in his neck. After a moment, he moved to the duffel and began rummaging through it.

"Is he . . ." Clark couldn't say the word. His own brother had wanted to kill him and China, but he couldn't ask if he was dead.

"Yeah," was Jackson's clipped response.

The sound of helicopters in the distance made them look up. Jackson pulled something from the duffel. Emergency flares. He set four on the ground around them as the helicopters grew closer.

"Are you okay?" Clark asked Jackson.

He nodded. "Broken arm, I think. Other than that, I'm fine." He fell to his knees in front of Clark, his haunted gaze on China. "Is she going to make it?"

"I don't know. Sh-she's lost a lot of blood."

Then they couldn't talk because the wind from the helicopters was too strong. Two choppers landed just in the clearing beyond where the SUV had turned over. Light flooded the woods, along with men toting automatic rifles.

"Medic!" Clark called out. "Over here! Medic!"

Men arrived with red crosses on their helmets, taking China's limp body from him. She was unconscious now, and his fear ratcheted up another notch.

"Her carotid's been nicked," Clark explained. "She's lost a lot of blood."

"We'll take care of her, sir."

Stretchers arrived for him and China. He didn't want to get on, but he wasn't given a choice. Jackson was helped into the second chopper by another medic.

They were putting an IV in his arm and blocking his view of China. He grabbed the arm of the medic taking care of him. "Take my blood," he demanded. "I'm O negative. She needs blood now."

The two medics conversed. Clark yanked him back. "I said, take my blood, goddamn it!"

"Sir, you're injured. It wouldn't be wise to—"

Clark grabbed the medic's shirt front and pulled him down. "Save her," he gritted out. "You think I give a shit about me? Swear to me you'll save her."

The medic didn't look rattled by Clark's vehemence. "I swear to you, sir. We'll save her. But we will need your blood."

Clark let him go. "Take it."

The sound of the choppers' blades was loud and lulling. Clark closed his eyes, listening. What was it China had said?

There are no atheists in foxholes.

So he prayed. He hadn't prayed since that night in Tripoli. *That hadn't turned out very well,* he thought, but he shoved the thought away. All that was left to believe in was what he couldn't see.

And the choppers' blades turned.

CH. 20

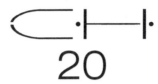

I'd had enough of hospitals to last me a lifetime, which was why I wasn't a bit sorry to see the outside of this one, though I should have been glad just to be alive.

It had been close.

I didn't remember much after the bomb and subsequent car wreck. Jackson and Clark had filled in most of the blanks, telling me what Rob had done.

He'd bled me. Slowly.

The thought still sent chills through me.

Jackson was waiting for me, his arm in a sling, as we walked outside to the waiting car that would drive us to the airport.

We'd laid my dad to rest yesterday. I'd gotten a pass from the hospital for the night, but had to return today for one last checkup before getting on a plane. Jackson had insisted on flying in Dr. Morris, who'd had a near fit when he saw I'd been in another accident, and had rushed me in for another CT scan. Though I was okay, he'd lectured me long and hard about "taking it easy" and giving myself "time to heal."

The funeral had been a solemn ceremony, not least because my brothers had been subjected to armed men in uniform coming to their door four nights ago to explain that no, they hadn't seen anything, and yes, their sister was just in town visiting for a few days.

Oslo and Bill had looked at the bandages and bruises with questions in their eyes. None of which I could answer. So I'd just hugged them and stood between them as they lowered Dad into the cold ground.

Heather was a godsend at the wake, handling the neighbors who came by with their casseroles and cakes, condolences and curiosity. They eyed me with my black-and-blue marks, Jackson in his sling, and Clark on his crutches. We offered no explanations, and the only one rude enough to ask was Old Widow Schaffer, who was too deaf to hear anything anyway.

I escaped to my room when I couldn't handle the prying and sympathetic eyes any longer. I felt as though I was hanging by a thread. My life was out of control, and nothing was what I'd thought. My father wasn't my father. Clark's dead brother hadn't been dead at all, but a psychopath intent on making Clark pay for the past using my blood. Jackson had been the one who had pulled the lever that had set the events of the past two weeks in motion . . . six years ago.

There was a knock on the door. "Yeah," I answered tiredly.

Grams poked her head in. "Can I come in?"

"Of course," I said, grateful it was her and not someone else.

She came in and sat down next to me. "I saw this downstairs on the counter," she said, handing me an envelope. "It's addressed to you . . . and it's in my daughter's handwriting."

I looked at her, a question in my eyes. "You . . . do you know? About me?"

"That your dear momma had an affair and you were the result? Of course, I knew, China-girl."

"You never told me?" I meant it to be a statement, but it came out a question.

"I promised your mom I wouldn't, and you don't break a promise made to your dead daughter. Not even for you, China-girl." She looked sad, but resolute.

There was nothing I could say to that. I looked down at the envelope in my hand. Grams patted my leg.

"I'll leave you alone to read that. You just let me know if you want to talk afterward, all right?"

I nodded, still looking at the worn envelope. I felt Grams press a kiss to the top of my head, then leave, quietly closing the door behind her.

My hands shook as I opened the envelope, and it was as though I could hear my mom's voice as I read the slanted, cursive writing.

My dearest China,

I know this must come as a shock to you, after all this time. The first thing I want you to know is that your dad—the man you know as your father and who raised you—is a good, good man. He loved me far more than I deserved. I was lucky indeed to have met him, and I didn't regret a day we spent together, or the two wonderful boys we had.

I didn't—until I met Mark.

He was everything I'd ever dreamed of. Dashing and charming. Exciting and dangerous. We instantly made a connection. The job we were doing was dangerous, which probably contributed to the intensity of our feelings. It was then that I regretted choosing security over a dream.

You were the product of our love, Mark's and mine. I would have done almost anything to be with him—anything except leave your brothers without a mother, and break your dad's heart.

I told no one but Grams what had happened, though of course your dad figured things out. He was never a stupid man. He should have divorced me, but God love his soul, he loved me too much. I wish I could have loved him as much as he loved me.

I think that there may be people who would like to use you for their own ends, my dear. Mark had many enemies within the CIA and other agencies. I've been worried, lately, that I may have been discovered here, in the backwoods country of Nebraska. Which is why I'm writing you this letter. Just in case I'm not around to tell you all of this. I hope I am, but the future is never guaranteed. I hope I've hidden you and your true parentage well enough.

Please take care, dear China, and know that while your biology may have been a falsehood, the love of those closest to you has always been true.

All my love,

Mom

I was crying so hard, it was difficult to read the last few lines. And since no one was there to see, I let myself cry. For my dad, my mom, and for me. This seemed like an excellent time for a pity party, guest list of one.

Rob's body had disappeared from the woods, as had all evidence of everything that had happened. Even the barn had somehow been fixed overnight, the Gemini symbol gone as though it had never appeared.

And now I watched from Jackson's private plane as Omaha receded into the distance behind us. I wasn't sorry to see the last of it. The nightmares I would have from what had happened I was sure would haunt me for years. Mia decided to stay through the weekend with her parents, and we made plans for her to fly back to Raleigh next week. I was glad she was getting along well with Oslo and Heather, but I already missed her. I needed her to give me random hugs that I wasn't prepared for, stay in the shower too long so I was four minutes late for work, and *ooh* and *aah* over the Winchester brothers with me.

A couple of hours into the flight, Jackson appeared and sat down next to me. He'd been in the back on the phone taking care of business calls. Now, he sighed and took my hand in his.

We hadn't talked much the past few days. Between the physical pain of our injuries and the emotional turmoil of the trauma, we'd spent more time just touching than talking.

Clark had left immediately after the funeral, after giving me a careful hug and a kiss on the forehead. Jackson had been gracious enough to provide a car and flight home before the plane returned for us. Being rich had its benefits.

"How are you?" he asked.

I looked up at him, my heart squeezing at the sight. He was so dear to me. And he'd saved me. Me *and* Clark.

"I'll be fine," I said, which was a true statement. I wasn't fine, but *time healed all wounds*. I was realizing, finally, why all those idioms were so prevalent. They were true.

"This has been . . . a helluva couple of weeks," he said with a tired sigh.

"I know. And I honestly don't know what I would have done without you."

Jackson just smiled and lifted my hand to kiss my knuckles, which made what I had to say next even harder.

"And I don't know what I'm going to do . . . without you."

His smile faded. "What do you mean?"

"I love you, Jackson, but not for the right reasons. I love you because you make me feel secure and safe. I can depend on you. I know exactly what our life together would be, and it would be picture-perfect."

"And what's wrong with that?"

I shook my head. "You deserve better. I deserve better. We shouldn't settle for what's safe and comfortable. Yes, we get along wonderfully and we understand each other. But I don't think that's enough to base a lifetime on."

Jackson looked away and cleared his throat. Then he cleared his throat again and straightened in the seat.

"A lot has happened," he said at last. "Too much to take in. Don't make a decision right now. Take some time."

"And keep you waiting on me?" I asked. "That's cruel. I won't do that to you."

"You'd rather break my heart now?" For the first time, I saw the crack in his composure, then he looked away again. "It's because of Clark, isn't it."

I'd known he would bring that up, and I was ready for it. "I know you probably think so, but no. Not entirely."

He looked at me, anger and disbelief in his eyes.

"I care about Clark, yes. He's definitely made me see a kind of man I'm . . . attracted to. But that doesn't affect how I feel about you, Jackson. I loved you and still love you. But I need time to figure out the kind of man I want to spend the rest of my life with."

"And what if you decide that kind of man is me?"

I gave a helpless shrug, trying not to cry. "Then I'll have made an awful, terrible mistake," I whispered.

Looking down, I worked the engagement ring off my finger. "Here," I said, handing it to him, but he stood.

"Keep it," he said, his voice flat. "This isn't over, China."

I looked down, tears dripping onto my lap. Breaking up was as horrible as I'd known it would be. And worse.

"I'm sorry," I whispered again, but he was gone.

He didn't appear again until we'd landed. Then, ever the gentleman, he escorted me down the air stairs to the car waiting.

"Lance, please take China to her home," he instructed. "I'll grab a cab."

"No, Jackson, please—"

"You're not the only one who needs some time," he said. He didn't look angry anymore, but the pain in his eyes made me want to take back everything I'd said, just so it would go away.

Lance took me home, and I gave him an impromptu hug goodbye when he dropped me off. I didn't say anything, but he wasn't an idiot. He knew. And he hugged me back.

My house felt emptier than it had in a long time. I set my luggage down and stared. Mia was gone. Jackson was gone. Clark was gone. Even the Doctor was floating in his tank. Again.

I'd cried enough to fill ten buckets, and I was done. No more.

It was a Friday. Chinese night. I ordered my usual pre-Mia menu, unpacked, and went through my e-mail. I ate two Fig Newtons before bed and was under the covers at precisely ten thirty. Just like I had before . . . but I felt much different now. Usually my routine made me feel warm and fuzzy inside. Tonight I felt . . . as though I was missing something.

◆ ◆ ◆

Saturday I decided to do something unexpected, which made my nerves dance and the butterflies in my stomach set up a hoedown.

Around noon, I pulled my Mustang into Clark's driveway, heading toward the beautiful log cabin in the woods that he'd shown me months ago. I wasn't even sure he was there.

I tightened my ponytail and pushed my glasses up my nose before I got out of the car, too late rethinking my *I Want to Believe* T-shirt. But it wasn't like I could back out now. If he was home, he'd likely seen and heard me drive up.

Retrieving the bag I'd brought from the back seat, I headed for the front door. I almost tightened my ponytail again before I realized I didn't have enough hands for it. Reaching out, I rang the bell, then winced. It sounded really loud.

I shifted from one foot to the other, waiting, and rethinking this whole stupid thing. But before I could run from the porch back to the safety of the car, the door opened.

Clark stood there with one crutch, eyeing me. He wore loose cotton pants like sweatpants but thinner, and a worn T-shirt that fit him like a second skin. His hair was tousled, and his eyes were as blue as I remembered.

Neither of us spoke for a moment.

"This is . . . unexpected." His lips lifted on one side.

"I . . . thought you might need cheering up," I said, talking too fast. "So I brought you something. But it's stupid. You probably don't want it anyway. Listen, I'll just go. Sorry for bothering you." I was halfway down the steps by then.

"Whoa, whoa, hold on, wait," he called out. I stopped and turned. "I would *love* some cheering up," he said. "Come in."

I followed him inside to the bar in the kitchen.

"Have a seat," he said, gesturing to the bar stools.

I climbed up on one, wishing I could do it more gracefully, but it was what it was.

"Um, here you go," I said, handing him the bag. I noticed he took a long glance at my bare left hand.

He set the bag carefully on the counter and reached inside, pulling out the cardboard container.

"Open it," I said.

He did, revealing half a dozen freshly made cannoli. He looked at me, his brows furrowed in question, and I cursed my stupid idea.

"Um, it's dessert," I said weakly. "You know, dessert first. You're not supposed to . . ." My voice trailed off as my utter mortification reached its peak. I was awful at this sort of thing. I didn't know why I'd tried. "Never mind."

I hopped off the stool. "Anyway, I thought it might—"

He yanked me toward him until our bodies met, cutting me off midsentence. I looked up at him in surprise.

"Yes, please," he said, his lips curving into a smile. "I would very much like to have my dessert first."

Epilogue

"You should be resting."

President Blane Kirk glanced up from where he was sitting behind his desk, going through the stacks of briefs and memos that had piled up during his absence. His wife had entered the Oval Office.

As always, the sight of her momentarily took his breath away. A reaction he'd had from the first time he'd laid eyes on her in New York nearly ten years ago.

He'd been at a charity event—a fashion show with designers with names like Versace, de la Renta, Chanel, and more—that had drawn the very wealthiest of New York's elite. Anne was one of the models, and when she'd walked the runway—clad in a diaphanous silver gown, her dark hair cascading down her back, with eyes that were deep pools he could get lost in—he'd been unable to think of anything but meeting her.

She'd proven somewhat elusive. Born to an old-money family, she'd been wary of his interest. But Blane himself wasn't unfamiliar with those drawn to wealth and beauty. He'd persisted, even as she was finishing her master's degree in fashion design. They'd married in a New York cathedral—with more than five hundred of their closest friends—and honeymooned in France.

Anne had been by his side through his terms as senator as well as a grueling presidential campaign. The people loved her. She was warm and approachable, beautiful and kind. Then they'd had the twins and cemented their spot as America's Perfect Couple. Blane had lost track of the number of magazine covers one or both of them had graced, though he knew Kathleen—his brother's wife—kept track of them all. She was adamant about it, saying the twins would want to have copies of them when they were older.

"I said, you should be resting," Anne repeated, pulling Blane from his memories. "It's late." She settled one hip against the edge of the desk.

"I've rested enough. The work has to get done. Somehow, the business of running the country doesn't pause just because I'm a little under the weather."

Her eyebrows rose. "A little under the weather? You were *shot*."

Blane took her hips in his hands and slid her closer to him on the desk. "I've been shot before," he gently reminded her.

"That doesn't mean I have to like it."

"I know." Anne had been horrified at the shooting and had refused to leave his side in the hospital, protecting him like a wolf with her mate. She'd been adamant that he needed time to recover. Kade and Kathleen had been nearly the only ones she'd allowed in the room.

"Did they catch the man who did it?" she asked.

Blane nodded. He'd just been on the phone with Kade and been caught up on the events in Nebraska. "He won't be bothering us again."

"Did they find out who or why?"

"It was a soldier who'd been left behind on an op six years ago," Blane explained. "I was the ranking member of the Intelligence Committee at the time. Someone leaked the attack plan to Gaddafi. He must've thought it was me—"

"You'd never do something like that," Anne interrupted. "You'd never put soldiers at risk like that."

"I know that, but obviously he didn't."

"Do you know who *did* leak it?"

"No," he answered grimly. "But I think it's time I found out."

Anne sighed. "Always intrigue and treachery. Like Caesar, having to watch your back before the next person stabs you." She sounded bitter.

"That's politics," Blane absently replied. He was distracted by the way the light shown behind her, outlining her body through the silk nightgown she wore. Tall, thin, and lithe, her legs stretched on for miles. Laying his hand on her calf, he slid his palm underneath the fabric up the silken length of thigh.

"Excuse me, Mr. President," Anne teased, stopping his hand with her own. "You're not supposed to indulge in any rigorous activity until you're fully healed."

"Then I suppose I'll be lazy and make you be on top." Scooping her into his arms, the tinkling sound of her laughter in his ears, he carried her from the room.

◆ ◆ ◆

Kade Dennon stretched, the kinks in his neck and shoulders reminding him that sitting in front of a computer for hours wasn't good for the muscles. But he'd finished, and all the loose ends were satisfactorily tied up. Mostly. Danvers was still an issue. But he'd deal with that later.

Turning off the lights to his office, he set the house alarm and headed upstairs. He'd moved to DC during Blane's campaign, buying a house Kathleen had fallen in love with. An old Georgetown colonial, it was homier than it should be for its size.

Although he was certain he made no noise, Kathleen still stirred when he slipped into bed beside her.

"About time," she murmured, nestling sleepily into his arms. "Everything okay?"

"Everything's fine," he replied, stroking her long hair. "Go back to sleep."

"That girl . . . China . . . she's all right?" she persisted.

"Yes. Choppers got there in time." No need to go into the details of how close "in time" had been.

"Good." She yawned and sighed.

Kade lay awake, staring at the ceiling, his fingers gently combing through her hair as her breaths evened and deepened in slumber. He often did this. Lay awake in the still of the night, just holding his wife and doing what she'd call "counting his blessings." His life could've been very different had things not gone the way they had. And not a day passed that he didn't stop and take a moment to appreciate what he'd been given.

He hoped China would be no worse for wear after this. She was a tough chick, but even tough chicks had their limits. She'd deserved to know the truth about her mother and Danvers. Truth was often painful, but also freeing. She'd have questions, and she'd want to hunt down her real father, something they had in common.

Danvers couldn't hide from them both.

ACKNOWLEDGMENTS

A huge thank-you to my wonderful family for dealing with my mood swings, eccentricities, and unpredictable family-meal schedule. I'm so glad I get to spend time with my baby girls, who make me so very happy. I couldn't get through life without you.

To the friends who encouraged me and listened to my worries and troubles—Nancy, Marina, Tracy, Leslie, Rebecca, Jill, and Lisa. Friends come and go in life, and I've been supremely blessed to know all of you. Your love and laughter are the sparkles in my day.

To my editors, Maria and Melody, you both help me be a better writer. I am thankful for your support and enthusiasm for my work. I'm lucky, indeed, to have both of you in my corner. You're both a true pleasure to work with. My day is made if I can make you laugh, Maria.

Thank you to Raydeen and Shannon for reading quickly and providing that essential feedback. For brainstorming and bugging me for more chapters. Thank goodness you're fast readers!

Thank you to all the Kathleen Turner readers and fans who enjoyed seeing their old friends pop up in this series. I love your enthusiasm to read about them again.

And last, thank you to MG for the plotting advice and assistance. As always, your insights and knowledge are invaluable to me. XOXO.